Rough Justice

For Richard

With best. wishes

Kw Watson.

23026831

Keith Watson

authorHOUSE®

AuthorHouse™ UK Ltd.
500 Avebury Boulevard
Central Milton Keynes, MK9 2BE
www.authorhouse.co.uk
Phone: 08001974150

First published by AuthorHouse 8/23/2007

ISBN: 978-1-4343-2837-3 (sc)
ISBN: 978-1-4343-2836-6 (hc)

Library of Congress Control Number: 2007905604

Printed in the United States of America
Bloomington, Indiana

This book is printed on acid-free paper.

The Court of Inquiry evidence in the book is true in every respect - even the statements of witnesses. Many of them are now dead but all their names have been changed. Named MP's in the book are real for they were in the public domain at the time. All other characters in this publication are fictitious and any resemblance to real persons, living or dead, is purely coincidental.

'For Maureen'

'For the countless numbers of National Servicemen who gave their lives for Queen and Country'

'For their encouragement'

My friends in the 'Blue Palms' group

Army Terms of Reference

Description/Abbreviations	Interpretation
Blanco	Application for colouring webbing
BTA	British Troops in Austria
'Canteen Cowboy'	Duty NCO in charge of NAAFI
Corporal	NCO – Two stripes
Compo	Emergency Rations (see hardtack)
CQMS	Company Quarter Master Sergeant
CSM	Company Sergeant Major
Firecracker	American Forces explosive simulator
'gonking'	Sleeping
'gundgy'	Dirty
'hardtack'	Rock hard oatmeal biscuits
'kate'	Kate carney – cockney slang for army
Lance-jack	NCO – Lance Corporal – one stripe
'mucker'	Mate
NCO	Non Commissioned Officer
ORs	Other Ranks
'picket'	Guard duty
RP	Regimental Policeman
RMP	Royal Military Police
Sgt	Sergeant
'snout'	Cigarette
'sprog'	Inexperienced soldier or rookie

Two I/C	Second in Command
TCV	Troop Carrying Vehicle
Thunderflash	British Forces explosive simulator
USFA	United States Forces in Austria
Webbing	Waist-belt, harness and anklets
WOSB – pronounced 'Wozby'	War Office Selection Board for officers

Foreword:

World War II had ended ten years ago. Austria was still occupied by allied troops from Britain, France, USSR and America. 'Allied' could not have been further from the truth. Whilst allied in victory, a 'Cold War' had emerged between east and west, with large concentrations of combat ready troops based throughout Europe and to a lesser extent, Austria.

Britain had just one infantry regiment in Austria, 1st Battalion The Middlesex Regiment. They were based in the region of Styria with their main barracks at Zeltweg. The southern border of the Russian zone was Fohnsdorf, just a few miles north. The Headquarters for British Troops in Austria, known as BTA, was at Klagenfurt in the south.

Each of the four occupying nations maintained a troop presence in the capital city of Vienna and took turns in guarding key installations for several months at a time. Whenever a change in responsibility took place, a grand take-over parade would be held in Helden Platz interpreted as Heroes Square. The retiring army would hand over to their replacement amidst great pomp and ceremony, their respective generals and Austrian dignitaries taking the salute. Invariably, up to two hundred men would be involved and large numbers of Austrian civilians would turn up to observe the spectacle, with both nations seeking to outdo the other in smartness and skill at arms.

In Vienna, the British maintained a force of Company strength based at Schönbrunn Barracks with frequent troop movements travelling north by train or south to their base camp at Zeltweg. This involved passing through the Russian sector and their checkpoint at Semmering where, needless to say, the Soviets were always suspicious regarding the numbers of men on the move.

The Middlesex Regiment, known as The Die-Hards, guarded its history jealously with its men disciplined to a high standard of smartness and efficiency both on and off the parade ground. Military manoeuvres were frequent and it was one such venture in the winter of 1955 that found the Battalion embarking on a joint exercise with its American Allies.

It is day five of Exercise 'Roundup' as the Company arrives at Mattighofen. The men are close to exhaustion. Lloyd Freeman, newly promoted Lance-corporal, takes up the story.

1

It was Saturday and the second time in less than twenty-four hours when our vehicles returned to Mattighofen, a small town, situated twenty miles or so north of Salzburg and close to the German border. Austrians stood watching us from a distance as stupefied with tiredness, we tumbled out of our transporters and formed up in three ranks. Company Sergeant Major Campbell, often referred to as Jock, the Gov'nor, or even the Führer, was unusually subdued as he consulted with the platoon commanders. Some distance away a local clock chimed the hour. It was midday.

In front of us stood a huge barn. We had been here before! We had stood in front of this same barn the previous afternoon and then the second-in-command had ordered a withdrawal and an all night foray.

Now, after thirty hours without sleep, we were frozen to the depths of our boots and totally exhausted.

The barn, higher than a house and more than forty yards long, was owned by a local brewery. It had a steeply sloping roof upon which clods of snow hung like a mosaic, glued with frost to the tiles beneath. A solid brick wall fronted the barn with two barred openings, high up on the left side, positioned just below the eaves.

Two large, wooden, double-doors, equally spaced, provided entrances to the building but one appeared to be locked. The other gaped open. In the depths beyond, the glow of interior lighting revealed hundreds of straw bales and the promise of warmth and comfort. At the far end of the building, on the outside, wrought iron steps led up to a first floor landing and a smaller door with curtained windows alongside. These were living quarters for the brewery manager and his family. Animals were stabled directly beneath.

Suddenly the sound of a Jeep approaching caused Jock to turn around and all heads followed his gaze. It stopped in front of the barn and an officer, Captain Clark, got out. "Not him again, I can't take anymore," mumbled Boozer, from the corner of his mouth, as Clark, swagger stick in hand, strolled towards the CSM. It was Clark who, the day before, had ordered the latest punishing all night diversion. Jock met him halfway with his customary snappy salute, acknowledged by the newcomer with the usual casual response.

"I can't stand that smug bastard," Paddy said, under his breath, as the two men out front decided our fate. Moments later, Campbell turned to face us, his jaws twitching, considering his next move. Like Boozer, all of us had had enough! A rifle clattered to the ground. Jock, unlike him, just glared at the numb-fingered, culprit!

* * *

The day before, we had arrived at Mattighofen late in the afternoon expecting a hot meal, shelter from the elements and sleep. We had left our base camp in Zeltweg five days ago for 'Exercise Roundup' but it had rapidly descended into 'Exercise Cock-up'. For days on end we had been crammed together in the back of unheated troop-carrying vehicles (TCVs) with inadequate clothing, footwear or sustenance. The daytime temperature had rarely exceeded minus six degrees centigrade.

Our convoy had journeyed a couple of hundred miles or so across the Alps travelling by day in a northerly direction through a circuitous route of mountain passes. At night we had rested in stables, barns or railway sidings and for the unfortunate few, in the open beneath a canopy of stars. Sleep breaks had been of four hours or less, staggered between guard duties. Morale was very low.

A few locals then had lingered nearby watching our Company, close to a hundred men, most of us conscripts, descend from our vehicles before shouldering rifles, whilst stamping our frozen feet and adjusting belts and berets, fearful of that man Campbell. The look on his face indicated he was impatient to get on. He looked smart enough, more erect and stiffer-backed than usual with his tongue sharpened to a new edge, clearly enjoying the Austrian audience. He hadn't been doing any all-night guards or sleeping in the open, like us.

"Fall in – in three ranks!" he growled, as sullenly, with heads bowed and shoulders sagging, we reluctantly obeyed. "Come on move!" he rapped, as stragglers hurriedly fell in.

This was the American sector and the first time Austrians in the north had seen the British occupiers, so Jock was determined to show them we could outshine the Americans, despite the fact our boots were filthy, our uniforms like sacks, our webbing streaked and brasses tarnished. Within minutes he had us perfectly aligned and facing the front in good order, with our shoulders pulled back and heads proudly held high, playing to the gallery ourselves.

A Jeep drew up behind Jock and Captain Clark, tall, hook-nosed and haughty, alighted from the vehicle and stood waiting. Jock took his time, called us to attention, then swivelled around like a ballet dancer and marched up to Clark. The Captain looked bored as Jock sprang to attention with an explosion of metal studs on concrete whilst his right arm, flayed the air to its fullest extent, moving outwards and upwards in a wide arc to salute, before being returned smartly to its side. 'The longest way up and the shortest way down,' he called it.

The locals were obviously impressed as Captain and Sergeant Major exchanged quiet words. Jock saluted again, turned about and returned to face us with jaws twitching, a mannerism of annoyance he had demonstrated on countless occasions as the Jeep spun around and headed back out of town.

The Gov'nor stood us at ease then flipped his head back a fraction, beckoning Sergeants Legg and Eames to join him. Like eager puppies they bounded across to receive their orders: words were exchanged before they turned and re-joined the parade. Sergeant Legg, or Leggy, our regular platoon sergeant, who had been acting as platoon commander for the duration of the scheme, ordered us, "Saddle up! Get back on the vehicles, we're moving out."

Hagley, one of the hard nuts, cursed under his breath, as he shuffled forward, "What a game of soldiers!"

Then Bins, ex-dustman and likeable cockney, unusually bolshy, pushed his beret to the back of his head, "Officers! I've shit 'em!"

Paddy fumed, rebelliously, "Where are we off to now then, for focks sake?"

"Quiet in the ranks!" That was Leggy, his tone more advisory than commanding – a man with feeling and much respected by us all. "We'll do our best to get you some grub later," he said.

"The mushroom theory has prevailed," said Nigel, nodding his head wisely, as the vehicle pulled away.

"What's that then, Nigel?"

He chuckled, "Keep them in the dark old boy, and regularly throw shit over them!" Nigel Pallister, ex public school and six-foot-three tall, with the looks of a Greek God, was a fellow NCO who had qualified, on the same cadre as myself, a few weeks before the manoeuvres had begun. We had become good mates during the scheme. One night he had become unusually talkative, confessing to me how he had failed the selection board to become an officer. But that's another story!

The temperature had dropped like a stone with the sun in pursuit as the convoy trundled back down the same road we had come in on, leaving everybody confused and even more fed up. The men began complaining, to each other at first, until Hagley decided to take it out on me, a green horn or so he thought, as he thrust his face into mine, threateningly, "What the fuck are you lot playing at, we're starving?" I shrugged and shook my head despairingly – he was always challenging authority and, I must admit, I didn't know how to handle him. Suddenly his patience broke as he slammed the butt of his rifle on the metal floor and looked around at the others, "What's the matter wiv you lot, are you fucking scared or summat? I've had enough, we don't have to put up with this crap!"

Boozer, older than most of us and a loyal member of the section, came to my rescue as he leaned forward, scowling, "And where will you go, out here miles from anywhere dick 'ead? There's nothing the NCOs can do about it – they take orders, same as the rest of us – they can't change things."

"And frankly, they tell us nothing," said Nigel, defensively, "Getting all worked up won't solve anything!"

"Oh! Get you!"

"Shut up the lot of yuh!" It was Corporal Flynn, referred to out of earshot as 'Chopper'. Silence descended making us aware once more of the flick-flack of wheel chains on the hardened snow. Flynn, a tyrant, was senior in rank and much feared by the men. Throughout the scheme he had remained seated up front in the depths of the vehicle, his back against the driver's cab, closest to Sgt Legg who sat alongside the driver. "Sarge says, keep the noise down," said Flynn.

It was dark by the time the vehicle stopped and all eyes turned outwards looking nervously for some distinguishing feature beyond the vehicle canopy. Long white snow-covered plinths laid horizontally and stacked high, interspersed with deep regular thin shadows, laid parallel with the road, told us we were parked alongside a timber yard of some sort. Beyond, snow-covered mountains rose up either side with little frozen outcrops of rock glistening in the infant moon. It was strangely quiet as Sgt Legg appeared in the road at the back of the vehicle fingering the catches on the tailgate.

"All out!" he mumbled, "we've heard the opposition are close. You know the ropes, take up defensive positions," he said, waving the palm of his right hand in a wide sweep towards a snow filled ditch. One at a time, we slid silently from the back of the TCV into the snow. "Corporal Flynn, get your section and come with me."

The rest of us ran crouching along the ditch and dropped into the snow five yards apart, pointing our rifles outwards, watching back up the road. Leggy beckoned the two American wireless operators accompanying us to join him, then took Chopper's section of men up a steeper incline to the rear. Chopper, a regular soldier, had served with Leggy in Korea.

The TCV moved off in the same direction before its engine cut out, the driver seeking a gully or natural hideaway to glide forward and conceal its location. From somewhere below us came the sound of a river tunnelling beneath the snow and coursing its way down the valley, unhindered by the intense cold above. There was no sign of the other platoons – they had probably been diverted elsewhere. Nigel's mushroom theory had haunted us all week.

During the next ten minutes our eyes became accustomed to the moonlight and shadows thrown up by every rock, tree and crevice. My only thought right then was of my own stomach churning; it hadn't been serviced for several hours. In the eerie snowbound silence I could hear the rest of the platoon munching hard tack (dry oatmeal biscuits as brittle as dog biscuits). I reached into one of my ammunition pouches for my own emergency supply. Once salivated and swallowed, the biscuits seemed to expand, persuading our stomachs that satisfaction was merely physical.

We remained lying there for what seemed an eternity until a messenger from Chopper's section dropped in the snow beside me and breathless, announced, "Sergeant says we've gotta remain here for awhile – the Yanks are either side of us. He's on his way. When he gets back, we'll fucking give it 'em!" He rose to leave.

"Hang on! What does he mean, Yanks either side of us? Is it either side of these mountains, or either side of this road?" I felt scared.

"Don't know – just stay 'ere like he said." He then moved along the line telling the others.

We remained in that spot, soundlessly, for another hour or so during which time our body heat had melted little hollows in the snow in the exact shape of our packs, belt, legs and boots. I felt my arms crack as I raised them to remove my gloves, then blew into my palms in a desperate, yet pointless, attempt to restore a degree of warmth in my fingers. Devoid of blood, my fingers shone like uncooked sausages in the darkness. After awhile I began to feel sleepy – drifting – drifting – imagining myself soaking in a warm bath!

Gradually, I became aware of being shaken. I rolled over and through snow-caked eyelashes recognised the silhouette of Sgt Legg with a bulbous moon perched on his left shoulder. The TCV was back. Parked on the road alongside, it was pumping out noxious fumes that appeared like smoke in the night air. Beyond, I could see shadowy shapes of men clambering into the back of the vehicle. I tried to smile but my face muscles refused to operate. He shook me again.

"Get the rest of your men back in the vehicle, Lloyd, old son!" He had never called me that before and in such a friendly way too – old son indeed!

I attempted to respond with, "Okay Sarge." My lips must have moved, though I couldn't feel them and words refused to escape. I pulled myself up and fell back again, with cramp in my legs. I rose again, gripping the ice cold steel of my sten-gun and grimaced as momentarily, my hands stuck to the metal. I stamped my feet, shook myself and stumbled forward along the gully looking for bodies and gently kicking each bundle of my section, like side-footing a football, as I ordered the frozen hulks back to the truck. Suddenly I felt a stab of pain in my calf-muscle as one of the lumps came to life and lashed out with his rifle butt, cursing me, with, "Fuck off!"

It had to be Hagley. He had been making trouble all that week. Now it was just the two of us, alone. I leaned forward, hissing in his ear, angrily, "Get up or freeze up, idiot."

"Fuck off, I'm staying 'ere!"

Orders were orders and this was one order I now relished, as with teeth clenched, I again ordered, "Get back on the lorry!" The impossibility of making out a two-five-two charge sheet for disobedience, in the dark, at minus ten in the middle of nowhere, made me smile. I winced with pain as my split lip opened up some more. Again he refused.

"Fuck off will yuh!"

My temper now took over as gathering all my strength, I grabbed hold of his shoulder straps, hauled him to his feet and with our faces inches apart, shook him like a rag doll, "Get in that fucking lorry, now! Uugh!" My lip was bleeding and I felt like hitting the man who had brought on such pain, as I dumped him back in the snow.

Hagley, his face plastered with snow and ice, rose to his feet and ran some twenty yards before throwing himself aboard the vehicle. I checked that the ditch was clear and staggered after him, feeling a warm glow of satisfaction. The confrontation had relieved me of the pent up anger of the last five days and nights but the emotional upset was already preying on my mind and I could feel my hands and body trembling as I levered myself up onto the truck.

Too cold to talk and too cold to sleep, we sat in the lorry, twenty or more of us, huddled together for warmth. We had compo rations consisting of chocolate and hard tack to chew and shared these throughout the night, experiencing camaraderie in its raw state. That night, praying came easy for some, the hardest men included, and there is little doubt that our combined body warmth prevented hypothermia setting in.

As dawn broke a supply truck arrived with breakfast. Haversack rations they called it, but it was the basic selection of compo, cheese and margarine, that needed no cooking and we were sick of that after five days of eating little else. However, the vacuum flasks of strong hot coffee, laced with a generous helping of rum, were most welcome and it warmed our insides. Next, we heard the welcoming sound of our driver swinging the starting handle and the engine coming alive before setting off – this time following a route already familiar to us. We were on our way, back to Mattighofen.

2

Now, back at Mattighofen, in our dreamy state, we wondered what Captain Clark had organised for us this time. Jock was in an unusually passive mood as he ordered, "Collect your sleeping bags from the vehicles one platoon at a time and come back here – right seven, on your way." I felt confused. Sleeping? In the middle of the day? I watched Captain Clark as he consulted with two officers, the platoon commanders of seven and eight, who turned and followed him into the barn. What are they up to now, I wondered? 'Why isn't Leggy joining them?' Bins had noticed too.

"I fought Leggy was s'posed to be an officer now? Wouldn't you fink…."

"Shut it, Harris and move yourself."

We returned with our sleeping bags to await further instructions.

"Okay!" Jock announced, in a conciliatory tone, "When I say the word, make your way into the barn in single file and bed down in the areas allocated by your platoon commanders." I breathed a sigh of relief; sleep at last, precious sleep.

All eyes now turned to Jock who threw his head back and stuck out his chin to emphasise the importance of his message, his tone deadly serious, "A word of warning. The barn is filled with hay – a fire risk. There will be no smoking. Anyone smoking will face a court-martial. Right, in you go."

All we wanted right then was warmth and sleep as we trudged into the building in an orderly fashion with seven and eight platoons in the lead. The two leading platoons were led up steps to an upper floor behind the family residence. This floor was split in two, with one side covered in layers of warm hay, two or three feet deep and completely open, providing a panoramic view of the barn interior. The men of eight platoon quickly settled themselves in this half.

The other half was enclosed, with entry to it through a small brick built arch, which seven platoon and two men from the American attachment, entered. This room had two barred windows on the outside walls, sealed tight, one at the back and another at the side. There was very little straw in this room, just loose grain and dust but seven platoon must have been jubilant seeing this as the most comfortable option – warm and relatively draught free.

As we entered the barn we could hear the other two platoons chattering excitedly and we too were lifted, gasping at the sheer magnitude of it as we looked around relishing the smell of warm hay.

I could see two doors opposite the entrance positioned at the rear of the barn. These were locked. In front of them were numerous farm implements including an old wooden cart and a plough of some sort. To the right, as we entered, was stabling for animals and the steps leading to seven and eight's accommodation. The platoon commanders, both of them officers, had already ordered their men to settle down and the men had commenced laying out their sleeping bags in the warm hay as the officers departed. Some, were hardly bothering to unzip their bags properly but leaving the nylon lining to take the strain as wet hobnailed boots were slid to the bottom of the already wet interiors.

Powerful lights in the cavernous roof illuminated the interior, as big as a dance hall, providing storage facilities for the previous summer's harvest. On the ground floor, our location, bales of straw were stacked two to three feet deep, with an abundance of loose strands strewn all around and a huge pile of loose hay, nine feet high, stacked to the left of the entrance, just inside the door. The officers' batmen were ordered to sleep alongside this heap just beneath a flight of wooden steps that led to an upper floor; this too was piled high with loose straw.

Apart from the men in my section and the rest of nine platoon, the general morale had been virtually restored as the excited chatter rose to a crescendo. We were still awaiting the order to bed down. From the floor above, members of eight were sitting up in their sleeping bags and pouring scorn on our lot below. I turned watching the men above, like an aggrieved orchestral conductor in the pit, looking up at the fun-loving players on stage.

There was no sign of Leggy and our platoon was becoming restless until Sergeant Eames appeared. We had seen little of him during the scheme for he had been more involved organising our meals than performing the tasks of platoon sergeant. He was over six feet tall, with an imposing figure, open face and pale complexion. Younger than most of the sergeants in the Battalion, he was very smart with a commanding voice. He ordered us to select spaces where we stood amongst a sparse layer of hay that littered the concrete floor and spread as far as the entrance and the open door. A gale was already being sucked in through the opening like a wind tunnel, unavoidable on account of the barred openings high above on the outside wall. Our platoon had been given the coldest spot in the barn..

"Well, it makes a change from gonking in pig shit, I suppose," scowled Pearce, with sarcastic optimism.

"Yeh but what's he got against us?" grumbled Hagley, referring to the Sergeant Major, as he threw his sleeping bag down. It was his first utterance since our confrontation and I felt warmed by it, as I nodded agreeably in his direction.

"Those bastards up there are taking the piss out of us, look at 'em," shouted Fuller, one of Chopper's cronies, as he kicked aside some loose chaff.

"They've got the best spot of all," moaned Paddy, pointing up at eight platoon. Boozer and Bins, like seasoned warriors and uncaring, had already unzipped their bags and were sleepily easing their booted feet into the depths of the nylon envelopes.

"Why us Lloyd?" moaned Dave, as he laid his rifle down and discarded his packs. It was unusual for him to question anything. Since those early days in training he had become much more self-assured of late, and it was good to see. I liked Dave, a good mate.

"Look, Dave," I said advisedly, "Get your head down, mucker – we could be on the move again before we know it!"

On the floor above, they were still chattering excitedly. Some, thawing out, were conversing from within sealed bags whilst others, unchecked, had removed their boots for greater comfort, a chargeable offence! These could be seen, together with rifles and packs, strewn in the hay alongside them. Hagley might have chanced it to remove his boots had it not been for the fracas with me during the night. Still thinking of Hagley, I rubbed my aching shin.

Suddenly, we heard, "Quiet!" It was Jock, his voice sharp as a knife and painfully penetrating. The barn fell silent. "There'll be no smoking. Anybody caught smoking will …" I switched my mind off, as he droned

17

on but clearly he was warning that anybody found smoking would face serious consequences. I would have the occasional cigarette but smoking was furthest from all our thoughts at that moment. Extreme sleep deprivation had taken over and the warmth of our sleeping bags would soon have a hypnotic effect on all of us.

The lights were turned off and I watched them fade away as if powered by some kind of generator. Some of the men were already snoring blissfully.

Suddenly, the lights blossomed again; dull at first, then dazzling, reaching into every corner of the barn. I turned my head to see the Sergeant Major racing up the steps, shouting at the top of his voice.

"Everybody up – stand to!"

"Fuck! Fuck! Fuck!"

Wearily we sat up and began unzipping our bags, just as Captain Clark, laughing aloud, called out in his plummy voice something like, "No, no Sergeant Major – I was only joking." We all heard it. There was a long pause. I could imagine the look on Jock's face; he must have been livid.

"As you were!" roared the Gov'nor.

Another officer could be heard in the background, chortling. They were in high spirits. Had they been drinking, I wondered? Such friendliness was not like them and they wouldn't dare embarrass the

CSM like that normally. The illuminations died once more and all around me snoring began in earnest.

I could have cried with the pain in my hands as the circulation returned. My nose and ears were frozen with the gale blowing through the open door. I considered zipping my whole self, head and all, in the bag to avoid the draught but dismissed the idea. I had tried it once but it made me feel claustrophobic, apart from which I knew that the others had found it difficult to unzip their bags from the inside on waking.

I could hear the mumbling of voices coming from outside and guessed it must be whoever was guarding us. The army never sleeps without a protective guard. I thought I heard Jock's voice outside at one stage.

"You awake Lloyd?" It was Nigel.

"Yeah."

"I can't sleep. I wish they'd shut that farcking door, don't you?"

"Me too. My hands are warm at long last but my nose is frozen. Do you think he's got it in for us, Nigel?"

"Why? Oh yes – Jock giving us the ground floor. I'd much rather be up there in the hay, lovely and warm."

"There's plenty of hay around us," I chuckled, "if you can catch it!" I felt physically sick with the cold. These manoeuvres can't last forever, I thought. I was angry too, with the Sergeant Major for having given our platoon the worst spot. I felt low at that moment with thoughts that I would have to tolerate this wretched man for another year or more.

My first meeting with Sergeant Major Campbell was when I had arrived at Schönbrunn barracks in Vienna five months earlier – a long time ago.

3

After my initial training I had attended a PT Instructors course and on completion was given a stripe and sent to Austria to join the main Battalion who were based in Zeltweg. At that time the men of 'C' Company were serving a spell in Vienna, performing International guard duties as part of the occupation forces of Britain, France, Russia and USA. The 'Cold War' was at its height and fear was a constant companion.

After an overnight stay at Zeltweg, I gathered my kit and reported to the guardroom for transport to the station and onward transit to Vienna to join my Company and Jock Campbell, the most feared sergeant major in the Battalion.

The provost sergeant, a fat brute of a man, flat nose, cauliflower ears and a vile tongue handed me a rail pass; then, pushing his huge jowls into my face, his foul breath, a mixture of garlic, cigarette smoke and beer, announced, "A word of warning, sonny – the train'll stop at Semmering the Russian checkpoint. Don't stare at 'em, do you hear. We don't want any trouble."

Outside a truck waited coughing out thick clouds of diesel exhaust in the cold morning air. The driver, short, thick set, waited impatiently, a cigarette stub hanging from the corner of his mouth - a mauve smudge in a leathery weather-beaten face, revealing a special toughness that demanded respect, as he growled scornfully, "What kept yuh?" In his early forties, the double rows of campaign ribbons were proof of a lifetime of active service that had earned him a red bulbous nose etched with a purple vein for every river crossed in battle.

Remaining cool, I threw my kit bag into the back of the vehicle, then picking my feet up gingerly in the soft snow, made my way round to the passenger side and levered myself onto the cold hard seat. Staring directly ahead, I slammed the door shut sending slithers of snow cascading to the ground. The driver meanwhile, sat at the wheel in silence, his door window down, scowling for having delayed his breakfast.

Ignoring him I ducked my head and looked out at the two-storey buildings, now punctuated with rectangular blocks of light, encircling the cookhouse like a giant horseshoe, their eerie silhouettes outlined by a halo apparition against the cold black starry sky, as the Battalion came to life. Beyond, I could just make out the dark irregular shapes of the mountains, their snow covered peaks glistening white in the dying moon.

"Right, let's go," the driver snapped, and without removing his cigarette, blew surplus ash at the windscreen, slammed the gear stick forward, and drove the truck out of camp.

Zeltweg, a tiny hamlet in central Austria was situated on a small plain close to a main north-south trunk road. Protected all round by high mountains, it had been an ideal base for the German Luftwaffe. That was nine years before. Now the airfield and surrounding buildings provided a perfect site for the Regiment.

As we left camp, I could feel goose pimples on my buttocks as I studied the older man driving and smiled at my own wicked thoughts; he reminded me of Punch. I wondered whether he had a Judy at home? Huge flakes of snow were silently changing the landscape and I shivered, cursing my stupidity for packing my overcoat in the kitbag. I yawned aloud and pushed my back further into the seat before rubbing my hands together vigorously and blowing into them, with my breath clouding the air.

"Ain't you gotta great coat?"

"Yes, but I packed it away."

"Feeling tough eh ... it'll be colder than this in Vienna." The driver closed his eyes momentarily, spraying ash onto his chest as he reached forward clearing condensation from the windscreen with his outstretched palm. "Here," he ordered, handing me a filthy cloth, "wipe your side of the winda."

The truck slewed to one side as it hit a frozen rut, accompanied by curses from Punch. He blew his cigarette butt out of the open window, coughed aloud and despatched a globule after it. "Have they warned ya 'bout the Ruskies?" he asked, more friendly, as he glanced first in the rear view mirror, then at me.

"Yes, I was told not to stare at them once I reach the border."

"Too right, their 'burp' guns are loaded. They'll turn the fucking train over if they 'ave to."

"Really?"

"They're ruthless, those Ruskies. First chance they get, they'll try 'n starve us outa Vienna, same as they did in Berlin, you see if they don't." He let out a blast on the horn, "Get out the way, kraut dog," he shouted, as he braked heavily and skidded. "Where was I? ... Oh yeah ... I tell ya - if the balloon goes up, we'll 'ave no chance."

"Blimey!"

He spun the wheel as his right hand reached into his breast pocket before removing a packet of cigarettes. Flicking it open with his forefinger and thumb, he tapped the packet and a tip emerged. Whilst holding the pack, he placed the tip between his lips and removed it before returning the unfastened pack into his breast pocket.

"Listen," he said, as his thumb rotated the wheel of his lighter against flint, "on the train, don't sit on ya own – we're s'posed to have guards but ya never see any!" The lighter flared, illuminating the cabin, as he drew hard on the cigarette. "The red caps are like coppers back 'ome – never there, when ya want one." The truck skidded to a halt and Punch nodded his head for me to get out.

I felt reluctant to move, as I peered through the windscreen at the blackness beyond. "Is this where I get the train?"

"What do you expect, fucking Kings Cross Station?" The driver threw the door open and slid out into the snow.

A layer of ice had formed on the side window as I pushed the door open and jumped out before slamming it shut behind me. The snow, softer and deeper than I had seen in recent years, threatened to cover my boots as I stamped my feet and adjusted my beret. All around, it seemed so quiet.

The driver's head appeared from behind the canopy, "Come on, lightnin', we ain't got all day."

In the darkness beyond I could just make out the rail line snaking away into the gloom as I slithered round to the back of the truck. Punch dropped the tailgate and nodded for me to retrieve my kit bag. Unspeaking, I hoisted it onto my shoulder and half turned to face the track. It was totally deserted. The driver laughed aloud as he slammed the tailboard shut.

"Give my regards to Jock."

"Jock?"

"Yeah, Jock Campbell the CSM – a right 'ard bastard 'im!" He chuckled as he saw the quizzical look on my face in the half-light. "We 'ad 'im wiv us in Korea. You'll never see anyone as cool as 'im under fire!"

"Oh!" I gave him the thumbs up sign and sauntered across to the makeshift platform. Behind me, I heard the rear wheels screech as the truck executed a brake-turn before speeding off, leaving me standing alone with my one-way pass to Vienna. At that moment, I felt the loneliest person in the world.

The train came to a halt with a hiss of steam. I climbed aboard, walked the length of the corridor of the empty train and threw my kitbag onto the overhead rack in a rear carriage, and shivering, slumped into a far side corner seat by the window. Silently, the train edged out of Zeltweg and gathering speed, headed north.

I had not yet recovered from the initial excitement of the long train journey the day before. Mesmerised by the scenery in the Alps, I had spent most of it staring out of the window. Resigned to doing the same on the journey to Vienna, I was nonetheless overcome by the warmth of the compartment, combined with the gentle rocking of the train and lapsed into a deep sleep.

A change in momentum woke me – the train was slowing. It was daylight. I rubbed my eyes and looked out of the window to find a dramatic alteration to the landscape. I could almost touch the mountains on my side of the train and the whiteness of snow was blinding. Looking out beyond the corridor to the other side, it was just the same. We were labouring through a mountain pass it seemed with the train slowed to a crawl. I lay back, eyes half closed, conscious of my head gently rocking back and forth, weightless, as I succumbed to sleep once more.

Suddenly I awoke with a jolt! Was this it? Sitting bolt upright, I turned my head to peer out of the window once more. The station sign read Semmering – the provost sergeant's words came flooding back. The platform appeared deserted. The window felt like ice against my face as I strained to look ahead along the full length of the train. Suddenly, as if from nowhere, two Russian soldiers appeared close to, walking slowly towards me, occasionally stopping and peering into each carriage. I remembered the advice - not to stare at them, they might re-act. How, I wondered? Right then, they were far enough away for a more detailed appraisal.

Their peaked caps appeared huge as they stood there, in black wrinkled boots, carrying short-barrelled automatics with circular magazines of ammunition. Were these the 'burp' guns the driver had mentioned? They were slung over the Russians' shoulders but I was in no doubt they were loaded. Their unsmiling faces looked pallid – their dull green overcoats, too long and surprisingly shabby. They drew level with my compartment and paused leaving me staring straight ahead pretending I hadn't noticed them. They moved on. I relaxed, breathing more easily.

The train remained stationary for what seemed an eternity, the heart-beat of its engine silent, as the temperature began to drop, with sounds of contracting metal all around me. I could hear myself breathing in the silence of the carriage as I watched the two Russian soldiers standing several yards away, in deep conversation. They were still there when I became aware of deep-throated mutterings and a scraping of boots coming slowly along the corridor from the front of the train.

Not more Russians surely? I began to wish I had chosen a different compartment – one nearer the front. Surely there are British military police aboard? If they question me, I thought, I can't speak a word of Russian.

The sound of boots was getting ever closer, as the wearers paused at each compartment opening the doors. My throat locked, my tongue dried up, and I caught my breath as suddenly two huge Russian soldiers loomed in the corridor alongside my own compartment. The door was thrown aside unceremoniously and the two men stepped into the opening, their demeanour far from friendly.

Nothing was said as they stood, rooted to the spot, scrutinising my luggage, the solitary stripe and the crossed swords on my jacket, insignia of a Physical Training Instructor. Could it be the similarity with the crossed scimitars of their own fearful Cossacks, I wondered? Struggling to control my emotions, I raised my head, half nodding, struggling to appear unafraid whilst avoiding eye contact?

They stood motionless, unspeaking, looking down at me. Time dragged – there was no air – I couldn't breathe. My mouth hung open and I felt my head tilting backwards. What were they thinking? I could contain myself no longer, when suddenly the Russians stepped back into the corridor, turned, and with great deliberation, and yet more scraping of heavy boots, moved on.

I lay back, took a deep breath and closed my eyes, not daring to look at the men on the platform for a second longer. A door slammed from way down the train, followed by an eerie silence once more, as I strained my ears for a comforting sound. Nothing! I was really scared. Total silence. It seemed to last forever as doubts clouded my mind. I shivered as a draught swept through the inner door of my compartment from somewhere beyond. Could I be on the wrong train? Had the carriage been uncoupled, I wondered? I prayed for the sound of an engine. Any sound. Civilization. My heart was hammering at my rib cage to escape.

From the corner of my eye, I thought I saw a shadow slip past on the station. Was it imagination? Then I felt it? The nerve ends in my spine iced up as ponderously the train slid forward, couplings creaking. My mouth involuntarily dropped open releasing a deep sigh of relief. We were moving.

Confidence restored and feeling bolder, I turned my head studying the men in olive green standing alone on the platform as they drifted by in the opposite direction. They too, were very young men.

It was early afternoon, with overcast skies and the threat of more snow, when the train pulled into Mödling station. A truck, my transport, stood waiting. Painted on each door were distinctive British markings – a nine-inch square Union Jack and a dark blue shield with a white cross, symbol of the eighth army. A friendly looking Lance corporal, wearing Korean ribbons, took my kit, tossed it into the back of the vehicle and invited me to climb aboard. How different, I thought, to the reception at Zeltweg, as I settled back to enjoy the city.

It looked a little like London, but less drab, with its magnificent buildings and statues topped with snow. The trams, a new experience, were thronged with people laden with Christmas gifts. The streets, wider than at home, were lined with young trees, leafless but pretty, with the tiniest white lights, twinkling like diamonds, amidst their snow-covered branches.

The driver looked at me, as he stopped at traffic lights, "How long 'ave you done?"

"Seven months – I went on a PTI's course straight out of training."

"Aldershot?"

"Yup - never felt so fit in my life." I smiled to myself, recalling the early morning jaunts across the sports field to the gym and the first strenuous exercises of the day. Working in a six-man team and wearing shorts only, we would spend the first hour of the day tossing miniature, smooth telegraph poles, to and fro, developing our lateral, pectoral and abdominal muscles that rippled and steamed in the frosty air.

"Was there much bullshit?"

"Yes, but different to Mill Hill, we weren't bullied. We were all very keen anyway. Every Saturday we'd get a weekend pass, after we'd scrubbed the gym floor. We'd be given a tin bath of hot water, a bar of Sunlight soap, a scrubbing brush and a flannel. Then with a yard width each and, in a line across the gym, we'd scrub it, the full length, from one end to the other. It took us the whole morning but the floor boards were white when we finished."

"A whole morning for one gym?"

"You should see Fox Gym – it has three basket ball courts across the width alone, not counting the balcony at one end." It was the first time I had talked about my experiences and I felt proud of my achievements.

Just over six feet tall and weighing thirteen stone, my body was honed to the peak of fitness. Called up for National Service, I had joined the army with the ambition to become a PTI but in spite of achieving this goal, the bullying during induction training and the petty discipline experienced thereafter, had destroyed my enthusiasm. Now a Lance Corporal, I was looking forward to an easy passage for my last eighteen months, doing the things I loved most, as a Physical Training Instructor.

The vehicle turned off the road and stopped at a barrier in front of a magnificent arch, much like a miniature version of Admiralty Arch in London. Alongside this was a smaller one for foot traffic. A guard, standing alongside his sentry box, yelled at our approach and an NCO emerged from the guardroom, winked at the driver, and raised the barrier.

Beyond, I spotted the parade ground, the size of a football pitch. To the left was a large barrack block three storeys high, as long as the parade ground itself, with a steep slated roof and an arch in the centre, identical to the entrance through which we had just driven. The road skirted three sides of the square and then, joy of joys! I spotted the gym at the back of the square.

"They built these barracks before the War – for the Gestapo," said the driver, as he stopped, opened the door and jumped down. He had already hauled the kitbag from the back and was dumping it on the ground as I joined him and the guard commander.

"Corporal Freeman, is it? We've been expecting you. I'll sign you in and get someone to take you across to the orderly room – the Sergeant Major wants a word, I'll let them know you're here."

The door burst open and the Sergeant Major, heavily built, about five-foot-ten in his boots and in full uniform, entered the room frowning. The crown on his sleeve, the cane and cold stare brought about an instant reaction as, instinctively, I leapt to attention. He remained silent as his piercing eyes slowly roamed my being from my boots upwards, taking in my gaiters, trousers, belt, jacket and beret, before settling on my eyes.

Campbell's eyes were dark and angry, smouldering beneath thick black brows. His face was tanned, the bone in his nose threatening to surface. I returned his stare, self-consciously hazarding a guess at what he was thinking. This newcomer hasn't bulled his toecaps since training! His trousers need pressing! The brasses on his cap badge, collar and belt are filthy! His belt and gaiters need fresh blanco!

In his late thirties, possibly older, he wore a double row of ribbons including the most recent, the Korean Campaign Insignia. With

33

jawbones twitching slightly, his eyes looked accusingly into mine. I held his gaze, determined not to wilt under this mental assault but I felt myself shaking, as he extended his arm sideways gesturing for the clerk to hand him some documents. I hoped mine – a report on my achievements at Aldershot perhaps? I wanted to sit down.

He softened, "At ease, man!" I obliged, as he placed his cane on the desk and thumbed through the papers. He handed the sheath back and looked at me with a grudging smile, "Welcome to 'C' Company, Corporal Freeman."

"Thank you, sir." Could it be the report that made his face crack, I wondered?

"So you're a PTI? We can use you." I felt good. It was the first time I'd been acknowledged as a PTI since leaving Aldershot. Ten minutes before, surveying the gymnasium from a distance, I had imagined the joy once more of hand balancing, hand-springs and routines on the parallel bars. He went on, "There's always a need for PTIs but the battalion has one already."

Why not a PTI company based, I thought, optimistically, it would suit me? He seemed to be reading my mind, as he concluded, "We're a rifle company and you must prove yourself as a rifle NCO first." I was confused – what was he talking about?

He continued, "We'll arrange for you to attend an NCOs cadre as soon as possible. In the meantime, remove your stripe and watch out for future duties as they arise on Company Orders." He turned to the Orderly Room NCO; "I'll leave you to brief him on the camp lay-out, daily routine and his platoon." With that, he grabbed his cane, turned and with a measured step, strode out into the snow, chin in, chest out, back erect – not quick but steadfast.

Oh, how I had hated CSM Campbell at that moment.

4

Laughter! Spirited laughter interrupted my reverie and then, **BANG!**

I awoke trembling – was it an attack? More laughter! My ears were ringing as I turned on my side to see Nigel, sitting up, alarmed. "What the fuck was that?"

"Sounded like a thunderflash."

"That's what I thought." Next moment, we heard, **VROOMFF!**

"Fire! Fire! Fire! Get outside now! Pick up your weapons and get out!" It was the Sergeant Major, his tone urgent.

Bins, unzipping his sleeping bag, sat up, "S'pose he finks that's funny!

Nigel exploded, "This is no time for wise-cracks – get moving!"

"Fire! Fire! Fire!" Jock was off again. Smoke was spiralling upwards alongside the opening, as I dragged my legs and sodden boots out of the sleeping bag.

"Oh! No! Oh my God!" Suddenly, flames were crackling through the pile of straw beneath the stairs and spreading up inside the barn wall with great clouds of black smoke pouring into the loft above.

"Fire, fire, pick up your rifles, MOVE!" Campbell's voice was urgent but controlled, as he rasped aloud, "Grrab your rrifles and get out - NOW! Don't leave your weapons behind." Jock, professional to the core, was concerned for the guns. Your rifle's your best friend – that was drummed into us in training. "Get out! Get out! MOVE!"

Keep calm, I told myself; small pack, gun, sleeping bag, have I got everything? I looked up – my escape route, the open door, was clear and then, "Bloody hell!" Someone was trying to beat the flames out with a pitchfork – sparks were flying in all directions as burning straw rained down. "Stop him, for Chris' sake, he's making it worse!"

Now everybody was yelling, '**FIRE!**' Straw was igniting all around creating a sound like the roar of a modern day jet plane as it speeds up the runway before take-off. Flames leaping high in the air – out of control – men were running. Some were remarkably calm, Nigel for one.

He was coolly stamping out the flames and kicking prostrate bundles of men who were struggling to free themselves from their sleeping bags. "You heard what he said, let's get out of here!"

I looked down. A dull green chrysalis, surrounded by burning flotsam, squirmed at my feet as the occupant trapped inside clawed at the zip. I dropped my kit and trembling, inserted two fingers, then my hands and ripped it apart cursing as Boozer's head popped out, grinning. He could take care of himself, now.

I reached down and grabbed my gear just as Dave, still in his bag, surrounded by flames, was dithering. I kicked his feet, "Get out you dozey bastard!" Coughing and sputtering and urging my section on, I ran forward bumping into a guy from eight platoon as he jumped, like a lemming, from the upper floor. He went flying. I helped him up, "Where's your rifle?"

"I couldn't find it, Corp."

I turned for the door. Above and to my left men were pushing each other down a flight of steps. It was now every man for himself as I charged through the open door, almost colliding with a driver.

"What happened?"

He looked stricken, "It was Major Appleby – he threw a thunder-flash."

Outside, a woman, wrapped in a shawl, clawed at her lips with trembling hands, wailing uncontrollably. All around her, women with shawls were sobbing. A church bell was tolling – others more distant could be heard now, as I stopped running and looked back.

"Come on Lloyd, don't hang about!" It was Nigel, breathing heavily, "The others are over there." Fifty yards ahead, I could see our men congregating. Behind me, I heard one of our lorries start up.

I felt myself shaking as I looked at Nigel, panting, "The animals are in there – they'll die!"

He seemed calm, "And their home – they can't save that."

I choked up, "Poor devils." We heard more bells as a couple of ancient fire tenders arrived with civilian auxiliaries.

Nigel seemed relaxed, as we stopped and looked back. "The animals should be okay, Lloyd – there you see, they're leading a horse away now."

"We had eighty or ninety blokes in there, Nigel – do you think?" I choked back my fears, looking up, as the air filled with thousands of fiery smuts, floating down feather-like and turning black as they settled in the snow. Another TCV started up and moved off down the road; "I hadn't realised, if they explode, the whole lot'll go up!" There was a pungent smell in the air, like burning rubber. "I can't drive, or…"

"Jock was driving the first one," shouted Boozer, laughing, as he ran past.

"Oi, Boozer! Where's your sleeping bag?"

He looked back, chuckling, "You tore it apart - remember?"

39

Looking back, inside the barn, I could see it was a blazing inferno. I shuddered at the thought of what might have been – another minute and we would have fried. Ahead of us, Austrians, heads bobbing, watched a barred opening high above from which black clouds of smoke and sparks were pouring out. Suddenly, we heard an audible gasp.

"Look! Who's that waving?" Blackened arms poked through the bars waving frantically. Behind, a mask hovered, screaming - high pitched, like that of a caged animal.

"They need a ladder for focks sake," shouted Paddy.

"It's in use round the back!" It was Leggy. "Corporal Flynn, grab your section – come with me." Then over his shoulder, "Corporal Freeman, check your men, and you Pallister."

Trembling and feeling sick, I looked at the sea of faces around me. Who was it behind the bars? The newcomers – Storer, Paddy, Pearce – they were there. Trouble makers, Fuller and Hagley too. My old muckers from training, Boozer, Bins – they were okay. No Dave Allen?

"Where's Dave?" No answer. My guilt-ridden thoughts registered aloud, "He was awake when I left!" I remembered kicking him – he had seemed confused. Anxiously, I looked around at the vacant faces pleading, "Has anyone seen Dave?"

"Some of our blokes must be trapped in there – they couldn't of all got out."

"Don't say that!"

"That driver reckoned he saw him do it."

"Who was it?"

"Major Appleby."

"Where's Dave?"

"He ain't been seen since the fire started."

"Who, Dave?"

"No – the fuckin' driver what saw 'im do it."

"He weren't a driver – he was a signaller."

"He drives don't he – I've seen 'im."

"Where's Major Appleby, anyway?"

"Has anyone seen Dave?"

Next, I heard crackling sounds from within the barn. "Guns! What do you think, Nigel?"

"Could be blanks, some of the silly buggers left their rifles behind – it might even be roof tiles exploding with the heat." Volumes of smoke could be seen pouring out of the windows and between the roof tiles but little sign of flames.

I had other worries, as I called out again, in desperation, "Where's Dave?"

"I'm here, Lloyd," he said, as he popped up alongside me, grinning.

41

I coughed and wrapped my arm around his shoulders, "The last I saw, you were…" Words failed me as embarrassment took over, "Where were you anyway – you should have kept up with the section?"

"I went round the back to see if I could help. They've put a ladder up the wall and broken through the bars. Austrian firemen have gone inside. They are," his voice faltered, "getting blokes out – they look!" His eyes filled with tears.

"Take it easy, Dave!"

He spat the words out, "Ginger Parker went back in …. they told me, he's still in there."

"Oh!" My throat locked, choking back my own tears. Ginger too had been with me in training; the next bed in the same room, in fact. It had to be someone else trapped behind the bars. Please, not him!

"I blame Campbell," said Paddy, "pick up your rifles, he kept saying – some of the poor bastards couldn't find 'em - wastin' toim groping around for 'em in the hay, they were. That's why they were trapped in tharr."

"It wasn't that, they couldn't undo their zips and could have been trapped in their sleeping bags. *He* tore mine apart," said Boozer, as he looked at me, grinning, "They'll charge *you* for damaging WD property." I glared back at him, in no mood for jokes.

"Hey look! Here come the cavalry!" Shouted Nigel, as the clack, clack, clack of an American helicopter was heard overhead before dropping down behind the barn. Within minutes it took off again just as another arrived. The first one, as it flew back over us, had what looked like bodies on stretchers strapped to the skids beneath.

Sergeant Legg, reappeared, his face drained of colour, "Listen here the lot of you - if anyone asks questions about the fire, you know nothing! Understand?"

It was later when Leggy came back and checked the numbers again. Nine platoon, my platoon, were all accounted for as he ordered, "Right men – saddle up!"

We moved forward in line following one another in silence, struck dumb by what we had seen and unsure who had been taken away on the helicopters.

Satisfied that all in nine platoon was accounted for and safely aboard the TCV, Sergeant Legg secured the tailgate and climbed up beside the driver. It was dusk when we left Mattighofen for the last time to the mournful sound of slowly tolling bells. We were also leaving behind a smouldering shell, a ruined Austrian home, many distraught Austrians and a lot of unanswered questions, but most important of all several dead and many others, severely burned, soldiers. They had been transferred to American Forces hospitals for emergency treatment. Our destination was Camp Roeder, an American barracks in the Salzburg region.

At short notice our American allies were already preparing to receive the remnants of our grieving company, Charlie Company, the best in the Battalion. I turned my eyes to scan the faces of the men seated opposite and beyond in the depths of the vehicle. Totally subdued, they were trying to blank out the events of the last couple of hours. For them, their only counselling was the whine of the engine.

At Camp Roeder, we were met by a couple of Americans NCOs. Mumbling words of sympathy, they led us into a centrally heated camp theatre with lines of camp beds and a stage at one end. We all craved for a hot bath but with our meal ready and sleep beckoning it would have to wait, as we discarded our kit and blindly followed another American NCO to their canteen.

An hour later, with full stomachs, we released our sodden feet for the first time in a week and propped our wet boots in lines beside the radiators. The stench of wet socks, stinking feet and sweat was overpowering as we lowered our aching limbs onto hastily erected camp beds. My own feet had been too cold to sweat but now, upon warming, they caused me stress, with a feeling of pins and needles, especially in my heels. By morning our ammunition boots, that had been totally ineffective in keeping out water and snow, would be baked hard and smothered in irregular white stains.

The main lights were extinguished and fitful snoring commenced. It was then I noticed the Guv'nor, sitting on a chair, centre stage, unspeaking and seemingly in shock. I had too much on my mind to sleep as I lay there watching the stage above, where Jock, head bowed, alone with his thoughts, sat chain-smoking, keeping vigil like a mother would for her sick family. We were like a family in Charlie Company and we all looked upon Jock as head of the family, even though we detested him most of the time and I am sure he felt the same about most of us, particularly the lower paid National Servicemen.

That night, we knew that some of our mates had died but it was only through rumour and we had no idea of the number. The loss of men had obviously affected Sergeant Major Campbell and in spite of my hate for him, I was convinced he had prevented even greater loss of life by his prompt action in rousing us at the outset. That and his swift action organising and removing vehicles from the front of the burning barn, would have prevented further loss of life including some of the civilian onlookers.

I awoke from a deep sleep and looked at my watch. It was 0500 hours at camp Roeder the morning after the fire. All around me men were snoring. I looked up at the stage. Sergeant Major Campbell was still there; sitting in the same position, head down, chain-smoking. He appeared to have taken the events of yesterday pretty badly and looked as though he had been awake all night.

I had thought him heartless once or twice, particularly on the parade ground but having slept and seeing that tough man in grief, I felt confident that he would insist on a thorough investigation into how the fire started and even if an officer had been involved, he would demand answers.

5

At Camp Roeder I rose early. Jock was still there puffing his cigarettes up on the stage as I sat up, stretched and massaged my stiff neck – the result of using my respirator as a pillow. My first thoughts were for the poor soul trapped behind bars in the barn the day before. Who was it, I wondered? And that scream? I felt my head tremble involuntarily as my jaws tightened and knuckles cracked, suddenly angry and still wondering whether it was Ginger Parker I had seen.

I felt guilty to be so concerned for Ginger and no one else at that moment as I gathered up my shaving kit to beat the rush for the washroom.

Over breakfast, rumours spread that four men including an officer, had perished and many more were dangerously ill but by the time we boarded the lorry to return us to our own camp, we had learnt the full story. Gerry Parker was dead together with three others including an officer. Seven more men, including a corporal, were dangerously ill and an eighth was receiving treatment.

Furthermore, it was confirmed that many more would have been killed had it not been for the bravery of Austrian fire-fighters who entered the burning building to rescue them and the tireless efforts of a member of Support Company and an American sergeant, who administered artificial respiration at the scene. Typically, Gerry could have walked away unscathed when the fire started, yet he had been seen re-entering the burning building to warn others. He paid for it with his life.

I reflected on those early days when I had joined up almost a year before. The army food during our basic training at Mill Hill had been awful but Ginger had made those ten weeks more bearable with his generosity, willingly sharing his mother's food parcels with us. I think she must have felt sorry for all of us because throughout the ten weeks of training, Gerry's mother kept up a generous supply of wholesome food encouraging him to share her home made cakes, chocolate bars and fruit, with those of us who shared the room with him.

Over-weight and not the fittest of men, Gerry found the rigours of army life especially gruelling and having eventually found his niche as a batman, it was sad that his life ended prematurely in that way. In training he had told us unabashed that he was in love and what a wonderful girl he was engaged to, that once demobbed they planned to marry.

As we left camp Roeder to travel back to Zeltweg, the gossipers were indicating that 2nd Lieutenant Rawlings had somehow been implicated in the fire outbreak. Still grieving the loss of Gerry, I pondered over Leggy's warning the day before, as we watched the fire raging. 'If anyone asks questions, you know nothing,' is what he had said. I couldn't get that out of my mind. Surely, if Major Appleby started the fire, he would be held accountable for it! 'It was Major Appleby – he threw a thunder-flash.' That's what the driver, or signaller, had said. Whoever it was, we all heard him. Surely, he would be a key witness!

I remembered how the huge bang had awakened me. No! On reflection, I had heard laughter before the explosion. So I must have been awake before! Then Jock started yelling for us to get out. Next thing, I saw that idiot trying to put the fire out by beating it with a pitchfork. It had all happened so quickly. Whoever was beating the flames could have been involved from the start but I couldn't see who it was! Someone in our platoon must have seen something?

The driver double de-clutched and the TCV took on a high-pitched whine as it began a fresh ascent. The men, seeking warmth, had shrunk into their wind-proofs in silence, immersed with their thoughts; no doubt they too were ruminating on the past twenty-four hours. I turned to Nigel sitting beside me and quietly, asked, "Appleby was only with us for the manoeuvres wasn't he?"

"Yar." I might have guessed Nigel would know that. He knew everything about anything.

"Of course, I can see it all now." I said, struggling with my emotions, "when Appleby threw the thunder flash and the hay caught fire, Ginger would have wanted to help get his boss out of trouble." I felt my emotions threatening to spill over yet again, probably on account of my tiredness. Major Appleby could have been indirectly responsible for Ginger's death. "Poor old Ginger – trapped . . . Was it him trying to put the fire out?"

Nigel looked to the man on his left then back at me, as he lowered his voice, "I've no idea!" He went quiet. The men were stamping their feet now to keep their blood circulating as they had done throughout the last week on the scheme. All at once, Nigel announced, "Major Appleby's very popular in the Battalion, you know." He sounded almost forgiving.

"So?"

"I believe he shot for the Regiment at Bisley," he said, nodding his head as if to say, we can't punish him too severely. Nigel's attitude annoyed me at times.

"You told me before, that Appleby was a crack shot. A crackpot, more like – for what he did yesterday. What a stupid thing to do."

"Careful Lloyd, accusations like that could get you into trouble. You didn't see him do it – it's only hearsay." Then behind his cupped hand, Nigel added, "We all know he did it, but he's innocent until proved guilty."

Nigel seemed to enjoy influencing people and me in particular. Here he was, giving me a clear warning that I felt reluctant to adhere to, although tact had never been my greatest attribute. The TCV rumbled on. Deep in thought, I considered Nigel and his reasons for feeling the way he did. His background and associates, perhaps?

At the end of the NCOs cadre, we had both been promoted to lance corporal and returned to nine platoon, sharing the same room in 'C' Company block. For the purpose of the scheme we had been acting as section leaders, facing our first real leadership challenges, unaware of the dangers we would have to face.

Nigel Pallister would have been an ideal candidate for an officers' training course at Sandhurst. He was well over six feet tall, with a high forehead and straight black hair, parted in the middle. He had a straight nose, full mouth and fine teeth. His skin was permanently tanned and he had a strong chin and thick lips – good looking, not unlike Gregory Peck, I thought. He had large hands, with well-manicured nails.

Surprisingly, in spite of his cultured background and posh sounding voice, the men respected him because he had the maturity of an established regular soldier and a lot of common sense. He had actually signed on for twenty-two years with the option to leave after three if dissatisfied. A big man, he was quietly spoken and soft on the outside but it was apparent, especially in the moments following the fire outbreak, that he possessed a hard core and a calculating mind.

His great interest was psychology and he enjoyed the challenge of analysing people and their motivations. It is true to say he had a great influence over me, yet I enjoyed the challenge of intellectual duels with him. Before the manoeuvres commenced, I had found out a great deal about Nigel Pallister but it was his confession on the third night of the scheme, when he was under the influence of drink that surprised me most. Afterwards, I had promised not to divulge his secret to anybody.

Nigel had just dozed off when Boozer broke the silence. "Wakey, wakey, Corporal! We're nearly home – you can slip between warm sheets and rest your head on a nice soft pillow tonight." Nigel lifted his head and smiled back weakly.

My ears clicked and the whine of the engine eased before adopting a more pleasurable sound as, leaving behind the sweet smell of pines, we descended to the plain. I felt relaxed as straining my eyes through the gloom to our left, I could just make out Judenburg whilst to the right, beyond the river, was the Communist town of Fohnsdorf. I smiled at the thought that news of our return to barracks would be filtering back to the Russian High Command by now.

I elbowed Dave in my excitement, "It'll be good to get back, eh!"

"Mmm!" He smiled up at me, weakly. We were all still very, very tired.

Back on the flat, the TCV began to gather speed on the snow-covered road, set hard like crystallised icing sugar, with the barracks at Zeltweg, unseen by us at the back, but what I knew would be a small black sprawl in the distance. The rest of the men were silent, their heads nodding, as I tugged at the drawstrings of my hood, suddenly aware of an incoming wind.

My head swayed uncontrollably as I stared back along the road through the open canopy, mesmerised, watching the parallel wheel tracks converging and the distant mountains shrink. Beneath us I could feel clods of snow smacking against the wheel arches to the constant flick-flack, flick-flack of the snow chains cutting into the surface. The driver also, seemed to be in a hurry to get back.

The lorry slowed and the sound changed, as the chained wheels connected with tarmac, before coming to a halt. The great sigh of relief was audible in the back of the TCV: we were home. Cocking my head around the canopy I could just see the entrance and the familiar

Regimental Crest painted on a bright background of maroon and yellow. A lance corporal, knife-sharp creases, highly bulled boots, white webbing, with a maroon armband and the letters 'RP', emerged from the guardroom and strode across to open the barrier.

It was the happiest I had felt in over a week. Thoughts of a hot bath, prolonged sleep and a decent meal were crowding my mind. The familiar 'C' Company lines were a welcome sight and the large 'C' Coy, painted on the pillar alongside the steps, all my own work, carried out during preparations for a past inspection. And the steps to the entrance, which we had dashed up on countless occasions to satisfy him, who had to be obeyed, Sergeant Major Campbell, were still intact and frost free, thanks to the fatigue party.

The prisoners, dressed in denims, with shovels and brooms, guests of the Provost Sergeant, could be seen in the distance; they had already cleared the roads for the Battalion's return under the watchful eye of a Regimental Policeman.

Nigel looked at me, chuckling, "What do they remind you of?"

I grinned back at him, rolling my eyes sideways towards Fuller in the back of the lorry "I was thinking the same thing."

It was only a couple of weeks before that Nigel and I had returned from Vienna for the NCOs cadre and seen Reg Fuller in a similar fatigue party. On that occasion he had been sent back to Zeltweg to face punishment for his crime – stealing a civilian's watch.

Everyone knew Reg was expert at removing watches from unsuspecting victim's wrists and I was sure that he had been responsible for stealing the American's watch during the scheme, but I hadn't seen him take it and it would have been wrong to accuse him without proof.

During my first few weeks in Vienna I had learnt that Reg Fuller, nickname 'Fingers' was one of the Company hard nuts – a man whose honesty could not be relied upon.

6

Reg Fuller had been one of the first men I met when I arrived at Schönbrunn Barracks in Vienna. After my, less than friendly, meeting with CSM Campbell, I had been given a briefing by the Orderly Room NCO before eventually collecting my bedding from the stores. Then I made my way to the barrack room on the first floor of the huge block that stood alongside the parade ground. As I entered the room, I was taken aback by the size and facilities within it. Bigger and more luxurious than any at home, it was centrally heated too.

It had twenty or more beds, in lines equally spaced on both sides, the foot of each facing the centre. Windows spanned the length of the wall opposite the door. Intrigued, I walked across to the only vacant bed, dumped my bedding on the open springs and looked out to see the new guard were forming up on the parade ground below.

Standing alone, I began unpacking my kit, aware of a group of men watching me from the far end of the room. Their reception, when I first entered, had been decidedly frosty – probably on account of my stripe! Feeling sore still, I felt no inclination to introduce myself as, removing my jacket, I opened the empty wardrobe alongside my bed, reached in for one of the wire hangers and slipped it into place. Then staring for a moment at the stripe and crossed swords, I was sorrowfully returning the hanger and jacket to the cupboard when from behind me I heard a warm voice of friendship.

"Hullo there!" I spun around, surprised to see a sergeant, and the first pleasant voice I had heard that day! That was my first meeting with Sergeant Legg as slamming my feet together, I pulled myself upright to face him. "Take it easy, Freeman," he said, smiling. A lump rose in my throat as like a drowning man, I grasped his outstretched hand. "They told me you were a big bloke, Freeman, now I know." I heard guffaws coming from the other end of the room.

Leggy looked eccentric the way he wore his uniform, but I took an instant liking to him, with his beret perched on his head like a chef's hat and his trousers tucked into his gaiters in a carefree manner. He didn't go in for shrinking his beret to the contours of his head, or wearing weights in his trousers to improve the fall, like so many, but his beret was well brushed and his toecaps sparkled. The ribbons on his battledress tunic told me I was in the presence of another Korean veteran.

"Sit down, Freeman," he murmured, "let's have a chat." He seemed laid back, mild mannered and very friendly, with an open face. "I'm Sergeant Legg, you'll be in my platoon – nine platoon. How're you finding things?" He said, studying my reaction.

I nodded, unconvincingly, "Fine thanks, Sarge,"

"We'll all get together tomorrow for weapon training, immediately after the morning parade. You'll recognise some of your mates from training," he said, with a wave of his hands towards the empty beds, "they're in nine as well," He seemed a caring man. "Shame about the stripe," he said, earnestly, "we'll put you on the first cadre in the New Year, it won't be long before you get it back." He had a genuine smile, revealing nice teeth, extra white against his tanned face. He raised his voice, chuckling, "So you're a PTI, we'll need you around with lay-abouts like these," he said, aloud, whilst tossing his head and looking meaningfully towards the other end of the room.

"Oh yeah!" Came a challenging reply followed by laughter. I was surprised that Leggy just shrugged off their flippancy, but I would learn in the course of time that the hardest nuts in the platoon had great respect for him.

Lowering his voice and nodding towards the empty beds, he advised, "These lads will be coming off duty shortly – they'll show you the ropes. Any questions?"

"No – thanks, Sarge."

"Okay!" He stood up, turned, marched to the other end of the room and had a quiet word with the hard men, before leaving. I felt pleased. In the time I had been in the room, quite alone, not one of them had condescended to speak to me but now I felt uplifted by his visit.

Sergeant Legg, a Cockney and a career soldier, in his mid-thirties, had a pleasant disposition and was never flustered, achieving commitment from his men through his motivational style and great sense of humour. That was why, at camp Roeder, the night of the fire, I still couldn't get it out of my mind – that warning from him, when we stood watching our mates fighting for their lives.

'Listen here the lot of you - if anyone asks questions about the fire, you know nothing! Understand?' That's what he had said – so unlike him.

With Leggy gone, and alone once more, I was conscious of being scrutinised as I continued unpacking. Slowly and self-consciously I looked up, tracing the line of tables and chairs in the centre, to where a couple of men sat on lockers at the foot of their beds, cigarettes drooping from their mouths, bulling boots. They looked up but my smile was ignored.

Recounting the chat with Leggy, I suddenly remembered, my stripe. I grabbed my jacket from inside the wardrobe, and began unpicking the chevrons with a spare razor blade, all the time fearful of slipping up and cutting the sleeve as I examined the fingers of my right hand. They were still scarred from the lacerations received one night in training, when Dave Allen and I had been forced to use an open razor blade to scrape the stains off the backs of toilets. I wondered whether Dave was one of those from training that Leggy had mentioned?

One of the men from the other end of the room, the biggest in the group, over six feet tall, pasty faced, narrow eyes and a cocky air, sauntered up. "Hi there, m' name's, Fuller." he said loudly, as he turned, winked at his cronies and extended his hand, "Reg Fuller."

"Hya," I replied, as my own hand was grasped quickly and deliberately in a vice like grip making me wince before, just in time, I managed to adjust my own grip and avoid a wet lettuce response. "Lloyd Freeman," I hissed, through clenched teeth, thankful I had managed to avoid having my knuckles crushed. He was a powerful man.

"Do you wanna buy a good watch, Freeman?" asked Fuller, retrieving his hand.

I dropped my own throbbing hand, "You kidding, not on my money!"

"Okay – suit yourself." He turned about and ambled back to his bed space, with shoulders rolling threatening to overtake his stride.

Casually, I crossed the room, switched on the lights and left seeking a cold tap. The latrines, centrally heated like the rooms, were furnished with gleaming white porcelain that included footbaths, so I thought? They were in fact bidets, the first I had ever seen. These enormous basins were higher than average at the front, with curved sides rising up and round at a thirty degree angle, ending in a huge sweep at the back. Obviously they were designed to accommodate huge bottoms. The SS must have been big men. Fat too.

When I returned, there was an excited babble coming from the room. I recognised one of the voices immediately as I opened the door – it was Boozer, so called because his surname was Boucha – pronounced Boozer in Polish. Six foot tall, he was as lean as a post and seven or eight years older than the rest us. I was so pleased to see him again.

Yanek Boucha had spent his youth in a Nazi labour camp but when freed by the allies had promptly joined up to fight the common foe. Returning to Britain as an ex-Polish serviceman after the War, he married an English girl, obtained British Nationality and was promptly called up for National Service. Unable to support a wife on NS pay, he had signed on for three years.

"Yanek! It is you – you old bastard!" I was the only one who called him by his first name.

"Hiya Lofty!" He shouted, ignoring my outstretched hand as he threw his arm around me in a fatherly manner, laughing, "Still as handsome as ever, with that Macleans smile of yours." It was the same old Yanek, always happy and very demonstrable. He hadn't changed since I had last seen him, a little older perhaps and less hair, but fatter than I had remembered from that first day we met at Mill Hill.

We had stood in the pouring rain, weighed down with bedding and feeling pretty miserable, but Yanek was the cheerful one. In spite of the bullying, with his blue eyes twinkling, he had given everybody fresh hope. His pasty face, sparse colourless eyebrows and blonde eyelashes combined, likened him to a white-faced circus clown. His lips appeared as thin purple streaks.

I heard a movement behind me and swung round to see Jim Harris. A dustman in Civvy Street, he had acquired the nickname Bins. I had first set eyes on Jim when he was one of a group of Teddy Boys, swaggering up Bittacy Hill towards the barracks at Mill Hill. Jim's head, large by any standard, with a pronounced forehead and heavy brows, seemed to diminish in size when the barber had got to work on his haircut. His hair was a little thicker now but bodily, he was still as big as a barn door with a neck like a bull. We shook hands: Jim's, a hand of bananas.

In the second week of training, Bins had suffered a personal crisis and attempted to solve it by going absent without leave. He was brought back to camp and punished, after which he secretly confessed to me, that his girl friend Maria was pregnant. Maria, it seemed, was a Catholic and had lost her own mother. The local nuns had offered her shelter and support but, the way they treated her, it was more like 'the workhouse' according to Jim and he was anxious to marry Maria and save her further suffering.

He asked me to help him by writing a letter to the Mother Superior confirming his love for Maria and willingness to marry and care for her and the baby. Bins told me what he wanted to say and I wrote it, amazed that he was such a romantic. One thing led to another and eventually the Training Sergeant arranged a weekend pass, on compassionate grounds, so that Jim Harris, Bins to his mates, could marry Maria before departing for Austria.

I asked him, "How's the old married man then?"

"Marv'lous, baby's due any time."

"I think he should get compassionate leave, don't you, Lloyd?" said Boozer. He, like the rest of us, had been surprised when the army had shown great understanding for Bins predicament whilst still in training. "Why don't you write a letter for him, Lloyd, like you did in training?"

"I would, if that's what he wants," I replied, looking at Bins quizzically. I was surprised he had told them of my involvement. The big man grinned back, nodding his head. "I'll have to get myself a typewriter at this rate," I added, laughing, "It could prove to be a good little earner."

"Can you type as well then?" Bins asked, his eyes popping.

"Better than that, I can touch-type," I replied, proudly, "over sixty words a minute – I was a Civil Servant, if you remember?"

"Christ that's a word a second, I can't even fink that fast. You could make a bomb typin' letters for the boys."

Little did I know then, my revelation that I could touch-type would have repercussions for me in the future?

I looked around for other familiar faces. "Is Dave or Ginger with you?"

"Dave's in nine too, he's on guard duty. Ginger's a batman now."

I felt pleased. We had all shared the same room and the hardships and heartbreaks together in training and a special camaraderie had developed between us in those ten weeks together. Dave and I had a lot in common. We had both worked in the City before joining the army – Dave in the bank and me a Civil Servant. Bins referred to us as 'gentlemen'. Dave's upbringing had been softer than most. An only child with older parents, he had been a 'mummy's boy' and army life had come as quite a shock to him.

Impulsively, I took Boozer to one side and quietly asked, "The bloke down the end? Fuller, what's he like?"

"Fingers? He's a right 'ard nut. I wouldn't trust him no further than I could throw him." I was reminded of my father's warning, on joining. 'There's a thief in every barrack room, they'll steal your last pair of socks'. Boozer continued, "Fuller is mates with Chopper – you need to watch those two!"

"Chopper?"

"Chopper Flynn! A lance-jack – tricky bastard, always threatening to chop our legs from under us – his favourite saying."

I realised then, that Sergeant Major Campbell had done the right thing in telling me to remove my stripe. The pressures for a rifle NCO in the Battalion seemed greater than for an NCO physical training instructor, particularly with hard nuts like 'Fingers' Fuller. On the PT Instructors course we had all been willing participants, eager to earn our coveted crossed swords, readily obeying each command by fellow fledgling instructors.

In the Battalion it was different to Aldershot, with men who had been to war; many of them had faced hordes of attackers and survived. The majority of men in Charlie Company were National Servicemen but there was a nucleus of regulars and most of these had served in Korea. The best had been promoted to warrant officers and sergeants but those that hadn't were hard men and difficult to control. I needed time to adjust.

I clashed with one of the hard cases at a very early stage. It was 'Chopper' Flynn, a man with a grudge.

7

In Vienna, a Private once more, I had been detailed for a twenty-four hour guard. It was New Year's Eve, the worst possible time for anybody to be on picket and I was determined to avoid it. Chopper Flynn was the lance corporal, second in command to the guard commander, himself a full corporal. Chopper was a regular soldier; regular also in the frequency with which he had been promoted and demoted, often as a result of fighting, usually whilst under the influence of drink and always on account of his temper.

I had been feeling quite proud of myself that morning, having bulled my kit and pressed my battledress to a high level of perfection, not without some help from my mates, hoping to be chosen for 'stick man'. The entitlement, indeed honour, meant exclusion from guard duty and I was determined to achieve it. The man selected would instead spend the day carrying out duties for the Sergeant Major or guard commander, far more preferable to spending hours in freezing temperatures throughout the night with loss of sleep.

The honour of 'stick man' was decided in the following way. One man, in excess of requirement, was always detailed for guard duty. The whole contingent would form up and the duty officer, in consultation with the duty sergeant, would select the smartest soldier on parade.

That day, as we gathered on the edge of the square waiting to be called on parade, Chopper picked on me, leering, "I see you're wearing weights, Freeman, take 'em out!"

I shrugged smiling and mingled with the others – he wasn't serious surely? My weights, the same as most of the men's, were tiny pieces of lead strung on a cord and held in the overhang of my thick serge trousers. This ensured the trouser creases stood out – much smarter. It was common knowledge that the use of weights resulted in undue wear and tear on trousers and was officially forbidden by the Army. However, the Regiment turned a blind eye to their use in the interests of all round smartness.

Chopper edged closer and rasped, "You 'eard what I said, Freeman – take 'em out!" To obey Chopper's order would mean, laying my freshly polished rifle on the wet ground, removing my gaiters, soiling the brasses on my buckles and dislodging my belt and jacket, just to re-arrange the tucks for my trousers – and certain failure to achieve the coveted award of 'stick man'. From the corner of my eye, I could see help approaching – the guard commander, a decent man.

Chopper too had seen him and moved fast as he stepped in front of me, his rifle slung across his chest menacingly as he looked up, snarling, "Yes or no? Don't push me – what is it?" The guard commander arrived at that moment just in time and ordered us to fall in. Chopper now turned his attention to the new arrival, pleading, "Freeman's wearing weights, Corp, I've told him to take them out."

The guard commander too was wearing weights as looking at his watch, he over-ruled, "We haven't time for that now, fall in."

Out of earshot of the guard commander, Chopper turned to me, threatening, "You'd better watch yourself Freeman. If you so much as step out of line, I'll chop your fucking legs from under yuh!"

There, I had heard it for myself – the famous threat: and the look in his eyes scared me. In his early twenties Chopper Flynn had been good looking once, but not now. His face looked totally repulsive due to a life-changing disfigurement. He had a deep furrow across his pug nose and left cheekbone where, it was said, a bullet had carved its path. A skin graft of some sort had left part of his top lip disfigured, which devoid of hair was bright pink in colour.

His scarring had left him with a permanent grudge frequently levied upon the men under his command. Some said he was lucky for having cheated death; others declared it was a pity the 'Gooks' in Korea had just missed him.

In spite of his appearance and disposition, he was a useful member of a fighting unit and as an NCO, was capable of selfless heroism. Swarthy, short in stature and broader than average, his dull brown eyes could pick out a target at three hundred yards as if it was a mere stones throw away. The badge on his sleeve, of crossed-rifles, confirmed him to be a marksman on the 303 rifle.

My stand that morning paid off. I was awarded 'stick man' leaving Chopper even more determined to 'get me' though he little realised his opportunity would come that same evening when, along with my mates, I celebrated the New Year in the NAAFI and received my first initiation to the evils of Gosser beer.

At ten pence-half-penny a bottle, the heaviest drinkers could enjoy a good night for less than five shillings, in old money. Three pints of it and my head was spinning as along with the others, I struggled to remain upright as we made our way back to the safety of the barrack room and a welcome bed. I had grown to respect Jock Campbell for some unaccountable reason and in my drunken state was praising his virtues – I minor blip, as I announced.

"He's a good 'un, I tell yuh!"

Boozer was not convinced, as we staggered across the square, through a flurry of snow. "Lloyd, you're pished. It's time for bed. If Chopper could see you now, he'd have you inside the guardhouse quicker than Bins could sink a pint."

"I'm not talking about that bastard – I mean Jock," I said, with a loud belch. "Anyway, I ain't done nuffin wrong." Then I remember falling and rolling over and over spitting out snow, fascinated with the taste – like coconut ice, a favourite of mine. I struggled to my feet and staggered forward.

"You're pished I tell yuh."

The 'Canteen Cowboy', the NCO in charge of the NAAFI, had just ejected us from the best bar in town but not until Bins and Boozer had managed to restrain me from doing something stupid. A night's drinking had obliterated all thoughts of homesickness but had revealed an aggressive streak in me I hadn't felt before.

I tried to stand up then staggered forward, clawed at Boozer and fell over again. Strong beer that Gosser! This time the snow must have had a sobering effect for I remember lying there on my back for an age looking around. During the evening the heavy fall of snow had changed the face of Schönbrunn Barracks and it was so quiet everywhere, so deathly quiet.

The pure white roofs looked stark, against the reflected glow of the clouds beyond – coloured lighting of Vienna nightlife. A moving spectacle of red and orange clouds merged and flickered rekindling sad memories of a distant past, the London Blitz. As a child, together with my brothers, I had watched the sky eleven miles to the south of us, a deep scarlet and yellow wash across the horizon, as the City of London burned.

I began to feel nostalgic as my thoughts turned to Christmas at home; Dad would have been playing the piano with the family around him drinking, cracking nuts and singing – 'Hometown', one of my favourites. I choked up – homesick again.

My eyes focused on the main arch of the barracks, clearly visible across the square, the underside illuminated by the streetlights beyond. A vehicle passed by producing flickering shadows on the wall and an impression of people entering. I imagined what it must have been like in the War, as visions of German armour and troops marching through the gate, the way I had seen it on newsreels, crossed my mind. I was drifting when I felt somebody grab me under the arms.

"Come on – you can't sleep there," Boozer's voice, announced, as he struggled to lift me.

"Leave 'im," shouted Bins, from behind, "It'll sober 'im up."

I made a supreme effort and rose up once more, struggling to stay upright, as a new inspiration warmed me. I began mimicking the Guv'nor, barking commands whilst goose-stepping across the square, shouting, "Git your feet up, soldier!" Then down I went once more with my feet flaying the air. I rolled over and peered through snow-caked eyelashes in the direction of the guardroom.

Suddenly a real vehicle was entering, then another, their lights dazzling. A hush fell all around and I realised the others had thrown themselves down alongside me. The weight of an arm pressed down on my back. "Was a' matter?"

"Shuddup, Lloyd!" It was Bins. He sounded worried.

The headlights swung across the square like prison camp searchlights as the vehicles rolled in. The first was a military police vehicle – completely white with four national flags printed on the front door. Usually a military policeman from each nation travelled in these. The second car was black – Austrian Police. I didn't remember anymore until . . . .

. . . . . . I heard Boozer, saying, "Grab his right shoulder, Binnsy, I'll take his left, let's sit him up." It was the first day of the New Year as my mates tried to wake me from my drunken stupor.

"I dunno, you'd fink by now he'd a' learnt to take his drink wouldn't yuh!"

"Turn that light out, it's hurting my eyes!"

"What light, there ain't no light! It's daylight!"

"Take his right arm, Binnsy, I'll take his left."

"Where am I? What am I doing in bed?"

"Fuckin' 'ell, he weighs a ton!"

73

"Give his face a slap, Boozer, we can't lift 'im until he's sobered up a bit."

"Wakey! - wakey! - come on dreamboat, it's time to get up!" Boozer was dangling one of Bins' sweaty socks under my nose and chuckling to himself, "If these don't wake him, nothing will."

I shuddered and screwed my face up as one eye opened and my hands went up to my temples, the pain almost unbearable. "Piss off Yanek, I wanna sleep!" My head felt swollen and too tender to touch. I closed my eyes, conscious of the cackling around me as mercifully I sank back into oblivion.

Boozer persisted, "Come on, Nancy Boy, stop shagging that pillow, Jock's called a parade!" There was urgency in Boozer's tone as he grabbed my shoulders, shaking me.

"Fuck off, Boozer, I wanna sleep for Chri' sake."

"Either you get up or you'll be on a charge," Boozer shouted, yanking the sheets off the bed, "We're on parade in half an hour, Jock's orders. Bins reckons there was a mugging in Vienna last night and one of our lot did it."

The name Jock had an immediate sobering effect on me as mechanically I swung my legs over the side of the bed and straightened up; those legs, they didn't feel like mine, buckled beneath me and I crashed to the floor. "I can't, I'm still pissed – hey! Where's my pants?" I was completely naked.

"Move out the way, Boozer, I'll lift 'im," said Bins. I was being mugged myself that morning as Bins hauled me to my feet, slung me across his shoulder like a bare doll and marched across to the door. Two minutes later I was dropped unceremoniously into a shower basin and the tap was turned on, ice cold, with the others laughing in the background – then silence.

All at once a gentler voice cut through the sprinkling sound, "Here, Lloyd, I've left your shaving gear on the side." I glanced up to see Dave. The way he looked at me, I thought he was going to cry – a real softie was Dave.

"I'm okay, Dave, don't look so worried, I'll survive. Ouch! That was my head." His appearance, completely dressed too, except for his belt and beret, was probably enough to trigger my recovery, as slipping and sliding around like an eel on a fishmonger's slab, I managed to stand up then showered and shaved where I stood, before practically running back to the barrack room shedding water everywhere.

"You'd betta move yerself, Cocker – we're on p'rade in fifteen minutes," announced Bins, throwing me a towel.

"What is it - a church parade or something?" I staggered to the window and looked out to see the snow had almost cleared: it was a dull morning and the parade ground looked wet.

"You weren't the only one making trouble last night," said Boozer, "The Austrian police are here – they want us to attend an identification parade. They're looking for someone. I bet Jock's mad, it's ruined his lay in."

"Who spiked my drink," I said, aloud.

"They all say that, Lloyd, you just can't take yuh booze – that's all I can say," said Bins, "I follared you outa the NAAFI and as soon as the air 'it yuh, you went down, like a sack o' taiters."

I shook my head as I reached for my jacket, my head spinning still. "Why the ID parade?"

"They reckon a Russian officer was slung in the Danube last night and they believe it was one of our lot that did it." Boozer sounded excited.

"No it weren't," interrupted Bins, "One of our lot done a 'queer' over and nicked his gold watch."

"Who told you that?"

Bins chuckled as he rolled his eyes towards the other end of the barrack room and tapped the side of his nose with his index finger. We all looked in the direction indicated as Bins threw back his head grinning. "If you're finkin' what I'm finkin'," he said, ducking his head from side to side and thumbing his nose, "Fingers went inta Vienna last night to celebrate, didn't 'e, and 'e ain't been seen this mornin' since breakfast."

"Celebrate – what for?"

"He told Bins he's been selected for an NCOs cadre in Zeltweg," said Dave.

I straightened my tie and choked; it felt tight on my throat. "Anyone got a drink, my mouth tastes like shit."

"Poo, your breath stinks like it, here, have a hair of the dog." Boozer handed me a half empty bottle of stale Gosser – it tasted awful but it felt like cool milk as I swigged it, soothing my burning tonsils. I secured the front buttons of my battledress, and then fastened my belt whilst closing my eyes to relieve the pain. I opened them and looked down.

"Shit!" I stood there in bare feet.

Boozer, laughing aloud, retrieved a sock from one side of my bed and another from inside it and bent over holding them as I slid my feet in one at a time whilst steadying myself on Bin's massive shoulders. Dave slid my boots across for me to step into before sitting back on the bed to lace them up. I then tucked my trouser bottoms roughly into the tops of my socks and secured the puttees that Dave had handed me. I looked up to see Boozer staring at me, laughing, his shoulders twitching.

"Stop taking the piss you."

"We've re-named you, Lucky Lloyd, after last night," he said, steadying me. "Hey, Lloyd, your jacket's pulled up."

"Why lucky?" I removed my belt and buttoned my trousers to my jacket at the back.

"You were lucky you didn't get slung inside – you refused to leave the NAAFI at closing time." Boozer tossed a cigarette across to Bins and then lit one himself. "The canteen cowboy wanted to call out the guard to have you forcibly removed."

"Why?"

"You freatened to stick one on 'im," said Bins, chuckling, "you reckoned he'd ruined a good night." I re-fastened my belt and looked at Dave for confirmation.

"It's no good looking at him," said Boozer, "He'd already gone back to bed – he knew when he'd had enough, not like some people, right Dave?" Dave nodded, sadly. I think I disappointed him that night.

"So what happened?"

"We finally managed to persuade you to leave quietly. Then you insisted on marching across the square, calling out orders, taking the piss out of Jock. You must remember all this surely? If Chopper had seen you, he'd have nicked you for sure."

"Chopper hates my guts for some reason," I said, as we made our way down the stairs.

8

That morning at Schönbrunn, after the mugging, I remember, Jock had been so determined to find the culprit, he made us all suffer – as if it was our fault we had a thief in our ranks! A professional soldier, he was wedded to the Regiment and would have felt ashamed I guess for what Fuller did – at least we were all sure that he had done it at the time.

The lads had practically carried me down the stairs and as I stepped outside, the cold air and Leggy waiting alongside the parade ground had an immediate sobering effect. It was then I remembered the cars entering the barracks the night before when we were cavorting on the square, pissed out of our minds. It had to be the reason for this sudden parade.

Leggy had looked worried. "Do as you're told men – we'll get this over as quickly as possible and you can get back on your beds." He was doing his best to lift our spirits whilst, on the other side of the square, the CSM waited angrily. We were late on parade. I could just imagine the pressure on Leggy. He had probably had a briefing in the mess beforehand with Jock dictating the sergeants' role. The Guv'nor would almost certainly have decided then to make us suffer for the disgrace the incident had brought upon the Regiment. At times like that he was brutal.

I had visions of him, standing alongside a Christmas tree festooned with baubles and lights, enveloped in smoke, grinding his jaws, with his sergeants talking excitedly about the rumours going around and the reason for calling the meeting. He hated speculation and careless chitchat, and his eyes would have been scanning the room for any negative feelings.

The parade had been called for ten-thirty but it was closer to eleven o'clock when the sergeants marched our platoons onto the parade ground; once assembled, they loudly declared the absentees in the ranks. We were all there until Sergeant Legg spoke up for nine platoon.

"One man unaccounted for, Sir," he bellowed.

Jock scowled, "His name, Sergeant?"

"Private Fuller, Sir."

Someone mumbled, "Fingers! He's inside most likely."

"Quiet in the ranks!" The Führer seemed angrier than ever, as he demanded "Is he in camp, Sergeant?"

"He hasn't been seen this morning, Sir."

Jock gave a cursory nod; so that was it, Bins had been right all along. Okay, I thought, 'just dismiss us – you know who did it'. But no, Jock had other ideas.

Jock Campbell had served in Aden, Palestine, Italy, France, Singapore and Korea, most of the time at war, so I imagined this posting in Austria had to be the most enjoyable; for him, peace at last and moments to savour in this, his sixteenth year in the army. A self-declared, fun loving man off duty, his actual sense of humour was sadly lacking, as far as we other ranks were concerned. He was, in fact, a harsh disciplinarian and the most feared and respected CSM in the Battalion.

Standing well back from the body of men, he eyed each of us as he passed along the front rank, before stopping; then leaning back slightly, he drew a visionary line along the heads of the front row and pointing at one man with his stick, he ordered. "You – change places with him," as he indicated another in the line – it had to be just right to satisfy him. Then, with great deliberation he marched several paces in the opposite direction, came smartly to attention and with a stamp of his foot, calmly turned about to face us. Was it a hangover or pride that produced the whimsical look on his face? The onslaught was about to commence.

Jock would have been annoyed that the best New Year party in a long time had been spoiled. The sergeants would have enjoyed themselves well enough with good food, ample drink and plenty of laughs. I could just see it, dear old Leggy, in fine form, playing 'Jingle Bells', clapping the spoons to and fro on his knees, amid a spontaneous rendering of the song with the sergeants singing their own words; words they had picked up in the ranks, no doubt.

The others would have excelled, balancing on upturned beer bottles, seeing how far they could stretch without damaging their wrists and many other party games; Jock, I've no doubt, would have been prancing up and down with his version of the Highland fling, not bad considering he would have been three parts gone. Yes, he liked his booze and on occasions, he had been known to enter camp the worse for drink, after an off duty visit to Vienna.

Jock, robbed of his lie-in, would have been feeling fragile, like the rest of us. He was a chain smoker: his first cigarette of the day was probably smoked in bed before rising and the last before switching out the light. That morning he would have already demolished half a packet by then, I'm sure. He was about to make us pay.

Now, Sergeant Major Campbell, the quintessence of a perfect CSM, took a deep breath and sucked in his stomach simultaneously.

Then he threw back his head and from the pit of his stomach, let rip with the first command, sharp, crisp, menacing, a foretaste of what was to come.

"Company!"

Then, bellowing orders and waving his stick like an orchestral conductor, he commenced a marching routine practiced a thousand times before, as the silence of Schönbrunn was shattered, exhausting us with left turns, right turns, about turns and worst of all frequent doses of marching on the spot with knees held high. Nothing hurts more, particularly after a night of boozing. The sergeants supported him, moving amongst us, belting out the timing of steps with their monotonous, "Left, right, left, right, left …" to maintain pace.

Prior to drill starting, my mates had more or less supported me physically until the cold morning air had eased my hangover. Now I was on my own with an empty stomach and a throbbing head, a lethal cocktail before a spell of square-bashing as I felt my energy dwindling with every step and a feeling of sickness in my gut. The Führer meanwhile, was determined to punish us on several counts – the mugging, getting him up early, and causing him embarrassment by being late on parade.

If his intention had been to turn us against the perpetrator of the crime, he had got it wrong for with each painful manoeuvre, the feelings of anger were directed at him instead. I especially hated him at that moment, as my own hangover took effect, but pride was about to take over!

Campbell was a perfectionist and apart from wanting to make us suffer, he was also showing off, giving an exhibition of drill to the group of civilians, on the far side of the square, who had just emerged from the Officers' Mess.

We too, had seen them and responded with renewed vigour, our cheeks flushed and chests heaving, in spite of our anger. Now the combined, Gosser-charged breath of eighty pairs of lungs could be seen drifting like smoke across the parade ground in the cold morning air, whilst our hob-nailed boots, stamping in perfect time, echoed off the buildings around the square, bang, bang, bang!

Finally, Jock called "HALT!" and with an almighty crash, one hundred and sixty studded boots hit the tarmac within a split second of each other, the men in three ranks, line abreast, in close order facing the Union Flag, lungs screaming for oxygen in the thin morning air.

The 'open order' command was given – not good enough – 'close order' – start again. That man was never satisfied, or was it that he wanted to show us off again for the visitors? At last, we saw that he visibly enjoyed the crispness of the last manoeuvre and a thin smile cracked his face. Then, glaring triumphantly, he stood us at ease, most of us completely exhausted, to await the inspection.

From the corner of my eye I could see the Company Commander, obvious by his paunch and bulging cheeks, leading the small body of men as they ambled onto the square. In the party was the second lieutenant, who had been duty officer the previous day, and three other men in civilian clothes, all fortified against the cold with schnapps from the officers' mess, no doubt.

The Guv'nor called us to attention, spun around to face the guests, crashed his nimble feet together, tucked his stick under the left arm, the fingers of his left hand stretched straight along the shaft, saluted, and in his usual clipped delivery, lied out loud, "All present and correct, Sir!"

We could hardly believe it! Clearly he was covering up for Fuller, or was it for the Company, or more importantly the Regiment and we were witness to it? Was the Company Commander aware he was hiding Fuller's absence?

The portly Major smiled, flicked his hand across his right eye in a casual way and quietly introduced the guests. I was not alone feeling the pain after the marching and felt on the point of collapse when the Major, with a cursory nod in the direction of the parade, said something to Jock who promptly turned about and gave the order for us to stand at ease and stand easy. I heard a murmur of discontent further down the line. Jock heard it too and with his face contorted in anger, growled, "Take that man's name, Sergeant."

Sergeant Carter was beside the culprit in a flash, notebook out and writing. I turned my head a fraction and caught sight of one of the visitors close up. Bins had been right, this one looked every bit a homosexual as he walked behind the rest, his eyes scanning the lines of men, whilst staring intently at each individual in passing. The others walked slightly ahead of the victim, a lonely figure who was impregnating the air with his perfume, a noticeably feminine one. A hard nut in eight platoon smiled and pursed his lips seductively as the man stood before him. Jock spotted him and pounced, "Eyes front soldier!" he rasped, the look on his face betraying his feelings.

The homosexual, quite flustered, quickly moved on to the next man and so on until eventually he paused opposite Bins who smiled and shot him a wink. Jock missed it but it provided a lighter talking point after the parade.

It was at this point in the proceedings that we saw a military police car stop at the barrier. A 'Red-Cap' alighted followed by Fuller who was then escorted into the guardroom. So, had Jock known all along that 'Fingers' was in custody when he announced to the Company Commander the men were 'all present and correct' or was there some other ulterior motive for the parade?

Finally, the fiasco ended – they had found who they were looking for, that seemed obvious, especially since Reg Fuller was the only one absent and he had been arrested. With the inspection over, we were marched off the square and once dismissed, began making our way to the barrack rooms. Dave caught me up as I entered the building. "Tell me Lloyd, what will happen to Fuller?"

"Fingers? If he did the mugging he'll get out of it somehow, I'm sure."

"What a bender," said Boozer, as we ambled back to our room, "I don't know what he had on, but he smelt like a brothel."

"I wouldn't know what a brothel smells like!" I replied, chuckling.

"I feel knackered after that," came a voice from the past. I spun around to see Gerry Parker, overweight and pasty-faced with plump cheeks and ill-fitting uniform, now an officer's batman.

"So they roped you in too did they, Ginger?" It was the first time I had seen him for days. "You're beginning to look round-shouldered Ginge – all that kit cleaning I suppose?"

"I couldn't get out of it," he replied, his eyelids blinking, an affliction it seemed.

"Makes a change seeing you on parade," said Boozer, as he took a step back.

Gerry sniffed, another habit of his, "Yeah, but I'm always too busy cleaning his kit, ain't I. I've gotta get back now and prepare his stuff for tonight – he's duty officer you know."

"You were always a dab hand at bulling," I said, "do you remember that night in training, Ginger, when you blancoed my kit for me?"

"Yeh! I remember," he sniffed, "when that bastard Levy put you and Dave on cleaning the toilets."

"Yes, with razor blades, remember?"

He shrugged and moved closer, talking into my face, "You never told me you used razor blades to clean 'em?"

"We did," said Dave, joining in the conversation, "our fingers were bleeding – I've still got the scars, here, see!"

Ginger winced as Dave proffered his hand, sniffing again, "Yeah, I remember now. Then after lights out, I went outside to collect our kit off the blanco table. It was bloody freezing."

Over dinner, Ginger, well informed, told us the identity parade had been called to find the second man involved in the mugging. He had acted as a decoy, distracting the homosexual, whilst Fuller stole the man's watch.

"Yeh!" he said, in glowing terms, "The queer hadn't been hurt at all. They reckon he fell in love with our bloke and that's who they were looking for." He laughed aloud, "Couldn't wait to see him again!"

"Err! Sick, ain't it," said Bins.

"But he didn't pick anyone out on parade did he?" Said Dave.

"No," said Gerry, "But I fink they've got a fair idea who it was – but I can't say."

"Eh!"

"Come on Ginge – you can tell us."

"No!"

We never found out the 'third man' who was supposed to have helped Fuller. The watch was never found and Fuller denied everything. He was charged with being absent without leave and returned to Zeltweg under escort to serve time in 'Jim's Guesthouse'. But, Fuller, aptly referred to as 'Fingers' never relinquished his jackdaw-like desire to purloin other people's property, watches in particular.

As for the 'third man', Gerry always refused to tell us his identity. Now he was gone, we would never know and even Nigel, in spite of his contacts was never able to resolve that one.

9

There were around nine hundred men in the Battalion, so it was inevitable that a nucleus of them were always available, serving detention for some crime or other, thus providing a ready source of supervised labour around the camp – cutting grass, sweeping roads, removing litter or painting kerb stones. This was the first sight on returning to Zeltweg – the fatigue party from the guardhouse cleaning up and they had done a good job.

The barracks looked immaculate with leafless deciduous trees, in neat rows fronting the barrack blocks. Yet more trees, equally spaced in the central area, lined narrow pathways, now cleared of snow and snaking like a giant fan, to link company lines to the cookhouse, NAAFI, cinema and adjoining buildings. These glowed pink in the dying sun welcoming our return.

Beyond the administrative buildings were the old Luftwaffe aircraft hangars and a vast plain, the size of six football pitches, stretching into the distance and covered in a six-inch thick blanket of snow. It had once been the airfield, stretching to the foot of the mountains beyond, maybe a mile or so distant. Part of it, an acre or so, situated just beyond the camp hospital, had been concreted over and served as a parade ground.

I smiled to myself remembering the first time we had spotted the aircraft hangars and the superb drawings of German aircraft adorning the walls, mainly Messerschmitts and Junkers. One of the aircraft enthusiasts had quipped, "I don't see any Fokkers?"

The training NCO, who must have been asked the same question many times, smiling, replied. "No, the Fuckers gave themselves up when we arrived in forty-four."

Beyond the airfield, the snow-covered mountains, a spectacular sight, were clothed in pink snow. I shivered, yearning for spring and warmer temperatures. My mind returned to the nightmare of the manoeuvres. It seemed a lot longer than a week since we had set out on 'Exercise Roundup'.

I had felt excited then as we set out on the scheme, a joint exercise, with our American allies.

* * *

Aroused at o'five hundred with the rest of the Battalion, we had stepped out into the darkness and shivered like dogs emerging from a dip in the sea. As I hurried across to the cookhouse, my nostril hairs were pricking like thorns and it felt as if the cold air would crystallise my lungs. All around I had seen shadows of men, distinguishable by their plates glistening in the camp lights, pouring out of their barrack blocks with the same objective, a hot breakfast.

To my left, lights blazed in the billets strung out in the shape of a crescent with the dying moon providing a luminous crest around one solitary unlit building, that of 'A' Company, the one that had replaced ours in Vienna. In the distance the mountain range looked cold and forbidding, their outline over that distance appearing like giant slag heaps, except that we knew they were more rugged and swamped in snow.

Suddenly I felt a tug, as Boozer, coming from behind and sliding in the light covering of snow, used my arm to steady himself. "Too important to walk with us now you're a corporal, I suppose," he taunted, laughing.

"Bollocks, I stopped you falling didn't I?" Years of living on a starvation diet in a Nazi concentration camp had left Boozer resilient to the cold, but he looked bigger than usual that morning on account of his extra padding. "I see you're determined to keep out the cold then, Boozer."

He chuckled, "Too True - It's going to be fucking cold in the mountains." Pointing to his camouflaged jacket, he said, "I'm wearing my pyjamas under this lot." The flimsy jacket, supposedly weatherproof, was anything but!

"Yeah, I'm wearing my thick greys under this lot, did you tell the others?"

"You kidding, they told me."

"I'm talking about the sprogs, just out of training."

"I told 'em," said Bins, as he drew alongside, "those jackets they gave us ain't gonna be much use and the uvver blokes ain't got climatised yet."

Alerted by the rumble of engines, we turned to see a convoy of TCVs using sidelights only, entering the camp. "I reckon they're for us to travel in, don't you?"

"You 'ave a way of comin' out with the fuckin' obvious," scoffed Bins, as he playfully nudged Boozer with his elbow.

As we walked into the cookhouse, Ginger came hurrying out. I confronted him, smiling, "Don't usually see you up this early – couldn't you sleep?"

"Bloody cheek, I'm always up early – *Corporal*," he replied, laughing as he emphasised the term. The other two moved on as Ginger, looking flustered, blurted, "Congratulations on your promotion, Lloyd."

"Thanks," I said, backing off a pace, "you've done pretty well for yourself I see. Batman to Major Appleby now – what's he like?"

"He's a bloody good bloke," he replied earnestly, his eyelids fluttering.

I smiled, looking sideways and pulling a face, disbelieving.

He sniffed, smiling, "No really, Lloyd, he's a very nice man – quiet, easy to please and he's very generous."

"You'll be all right then, sleeping in a gasthaus every night this week, I bet."

That was the last time I actually spoke to Gerry Parker.

Returning from breakfast that morning we could see the TCVs had already dispersed and were lined up in threes and fours in front of each building. Others were assembled out on the tarmac alongside the disused aircraft hangars, waiting to trundle forward, where shadowy figures were already loading a 'three tonner' at the Quartermaster's stores. Dodging between two vehicles in front of 'C' Block, we spotted the Sergeant Major directing operations. Quickening our pace, we headed for the entrance steps.

"Corporal Freeman!" Too late, he had spotted me – nothing escaped that man. The other two disappeared into the block laughing at my misfortune. "I want the men on parade in twenty minutes. Make sure they leave nothing behind. See to it!" His voice was unusually quiet and reassuring. I felt good. Is he treating me differently now that

I am an NCO? I lingered a while too long. "Well get a move on," he rapped.

Back in the room, I told Nigel the news that Gerry Parker was batman to the new Company Commander.

"Ginger's a lucky man. Major Appleby – he's a bloody good bloke."

"That's what Ginger said."

"He served with the Chindits in Burma in the last War. He won't be with us much longer though. I guess he's due for promotion soon. A staff role in the War Office no doubt."

"Nigel, you astound me at times," I said, adjusting my small pack, "How the hell do you know these things?"

Even then, I had felt troubled regarding Nigel. I didn't really know this man I shared my room with? Rumours about him had proliferated in the Company, some with substance but many, nothing more than speculation. His predictions were invariably ninety-nine per cent accurate and he seemed to know so much about what was going on in the Officers' Mess. It couldn't be an officer liaison – he was rarely out of my sight. Besides, officers and other ranks (ORs) were entirely different breeds.

Oh shit! Jock was calling us out on parade to assemble for the scheme.

"Get on parade!" My spine froze at the sound of his voice; it seemed more hollow than usual, with the beds and lockers cleared. The response was immediate, as men grabbed kit and rifles and fled outside onto the snow-covered road before lining up in two ranks for inspection.

The Gov'nor paused alongside one of the youngsters, fresh out of training, and with the faintest smile, advised quietly, "Lengthen your shoulder straps laddie and tighten your belt, you look like a badly wrapped parcel." He turned to one of the NCOs, his voice more brittle, "Give him a hand, Corporal!"

Sergeant Legg emerged from the empty barrack block and joined the parade. Jock looked at him, half-smiling, "You satisfied, Sergeant?" He seemed in an unusually good mood. It was all right for him, he enjoyed playing soldiers but most of us loathed it with a passion.

Leggy snapped to attention, his style respectful, in front of the men, "All present and correct, Sergeant Major."

Jock remained silent, his jaws twitching. Contemplating. Occasionally he would turn his head towards the guardroom and camp exit – waiting for some kind of signal, perhaps? We were all kept waiting, the cold beginning to penetrate the flimsy lining of our outer garments, so-called wind proofs. A loud fart erupted in the rear rank as a mumbled voice was heard, "Fall out the officers!" It sounded like Reg Fuller's voice – returned to the Company having served his time after the Vienna mugging.

Jock frowned. Eventually he spoke, his voice firm and reassuring, "Right - first vehicle, seven platoon, the next eight, nine take the last." He looked down at his boots, then back at the men, "Load up!" There was a mad scramble to climb aboard the TCVs, their engines still turning over. I ushered my section to keep together and checked them onto the vehicle before levering myself up and into the seat nearest the tailboard – my first error. It was to be the coldest spot throughout the journey and the week that followed.

My section sat in a line. The smartest by far was Fuller, the result of more than two weeks intensive bulling in 'Jim's Guesthouse', the affectionate name for the guardhouse. Jim was the Provost Sergeant, Jim O'Shaughnessy. I noticed that Fuller had moved deep inside the vehicle close to Chopper Flynn – two of a kind, I thought, at the time.

The rest sat in silence, immersed in their own thoughts, watching the officers and sergeants silhouetted in the dense fog of diesel fumes and vapours, looking more like red devils in the vehicle tail-lights as they conferred, synchronising their watches. The stench of fuel was nauseating. I removed my gloves, blew into the palms of my hands and rubbed them together vigorously, as I watched the "brains of the Battalion". I was already feeling the cold right through to my spine and we hadn't even begun.

The new Company Commander, Major Appleby, smart appearance, slightly built, thick brows and older than average, appeared for a brief moment and was greeted with reverence and then laughter by the two junior officers when he spoke to them.

"Well share the fucking joke with us then!" mumbled one of the men - greeted with nervous laughter from inside the canopy.

Nigel looked across from the seat opposite and mouthed, "What did I tell you? I said he was popular." He continued, speaking aloud in his cultured public school accent, "You know where they're taking us, Lloyd, don't you?" I shook my head – I didn't really care, I just hoped it was somewhere warm. He leaned forward in a confidential manner, "It's Camp Macauley, an American camp at Linz."

The Regiment were required to provide a full contingent of men at company strength in Vienna, so 'A' company had borrowed some of our NCOs. This practice, quite normal, had a continuous debilitating effect throughout the Battalion reflected in a general shortage of NCOs. So Nigel and myself, both newly appointed lance corporals, were to perform full corporal roles for the duration of the scheme. Even Sergeant Legg was acting platoon commander, an officer's role, and Sergeant Eames was performing two roles, nine platoon sergeant and quarter master sergeant.

Sergeant Legg, map in hand, emerged from the mist and addressed Nigel and myself, smiling. "Are all your men here, you two?"

"All present and correct, Sarge!"

He peered over the tailboard and into the depths of the TCV. "And yours, Corporal Flynn?"

"Skip!" replied Chopper, bobbing his head and laughing, like a child on his first outing.

I re-checked my men to make doubly sure. Boozer, Bins and Dave, were already well established together with Pearce and Hagley, all capable of looking after themselves, but I now had three newcomers – Fuller, the latest and a couple more fresh out of training, Paddy Molloy and Bill Storer.

The exercise started well enough and it was still dark as the convoy of fifteen or more vehicles, their engines in low whining gears, rolled past the guardroom and left camp. Nigel was right – our destination was Camp Macauley, the American army base camp near Linz.

Once clear of our barracks at Zeltweg, we settled down to a long cold journey in the back of the unheated TCV, but we little realised that we would spend most of the next five days doing just that, sitting in the vehicle unmoving, apart from stamping our feet and rubbing our hands together to kindle our circulation.

The TCV had a waterproof cover stretched over a tubular steel frame to protect us from the elements, with the rear end open. Much of the central aisle was taken up with bedrolls, backpacks and boxes of food, our sustenance for the journey. This consisted of tinned compo rations that required no preparation. These included hard tack, margarine and chocolate, better known as 'clacker' for some reason.

There were about thirty of us sitting, shoulder-to-shoulder, either side of the vehicle on long bench seats padded with the thinnest of layers for our bottoms and backs. Body heat insulation, partly fulfilled by the wiser of us, was achieved wearing army issue thick grey pyjamas beneath our uniforms. However, once the cold penetrated our outer garments, the woolly greys served, if anything, to retain it.

Nigel and I sat on opposite sides of the vehicle at the furthermost and coldest point, the open end, closest to the tailboard.

He looked across at me, "At last we are on our way. I can't stand sitting around." I nodded, anxious to avoid unnecessary chatter in the open air. Low temperatures were unsympathetic to my lips, besides which, it was difficult to conduct a quiet conversation across the void of the vehicle, what with the noise of the engine and the wind ripping at the shrouds.

In spite of my doubts, Nigel Pallister and I had become good mates. He had arrived in Austria a couple of weeks before me and judging by the condition of his uniform, the shine on his cap badge, his brasses and confident manner, he had already served much longer.

The engine whined as the TCV climbed higher and higher. Beyond the tailboard all we could see were pine trees and snow – no girls to whistle – no other vehicles to observe – the rest of the convoy had disappeared.

At this early stage of the journey, the cold had already penetrated the outer layers of our clothing and boots and the noise of the engine was exceeded by the rhythmic sound of stamping feet on the metal floor of the TCV, the only means of maintaining any form of circulation in our feet and bodies.

Around mid-afternoon the noise of the engine became subdued as the speed increased and we began to descend to lower levels. The temperature improved a degree or two and the mist lifted. A couple of lorries in our convoy re-appeared in the distance.

An hour later Camp Macauley came into sight and as we rumbled through the gates of the American camp, we realised immediately that compared with our own barracks, these were more like Buckingham Palace.

10

At Camp Macauley, everywhere looked newly built and organised on a grand scale Even the detention camp for felons from within the American's own ranks, dwarfed anything we had ever seen, more like a stockade. It was fenced in and topped with rolls of barbed wire, with armed guards manning look-out towers at strategic points within the compound. In the U.S. Army it seemed, the bad guys were much more dangerous than our own.

Feeling like paupers – bedraggled, blue nosed and shivering we lowered our frozen limbs from the lorries, shouldered our weapons, adjusted our berets, stamped our feet and looked around awestruck.

Faced with a, teeth chattering, half-frozen body of men on the road before him, Sergeant Major Campbell, proud and unbending, was determined to show American observers his men were made of sterner stuff. He turned to face us, steely eyed, jaws twitching, signalling danger for malingerers.

"Company! Com-pan-y . . . shun!" We sprang to attention, heads up, shoulders back, waists pulled in, looking inches taller. Setting a good example himself in deportment, he strutted among us, eyeing each man, criticising and correcting our postures in turn, daring anyone to wilt or defy him. Then facing us once more, he announced.

"We'll spend the night here as guests – don't abuse it. The scheme will commence tomorrow morning. We'll be moving out at first light. You'll be spending a great deal of time in the vehicles but be ready to de-bus for action at a moment's notice." The announcement was greeted with silence. Just then a couple of American NCOs, showing little respect, ambled up to our CSM and offered to show us around. How dare they when he was parading his men! He turned to face them – if looks could kill, they would have died on the spot.

We guessed what Jock must have been thinking, his jaws visibly grinding, as they slouched there, feet astride, one of them chewing gum, addressing him in a jocular fashion – the cheek of it! Suddenly his feelings registered with them as, mechanically, they dragged their feet together and rose to their full height before looking down spluttering at the disciplinarian with a crown on his sleeve.

We guessed afterwards what they had been suggesting when the Guv'nor swivelled around and grudgingly ordered us to follow the two

Americans. Over six feet tall, heavily built and much older than most of us, the two American giants led the way into a huge warm, well lit room, with camp beds placed in neat lines across the floor – our accommodation for the night, enough for the whole company of men and a few more besides.

"Okay guys, grab a bed, leave your kit and we'll show you to the canteen," announced one of our hosts, "you won't be needing your mess cans."

"Did you see that look Jock gave them when they ambled up, Nigel?"

He grinned, "Yah, if it had been one of us, Lloyd, he would have put us on a fizzer."

"That's what I thought. I bet he'd love to knock those two into shape – mind you, they dwarfed him in size, didn't they."

One of the Americans drawled, "Okay guys, let's go." Then, turning to Paddy, who was carrying his mess cans, "You can leave those behind, buddy." Paddy shrugged and tucked the handles into his belt leaving the tins flapping against his thighs.

Bins, risking an outburst, scowled at Paddy, "You deaf or summat?"

It was met with a grin. Paddy Molloy must have been feeling fragile. London born of Irish descent, Paddy, a regular, was like so many that had been cajoled into signing on, with a three-year leaving option. Paddy, pasty face, black hair and twinkling blue eyes, was quick-tempered but a lively individual. In the NAAFI, when tipsy, he and a couple of Irish mates had been known to launch into Irish Republican revolutionary songs. They were always met with approval by his London mates who, in most cases, were totally unaware of their significance.

At the self-service counter there were fresh clean trays with moulded compartments, a completely new innovation for us, as jabbering excitedly, we joined a fast moving queue in front of an array of appetising food and drink, the likes of which, until then, we had never seen in their lives.

"Orange juice! Do we drink that before or after our grub?"

"Just look at those eggs – Gord blimey and different hams, marvellous! I don't believe it!"

"Fuck me, look at the size of them steaks!"

"How d'ya like it done, bud?" Asked a big friendly black American, wearing a pure white chef's hat that contrasted with his teeth.

"Uh – what d'yuh mean?" Back home there were still degrees of rationing and most of us had never seen a steak in our lives, at least none the size of those laid out before us.

"Cream cakes ... That's never real cream, surely?"

"Hey, there's fresh fruit here. I've never seen a pineapple, have you?"

"Yeh, in a tin, not real ones!"

"Do they grow on trees?"

"No, they grow one to a plant, right in the centre – I saw it once in a geographical magazine."

"You're kidding, pull the other one!"

Big well-fed Americans, black and white, stood smiling, eager to please as they waited to serve. We Englishmen, lean and hungry, must have looked like poor orphans from another planet. Our hosts all looked so much older, better fed and more mature than most of us in 'C' Company.

Asked, "How do like your eggs bud, sunny side up?" I looked at Nigel and winked, before turning back to our benefactor smiling.

"Tell you what - make a hole in one of those thicker slices of bread, drop an egg in the middle and fry them together, please."

The chef looked bemused, "What, like this?" he said, as both egg and bread sizzled on the hot plate.

"Lovely. Now turn it over and do the other side, if you will. That's how my Mum does 'em, and we have it with spam," I said, proudly.

"Jees, I like that. What a great idea, how many would you like?"

I wondered why Jock had seemed so angry earlier when we paraded after alighting from our vehicles? Could it be that he felt the American hospitality would make us soft – and his job more difficult in future? If so, he need not have bothered – our admiration and respect for the Guv'nor grew still more after watching the American way of operating, but the food, well? That was something to savour and it would be a whole week before we would taste anything to match it.

That night our Battalion were entertained to a boxing tournament between teams from rival corps of the American Forces. Rumours spread that we had been invited to submit our own team but our CO had declined on the basis that we had not trained for it. However, judging from the boxing prowess of the American contingent, we were all convinced that our lion-hearts would have given a good account of ourselves, if we had taken part.

With full stomachs and a feeling of contentment, we retired to our camp beds for our last decent sleep before the scheme; it was an excellent way to commence joint manoeuvres with the Americans who were such generous hosts. Aroused at 0430 hours the following morning, we were given a huge breakfast and before dawn our convoy left Camp Macauley to commence 'Exercise Roundup'.

My own platoon was swelled with the introduction of two American radio operators, who joined us in the vehicle, as we were about to leave.

"Right," I ordered, "move along the seat – make way for our American friends," thinking to myself, two more heads and bodies might improve our insulation.

Nigel and myself, on opposite sides, pushed the others along the seats making room for the newcomers and their radio equipment.

From pure observation, I could see that their clothing was superior to ours. The Americans themselves realised this at once as one of them, a guy called Wayne, sallow skinned, thin lips and a blue chin, asked in a deep southern drawl, "How come you guys are not wearing warmer outfits?"

Pearce overheard, as shivering and stamping his feet, he yelled back in anger, "You've gotta be joking – this is the British army. We're s'posed to be 'ard and they don't give a fuck about us." Perhaps I had been correct in my assumption the day before, when I thought Jock was concerned that the American experience would make us soft? It had already affected Pearce – maybe the others too?

"Hey, there'd be big questions back home, if we were treated that way," said Wayne's mate, in a booming voice. This one, called Hank, a huge man with a treble chin and a hearty laugh, wore an abundance of jewellery consisting of three chunky gold rings and a very expensive looking gold watch. My eyes wandered from the watch to Fingers Fuller. Like a jackdaw, he had already spotted it, his face registering interest and excitement.

The Americans told us their equipment was designed for temperatures twenty degrees below zero. They wore fur-lined hats and padded wind proof jackets, trousers and boots. According to them, their equipment had been thoroughly tested in Arctic conditions. With jackets looking more like eiderdowns with sleeves, each of them occupied the space of two men, reminding me of the Michelin-man tyre advertising on buses back home.

"Yeah!" said Wayne, "Would you believe, my feet feel like toast in these boots." This guy was straight out of a western cowboy movie – skinnier than Hank, with a hawkish nose, thin mouth and nicotine stained teeth.

"Ya boots are more like the boxes they came in, I'd say," shouted Bins, making himself heard, above the whine of the motor.

Wayne looked at his pal and chuckled, obviously amused with our way of speaking. The Americans were a welcome distraction as Nigel and I discussed with them differences in customs and practices in our respective armies. It seemed that many of them commenced their army service much later than the British, due mainly to a more prolonged education. Many had attended college prior to call up, which on further investigation seemed on a par with our own Grammar school system back home.

The smell of pine forests was more noticeable as we climbed higher into the clouds once more, with the chain-clad wheels carving fresh tracks in virgin snow. The roads were becoming barely visible and the snow deeper as we spiralled clockwise up the steep slopes of the mountains. Reaching the pinnacle, we began a descent, slow at first but becoming faster and the engine noise quietened, as if we were freewheeling.

Our old roommate, Bins, always hungry, was busily sorting through a fresh supply of rations deep inside the truck. Chopper Flynn was running a card school and bragging about life in Korea and how much tougher it was there than in Austria. The TCV rocked as Fuller, complained that he needed more air and swapped places with Boozer.

Watching the wheel tracks left behind in our wake, I sensed danger. The parallel ruts seemed to curve outwards suddenly and then we all felt it as the vehicle lurched.

"Whoa there Trigger!" shouted Pearce, and we clung together, laughing nervously, as the vehicle began to slide. I smiled, trying to hide my fear as a rocky outcrop passed in the opposite direction – too close; suddenly, no trees and a sheer drop on our nearside as we all cried out in anguish.

"Slow down!"

"Easy will yuh!"

"Watch out!"

"Fucking 'ell!"

We held our breath, terrified, as the vehicle slewed first one way, then the other, with the driver wrestling at the wheel. At one point all I saw was space as a rear wheel flipped over the edge spinning.

"He'll never hold it!"

"Jesus Christ!"

"Help!"

I shut my eyes, expecting the worst, as we collided with each other amidst agonised shouts and bits of equipment flying through the air – then no trees, a sheer drop on the nearside and the TCV lurching sideways threatening to topple over, Kroomp!

Men, rifles, kit and stores were tossed around like toys and then instant silence. No more shouting. No cries. Eerie. Peaceful.

My first recollection was of a great weight on my chest and stomach. Afraid of what I might find, I opened one eye and swivelled it around to see I was lying on top of Hank – his eiderdown covering had softened my landing. Fuller was half-submerged beneath Hank having taken the force of the American's body weight. He appeared to be unconscious. There was nothing I could do to help: my left knee hurt and I couldn't move my feet.

Feeling scared, I opened the other eye, raised my head slowly and looking beyond the tailgate, gasped. All I could see was mist with the rear end of the lorry gently rocking up and down, weightless, silent, like a yo-yo on a string. Wayne, on his back, was stretched across both my legs. I felt too frightened to move now and was conscious of a horrible stench in the air. Pearce broke the silence.

"Who's farted?"

"Shut your face!"

No one laughed. No one moved. We were all too afraid to move.

Nigel was prone the other side of me, his head unmoving, facing the opposite way. It was then I realised that the outer skin and metal framework of the TCV was supporting all five of us. I heard a swishing noise outside in the snow just as Leggy's face appeared looking over the tailgate, his voice calm.

"Right men – keep still all of you!" I had never been so glad to hear his voice. "We're in a fix . . . Now listen carefully." Good old Leggy, so calm! "Right, I want you all to de-bus by moving along the top side of the vehicle but as gently as you can. Understand?" He released the catches on the tailboard and carefully lowered it. I could now see trees. They were vertical – I felt pleased. The pain in my knee had increased but I couldn't move it – I figured that one of the American's radio sets must have smashed into it.

Fuller opened his eyes. "What happened?"

"You alright, Reg?" His utterance seemed contrived? Somehow, I wasn't convinced he had been unconscious?

"Sure, if only I can get this big ugly bastard off my legs."

"Another fine mess you've got me into," Hank grumbled, with no particular person in mind.

"Sorry, Olly!" Bins whimpered – then laughter and more rocking, with the TCV threatening to tumble into the valley thousands of feet below. "I'd scratch me fuckin' 'ead, if I could."

Wayne turned his head and looked beyond the low corner of the tailboard to see that the ground beyond it had disappeared completely. "Holy shit! Take it slowly you guys or this fucking thing'll end up in the valley."

His warning came too late. Hagley had self-preservation in mind, as pushing Dave aside, he scrambled over the rest and hurled himself out into the snow. The lorry lurched and the low side dropped a couple of feet deeper into the snow.

"You tosser, do you wanna get your mates killed?" Leggy picked up Hagley by his webbing and hurled him aside.

Praying came easy to those on the low side now as our muckers eased themselves carefully along the high side, dropped down into the snow and clambered up the slope onto the road. I couldn't help feeling angry on hearing the escapees, once free, frolicking in the snow whilst the rest of us, back in the lorry, were wrestling our own fears. I was also finding it difficult to breathe as Wayne, unable to control his own movement, had rolled across my stomach.

Outside I could hear Bins saying, "We ain't got a fuckin' 'ope in 'ell of gettin' this fing out."

The rest of the men, unspeaking, began inching their way carefully along the high side of the sloping floor towards the exit whilst the rest of us remained still, not daring to move. I was beginning to feel hot for the first time that day, and my mouth had dried up.

At last it was Wayne's turn to move but like a beetle stranded on its back, he couldn't right himself. I took a deep breath, exerted all my strength and pushed him off. Wayne's feet slid from under him, his backside hit the sloping floor and then all at once he began to cavort with laughter.

"I need suction pads on my arse, to stop me sliding, man."

"Don't laugh, you're making it worse." I yelled, in desperation, as the vehicle became embedded even deeper in the snow. Hank groaned. I had forgotten he was beneath me – and poor old Reg Fuller, who seemed oblivious to the weight upon him.

"Sorry you two – hold on, we'll be out in a jiff. You okay, Nigel?"

"Sure." He didn't sound it. My tongue felt thick – glued to the roof of my mouth. I looked again at Nigel. The colour had drained from his face. The vehicle rocked a little as Nigel and myself eased our bodies to the high side followed by Hank then Fuller and one by one, we slid free.

The rest of the platoon, milling around on the road, were stamping their feet, laughing and running up and down on the spot, glad to be safely on terra-firma and oblivious to the danger they had all faced minutes before. Amazingly there were no serious injuries as we celebrated our survival, our voices echoing back up at us from the valley below, as we frolicked, like kids, in the snow.

I felt uplifted as I looked about me, marvelling at my survival and sucking in the sweet aroma of the conifers spreading upwards as far as the eye could see, before disappearing in mist. Either side of the road were five-foot drifts of virgin snow. The TCV had slewed into one of these on an uphill hairpin bend and the rear end had skidded and broken through one of the snow banks. A chopped down tree buried beneath the snow bank had prevented us plunging into the valley, hundreds of feet below, leaving the nearside rear wheels suspended over the edge of a steep slope.

From the rear it looked to me as if the chassis had twisted, unless it was the shock absorbers that had concertinaed on the offside and opened up on the nearside to give that impression. I squatted down on my haunches to inspect the rear axle and winced; my knee felt sore. Surprisingly, the axle appeared to be undamaged.

Visibility was little more than fifty yards and there was not another vehicle in sight.

Now we had to get the lorry back on the road somehow as Sergeant Legg ordered, "I want a dozen men over here." Nigel and I held back – guessing what he had in mind, as the men were directed to the valley side of the lorry. "Right," he said, "you lot get under that side and when I say heave, push upwards from beneath and give it all you've got."

"You won't catch me under there," mumbled Boozer, in Nigel's ear, "This lot's gonna end up down below, if e's not careful."

Leggy signalled to the remainder, "You lot push with all your might from the back." I joined them: at least there was an escape route if anything went wrong.

Leggy made his way gingerly along the nearside of the truck and addressed the driver through the open door, "Put it in a higher gear if you can and get ready to rev old son!" The engine spluttered as Leggy turned to us and in a loud voice yelled, "Hea . . . ve!"

The engine whined and the chained wheels spun, as the lorry, swaying dangerously, bit into the soil beneath and sunk deeper and deeper.

"Whoa a a l !"

"O a a l!" the mountains echoed back, then silence.

Sergeant Legg ordered, "Okay, we need to tip that compo on the floor; we need some cardboard!"

"You won't catch me going back in there," said Hagley.

Chopper Flynn, seemingly oblivious to the danger, gestured to one of the men to help him as he eased his body over the high side of the flapping tailgate and into the lorry. He could be heard in the depths tipping cans onto the floor of the vehicle then a moment later sheets of card were sailing through the air onto the ground at the back. Minutes later Chopper emerged triumphant as he eyeballed me, his face inches from mine.

"Feed some of those cartons under the back wheel, Corporal."

I shrugged and handed the last of the cartons to Leggy who was supervising the operation. I detested Flynn but couldn't help admiring him for his bravery in climbing aboard the lorry the way he did. Chopper seemed to detest National Servicemen, particularly the educated ones who stood between him and promotion. Having served eight or nine years of his twenty-two, I doubted that Flynn would progress much further in rank.

"Hey Sarge, how's about me callin' up support to get you out o' this hole?" suggested Hank, who was anxious to retrieve his abandoned wireless set.

"Thanks, but we'll give this a try." Leggy looked worried, as he began stuffing cardboard under both sides of the road-holding wheels of the TCV.

Meanwhile the men were lolling about the place - laughing, smoking, stamping and urinating, all bored but hopeful – could it be the end of manoeuvres? That would have suited most of us. All we wanted was some warmth. Bins prediction was right, we hadn't a hope in hell of moving that vehicle, as Sergeant Legg gathered us around like a rugby scrum and desperately shouted one last command.

"HEAVE!"

The rubber of the spinning wheels was smoking as sheets of cardboard were sent sailing backwards through the air. The lorry would not budge.

Up on the road, we stood around waiting for a miracle. Dave, nudged me, "Have you noticed, the Americans haven't used their wireless sets at all so far?"

"Come to think of it, you're right, Dave. They've done a lot of listening but no talking, strange! You seem very quiet – are you okay?"

"Yep." Dave Allen had always been quiet, a man of few words, different from the rest – a gentleman. A bit soft, and painfully slow, he had suffered miserably in training. The turning point had come when he achieved marksman on the three o' three rifle. Since then he had grown in stature and was well liked by those closest to him. Relative newcomers like Hagley and Pearce, two ignorant men anyway, had little time for him.

"Is something worrying you, Dave?" I asked.

He looked at his feet, then back at me, sad faced, "I haven't heard from Geraldine for over two weeks now – she usually writes twice a week."

We all heard it about the same time - one of those huge continental, long distance, haulage lorries, commonplace in Austria at that time, was trundling up the hill from below. All these juggernauts had sand hoppers cleverly positioned, one above each wheel, automatically dispensing grit and could clear the highest mountains effortlessly, as if they were just minor humpbacked bridges. The noise grew, the mountains reverberating to the sound. It was getting closer and as the lorry rounded the bend we could feel the road shaking beneath our feet. Sergeant Legg, smiling, waved him down.

He and the sad faced army driver, a corporal in the Royal Army Service Corps, approached the Austrian who sat at the wheel of his lorry, smiling. The three men conferred, whilst the remainder of us kept our distance. Leggy was beaming as he retraced his steps. The Austrian driver meanwhile, drove his vehicle on a little further before stopping and then, quietly confident, fixed a huge chain between the two vehicles. Minutes later the driver climbed back in his cab and with gentle revving and little noise from the powerful motor pulled the TCV back onto the road as if it was a toy.

The road was still vibrating as it came to a halt and the cheers of our entire platoon echoed off the mountain. The Austrian smiled and dropped down onto the road to unhitch the vehicles but his smile changed to joy when Leggy showered him with gifts of margarine, choc-bars and a few cigarettes.

"Right men, saddle up!" We climbed aboard once more and Sergeant Legg addressed us before securing the tailboard. "We're running late lads – the hot drink will have to wait, just help yourselves to whatever's in the back there. We've got to get moving." Miraculously the engine purred into life and once more we were mobile.

We had no idea what the schedule might be or what he meant by late – so far nothing had happened, militarily. Now the men began giving vent to their feelings by moaning about the food, especially since they had heard a story or two from Hank and Wayne who had yet to try British compo rations. On tasting our food, the Americans reaction was predictable.

"Hard tack anyone?" Bins yelled above the drone of the TCV. Situation normal! Replies typical.

"You know what you can do with that," shouted Paddy, followed by ribald comments from the rest.

"Margarine!" yelled Chopper, then laughter, "Who wants some fucking marge?"

"You can stuff that where the monkeys put their nuts!"

Hank rocked with laughter, "Marge – what is that, marge?"

"Oh you must try some of our marge," Pearce called out, aping the American drawl.

"Well, someone's gotta eat it," shouted Chopper. "Here give this to the big bloke on the end," he said, passing a small can down the length of the truck. Hank turned it over looking at it quizzically.

"It's a replacement for butter," I said, "It's all we could get during the War."

Hank took up one of our mini can openers, enthusing about the novelty of it and then, removing a glove, he opened the tin and rubbed a fat finger across the top of the tablet inside. It had shrunk away from the sides, was a faded yellow in colour and was rock hard. He sniffed it and then screwing his face up, pretended to vomit, before throwing it like a quoit into the wilderness. Then suddenly, pulling back his sleeve, he let out a yell.

"Holy shit, I've lost my watch."

"No, surely not," said Wayne, concerned for his friend, "Did you have it when we started out this morning?"

"I sure did,' he replied, optimistically peeling his sleeve back to check again.

"You could have lost it when we had the crash," said Nigel, "have you looked around?"

"That's what I was thinking," said Wayne, "try looking under the seat, buddy."

Hank looked devastated, as sinking to his knees, he searched the floor beneath the bench seat in the lurching vehicle.

"Check under your seats men to see if you can see Hank's watch will you," I shouted, "It was a gold colour wasn't it Hank?"

"It was solid gold," replied Hank, sadly, "my mother gave it me for my twenty-first."

I felt sad as I looked at Fingers Fuller searchingly, whilst a few men dived down, beneath the seats, fruitlessly feeling around the floor. Fuller, looking innocent, responded with a, 'I don't know what you are looking at me for,' face. There was no trace of the watch. I turned to Hank. "Was it insured?"

"Sure, but you'll 'preciate, it had sen 'imental value."

It was already dark as the vehicle, its engine rising in pitch, slowed to a crawl and eased its way into a small hamlet. There appeared to be more barns than houses. I stood up and holding onto the cowling, poked my head round to look beyond the front of the vehicle. Judging by the number of vehicles present, the rest of the Company had already arrived. The sweet smell of soup, or was it steak and kidney, warmed my nostrils long before I recognised the black silhouette of the Company supply vehicle, parked in the main square.

Our vehicle stopped with a jerk throwing me back on my seat where I remained awaiting the order to de-bus. The rest of the men were already on their feet anxious to get at the food. Through a gap I spotted several figures, presumably cooks, preparing the evening meal and a row of trestle tables illuminated by fuel burning arc lights.

In the foreground, by a frozen fountain in the centre of the square, stood the unmistakable figure of Jock, his back straighter than a plumb line, the hollow of his neck non-existent, watching us in silence. I imagined him as an executioner, silhouetted in the light of the power lamps, waiting to strike. He had the advantage too for he could see the expression on every one of the men's faces as they disembarked.

"The Fuhrer's waiting out there," I mumbled, "Pass it on."

Leggy appeared and disconnected the tailgate, "Right de-bus – take all your personal gear with you and fall-in on the road, in sections, in open order."

The frozen bone marrow of a hundred limbs stirred, warmed by the smell of hot food and pleasure awaiting us, as we lowered our aching joints from the back of the lorry and formed up in lines, shivering, as we faced the Sergeant Major. The two Americans, as if briefed beforehand, lugged their equipment across to the CSM who signalled them to join the activities going on behind him – no doubt for a nice hot cup of tea.

Nigel, Chopper and myself took up positions inspecting our own sections, as giving a knowing wink here and another there, we went through the routine expected, our backs to the CSM who, unspeaking, stood watching from behind.

Leggy appeared, "Whose small pack is this – left in the lorry?"

"Mine, Sergeant."

"Put it on then," I said, retrieving the situation. "And Molloy – straighten your beret, you're on parade." I stepped forward and adjusted Bins webbing, my back facing Jock, as I whispered, smiling threateningly, "Don't you dare grin, you bastard!"

Nigel and Chopper Flynn were going through the same procedure with their sections. Nothing missed Jock's gaze, like a falcon, waiting to swoop on its prey. Pretending to be satisfied, I took up a position on the right of my section.

Sergeant Legg, in front of the platoon, played the same soldierly game, "Are all your men here Corporal Freeman?"

"All present and correct, Sir." Better address him as Sir, I thought, with the CSM around. He is acting platoon commander after all's said and done!

Sergeant Major Campbell knew the score and he didn't fool easily but he expected the NCOs to operate this way, to show respect – I had learnt that much already. As the men stood at ease watching, Jock seemed to be fretting over something. No change there – a habit of his. His cheekbones appeared as shadows in the artificial light but I could still see his jaws grinding. Suddenly he reached a decision as he barked aloud.

"Sergeant Legg!" Leggy bounded over to him, his tail wagging as the Guv'nor gave him his orders.

Seconds later, Leggy turned about and marched back to face us. Since leaving Zeltweg we had seen very little of Sgt Eames, our acting platoon sergeant. He was busy in his other role, as acting CQMS, helping with the meals. We all preferred Sergeant Legg anyway so what did it matter - he had a knack of making bad news sound exciting as he returned, smiling and addressed us all with, "Nine platoon, stand easy – NCOs come with me."

Yes, yes, don't tell me, I thought sarcastically, he's about to show us to the local baths for a good hot soak, a rub down in hot towels, a change of clothes and a sumptuous meal. Well, I could always hope and a good hot meal later at least. As for the rest, dream on, Lloyd, I thought!

We were led to a dimly lit barn twenty yards away where, pointing to the hay and dung-strewn floor, he told us we were to sleep there overnight in between periods on guard duty. It wasn't just any old barn. I recognised at once – the pungent smell of pigs. It had no doors to help release the foul smell but it offered small mercy in protecting us from the elements.

Chopper turned his nose up, "Pooar! Is there nowhere else, Skip? We can't sleep here."

"There's outside in the open, if your men would prefer that?"

"How about you, are you kipping down here too, Skip?"

"You must be joking, I wouldn't sleep in this dump," he replied, chuckling, "at least the men will have a roof over their heads and they'll appreciate it later – it's going to get colder as the night wears on. Now get your gear, find a spot for your men and tell them grub'll be ready in half-an-hour." Then to Nigel and myself, he said, "Get your sections fed right away – they'll be guarding three positions on the west side of the village tonight. While they're noshing, I'll show you what's required." We went to follow him. "Just a minute," he said, pointing to a solitary hurricane lamp hanging inside, "I should warn you of the fire risk with all this hay around - that lamp should not be tampered with unless there's a major assault."

I remember distinctly how on the second night when Leggy had briefed us, he drew attention to the fire danger in that first barn.

11

The accident, earlier in the day, had delayed our arrival and apart from the fact that Sergeant Legg would have had some explaining to do with the Guv'nor, our platoon had lost out in bagging the best accommodation. This undoubtedly led to the major cause of friction that night. The moon, a full one, was already rising over the countryside north of our location and though I had no idea where we had ended up, it couldn't have been too far from Linz, our point of departure that morning.

I found the smell of the small barn quite repulsive and decided I would spend most of the night outside, if possible, keeping my limbs moving. I led my section into the barn and ordered them to choose a spot and prepare their sleeping bags. Paddy Molloy, I might have guessed it would be him, was the first to protest, as he stood horrified, reluctant to lay his kit down on the floor.

"I ain't fockin" sleeping here, "oi'v seen better pig sties in Oi'land – I tell yuh, it's not fit for humans." The rest of the section, holding their kit, stood waiting.

"You ain't ever bin t' Ireland, you liar," said Bins.

"I have too!" His eyes were flaring.

"Yuh from Camden Town, Paddy."

I was inclined to agree with Molloy but I was not in the mood to humour him. "You'll be gazing at the stars for some of it, on watch, Paddy, so stop bitching," I said, flinging my own sleeping bag upon the floor.

"Whad do yuh mean?" He said, reaching for his rifle.

In a flash Boozer grabbed Paddy's arm, his knuckles turning white, "Lay off Paddy, he's only carrying out orders." My friendship with Yanek Boucha had grown strong ever since those early days in training and I guess he wanted me to succeed in my new role. Yanek too, had quite a following of younger men who respected him for what he had been through during the War.

"You're on the first shift Paddy," I said, more friendly, "which means you can eat before the others, so make the most of it. You've got half-an-hour to get some grub down you! Just tell the cooks you're on first stag – so get dug out!" Paddy's anger subsided and I chuckled to myself having unconsciously used the same term that the training NCOs had, in those early days, back at Mill Hill. They had always been on about, 'get dug out', a typically meaningless expression, just one of many in the Regiment – this one meaning, to get organised.

Paddy's anger had subsided and with rifle slung over his shoulder and head down, he slunk out of the barn carrying his mess cans. Out of sight of the others, I gave Boozer a friendly slap on the back, "Cheers mate!"

The rest of my section, sulking, skirted around the CSM as they ambled across the square to join the 'priority first' queue. We three section leaders were about to join Sergeant Legg for a briefing when we heard Jock's voice, like a rifle shot, ripping across the square.

"Hey you – soldier, come here! Yes you man," he said, addressing Hagley, who shrugged and began to amble towards him. "Move yourself!"

Hagley ran the last few steps and came smartly to attention.

"Who gave you permission to remove your webbing?"

"Nobody, Sir."

"Get it on and keep it on – and where's your rifle?"

"In the barn, Sir."

"Get it and keep it with you at all times."

Hagley, head down, doubled back to the barn. I felt quietly pleased but equally embarrassed – I should have spotted it first. As an NCO,

I was responsible. I knew I would need to watch myself now, for Jock would almost certainly be aware that Hagley was one of my men.

Nigel and I posted the first pickets in their observation positions and then collected our own mess cans and eating irons from the barn. The smell of dung was everywhere, with loose straw and deep frozen ruts littering the snow, as we made our way across to the trestle tables, or open air dining establishment, as Nigel called it. With luck, we had a couple of hours before replacement pickets would need to be briefed.

The cookers were roaring away in the light of the lamps, where Sergeant Eames stood, supervising three or four cooks who were enveloped in steam rising from several large cauldrons. The aromatic smell of meat and onions surpassed that of the local stench and we were soon demolishing a scrumptious meal.

"The cooks have worked wonders with the compo, don't you think?" said Nigel, smiling contentedly, as he scraped the last particles of Irish stew from his mess can.

"Ahh, yes – I always loved Irish stew back home. My old Mum would add pearl barley to ours," I said, thoughts of home saddening me, "sometimes a few dumplings."

"Oh, dumplings – I adore them."

The cooks had supplemented the compo with vegetables and garlic, which they had scrounged from the locals. For dessert there was hot creamy rice, another compo special, and as we queued up for a mug of strong coffee and rum, one of the cooks handed each of us a bar of chocolate.

"It must be jolly cold to qualify for a rum allocation, Lloyd."

"I guessed it might be rum – we had some of that during our night scheme in training, do you remember? Oh, of course, I forgot – you weren't there. Bins, was in charge of the rum," I said, "so, you can imagine I did alright that night."

I was suddenly reminded of the night in training, when the permanent staff in the depot gave us their first taste of action in the fields of Ruislip, just a stone's throw from a London Transport bus route. It was really cold that night, in pouring rain in the middle of June, but it was nothing compared with mid-winter in Austria.

We returned to the barn feeling a lot warmer inside and grateful to 'Staff' and his cooks for a satisfying meal, their reputation restored, as the general morale soared for one brief moment. Nigel tossed a coin to decide shifts. "You jammy sod," I said, smiling.

"I'll take the first shift, old boy," said Nigel, grinning as he stubbed out his cigarette.

I cleaned out both sets of mess tins with a couple of handfuls of snow whilst Nigel posted the next shift. Those men not on guard had already cleared spaces in the barn, laid out their sleeping bags and climbed into them, but very few were asleep. Feeling sleepy myself, I changed my earlier decision not to use the barn and instead cleared a space for myself and laid out my bag.

Judging by the thickness of ice on the frozen fountain, the outside temperature was way below zero, yet once inside the sleeping bag, it felt like a sauna. Only my feet were cold as I lay there, with my nose protruding from the bag, watching the opening to the barn where anyone entering appeared as a black shape in the frame.

Sergeant Legg's silhouette appeared in the doorway, easily recognisable by his rounded figure but it was his beret that was the most distinctive, no style, more like a chef's hat. He remained there, with no intention of entering further. Who could blame him, with that smell?

"They're bound to attack tonight lads, so keep alert," he said, enthusing, "a 'stand to' could come at any time during the night. If the Yanks try anything, let's give 'em something to remember the Middies for."

"If they get a whiff of this place, they'll run a mile," said Chopper, followed by laughter from his admirers.

The pride of the Company and the Regiment was at stake, especially since Americans were the opposing force. We were required to remain fully dressed, including boots and gaiters, both on and off duty, even in our sleeping bags. Once feet warmed and swelled, the leather laces cut into our in-steps, causing a great deal of discomfort.

I couldn't sleep. Bored and in need of fresh air, I went out to join Nigel who was manning an observation post with the first shift. Nine platoon was dug in on a hillock with a commanding view of the snow-covered landscape in front and a field of fire covering a radius of a couple of hundred yards. The conditions were ideal to defend – good visibility, a starry sky and a lover's moon.

"At least you'll see them coming," I mumbled quietly, as I sidled up - we had learnt in training that the enemy can hear whispering in the dead of night more easily than low tones.

"Sure – not sleeping then?"

"No – I can't. That stench in the barn is too much for me."

"I thought you'd be writing to Jane," said Nigel.

"There's very little light in the barn, besides I haven't heard from her for a week." I shivered and tightened the cords on my wind-proof hood.

"You sound worried - here, have a bit of clacker," he said, handing me a piece of compo chocolate.

"No. I'm more worried about Hank and that watch. Do you think Fuller might have nicked it, Nigel?"

Nigel seemed surprised. "How could he? He wasn't sitting anywhere near Hank."

"That's true, I just wondered, that's all."

I returned to the barn and poured myself into my sleeping bag. My body wanted to sleep but my head didn't, as I lay there worrying about Hank's loss. He was American and I couldn't bear to think that an Englishman would do this when they had been so generous and kind to us at Camp Macauley.

At one o'clock in the morning I dragged myself out of my hot bag, stretched aching limbs and shivered before going out to join Nigel. My eyes had already accustomed themselves to the light as I stole up quietly from behind him, "Anything happening?" The poor man visibly jumped.

"Oh! I wasn't expecting you Lloyd! Boozer saw a fox, that's all. Oh yes, and a hare, so he thought." His face was a mask, "I'm frozen solid."

"You look it, Nigel. Why not take an early break? Was there anything else to report?"

"Yar!" He replied, struggling to form the words through frozen lips, "A guy in seven thought he saw something and fired off a blank."

"I thought I heard a bang earlier." We had all been issued with ten rounds of blank ammunition to repel an attack and strict instructions not to shoot until ordered to. Officers were equipped with flares to light up the enemy and thunder flashes to imitate a bursting grenade – all part of the grand defensive plan.

"The culprits platoon commander was hopping mad – said it would have given our position away. Someone said he'll be on a charge when we get back to Zeltweg."

"That's a bit harsh. Look! Go get yourself a mug of coffee and rum Nigel, they've got an urn on the go back there."

At two o'clock I returned to the barn to wake the next relief. One of them was Hagley, often referred to as 'Bear's Breath'. His reaction was predictable.

"Fuck off! I'm staying 'ere," he said, as I shook him awake.

"Get up you idle bastard – the others have done their stint." I tugged at the zip of his sleeping bag and the penetrating cold did the rest.

"You're too fucking keen you are," he said, as grudgingly he got to his feet and, with two of his mates, followed me to the frozen snow-covered slope.

Out in the open, the cold affected our men in their extremities, hands, ears, noses and feet, with boots that soaked up water like sponges. Shivering and stamping my feet, hopelessly trying to induce circulation, I remained in position with the men for the next two hours until it was time to change the guard once more. When I returned to the barn to wake the new relief, Nigel and the rest were sleeping like babies. Hagley, sulking, couldn't wait to get back to his 'den', the sleeping bag.

At five o'clock I woke the rest of the platoon – it was time to 'stand to'. In the square, Sergeant Legg and a couple of other NCOs stood by the cookers slurping hot coffee and rum. I went across. Flynn was there plus a couple more veterans.

"Are they awake Corporal Freeman?" Leggy asked, in his usual friendly manner.

"Yes Sarge."

"Right, I'll give it a few more minutes and we'll stand them to. Get yourself a drink."

It was still dark when the entire Company moved quietly into position around the perimeter accustoming our eyes to the changing light. An attack, if it was coming, could happen at any moment, the coldest time of day when the body resistance is at its lowest ebb. Silently we waited, nerves jangling as the stars dulled and the blue-black sky changed to grey.

The cold hurt. I was desperate for a pee. The noise of a rifle was heard being cocked, ready to fire. The sweet smell of coffee-impregnated urine cut like a laser into frozen snow. I grimaced, my hands a trifle warmer. Someone farted. A chuckle was strangled. I shouldered my weapon and folded my arms, hands under armpits, hugging myself for a feeling of imaginary warmth.

Now, the landscape began to reveal itself in more detail as the imaginings of the night took on a different shape. The shadows of advancing men were tree stumps – the tank turrets, hidden gullies. With the coming of the dawn the eastern horizon was a dazzling yellow whilst the facing slopes of snow took on a pinkish hue. A full hour we waited, holding our breath, watching the birth of a new day with the sky turning ice blue in the cold bright sun as the landscape revealed itself more fully. A miserably cold, yet magical hour had passed without incident.

"Right, stand down."

"The fucking Yanks ain't got the bottle to attack!"

"They've got more sense – they're laughing, tucked up in bed, I reckon."

"Right men, saddle up!" We clambered aboard the TCVs and once more, Charlie Company were mobile and the stamping of cold feet in wet soggy boots recommenced. The two American radio operators took up places alongside each other, their sets crackling, as they conferred. I winced, as turning, I caught my mouth on someone's harness. Nigel moved across to join me. Overnight I had developed a deep split in the centre of my bottom lip.

"A good breakfast, Lloyd," said Nigel, conversationally, his voice loud, full of self-confidence. We had just eaten lashings of fatty bacon, dried egg and beans, hot sweet tea and hard tack.

"Yes – I'm not a lover of fatty bacon usually, but I enjoyed it. A little sweet, don't you think?"

"Yar, I liked it but frankly, beans make me fart." I was reminded of how much Nigel spoke like a public schoolboy, or officer even. It was the way he pronounced, 'fart' that intrigued me.

"Where do you come from Nigel?"

"Harrow, dear boy."

I smiled, "Well, what a coincidence, we used to play rugby against a Grammar school in Harrow. Which school did you go to?"

He looked at me, smiling mischievously, "Can't you tell?" His thick lips seemed impervious to the cold, his teeth pearly white, perfectly formed, in spite of playing rugger. Many times I had found myself spitting out bits of enamel after a hard tackle when I played.

"Was it Harrow Grammar?"

"I went to Eton," he replied, his cheeks flushing slightly.

"That's a public school, how come you're not an officer then?"

"I'll tell you about it another time," he replied, smiling. His skin was tanned but his chin always looked darker on account of his rapid hair growth.

I thought Nigel was a good-looking man, yet I was surprised he admitted to having little feeling for the opposite sex. In fact, he frequently denigrated females and was always quick to admonish others if they expressed physical desire towards a girl. "There's more to love than just physical attraction," he would preach, "One must consider the spiritual side of a relationship." He had very little to say about himself. He wrote very little, yet received plenty of mail. I was intrigued.

A heavy smoker, Nigel was always charitable with his cigarettes, producing a silver cigarette case and opening it with one hand and a great flourish.

12

Back at Zeltweg, the big clean up had begun, with most of us left alone to sort ourselves out. The only exceptions were those detailed for guard duty but Charlie Company was excluded. Nigel was clipping his toenails as I walked in.

"You've been a long time!" He said, "What have you been up to?"

"I've had a nice long soak in the bath – going over the events of the past week, Nigel"

I felt good. Having had that bath, I felt I could better face the priorities that lay ahead. I had more pressing priorities, washing my socks, cleaning my boots, kit, weapons, webbing, brasses and last of all, the locker and room. As far as I was concerned, food could wait awhile.

"And what conclusions have you come to, old fruit?"

"What a waste of time and energy it was – and now we must pay for it."

"Ginger paid for it with his life."

"Don't!"

Nigel and I had our differences but I was fortunate in sharing a room with a man who nurtured the same degree of pride in personal cleanliness as myself. Occasionally we interrupted our tasks to visit the barrack room and make sure the others were doing the same for we knew an inspection was likely. Their room stunk of sweaty feet and damp uniforms drying on the radiators.

Sure enough, that evening Sergeant Legg appeared at our door. "Tell the men there will be a foot inspection tomorrow at twelve hundred hours – I want them on parade in plimsolls, with no socks."

*

During the scheme, we had all complained of pains in our feet and it must have been day four of the manoeuvres when I had raised the issue with Leggy during a stop.

"I'll see what I can do," he replied, sympathetically, as he turned to the driver, "Start 'er up!" Turning back to us, he breezed, "They'll just have to grin and bear it for the time being, there's no way we can stop here – we've gotta keep moving. Let's hope we can find better facilities tonight, to thaw out. Saddle up!" The men scrambled aboard whilst Leggy, securing the tailgate, whispered to me, "Get them singing, Corporal Freeman – it'll cheer them up and take their mind off things."

The snow was falling in flakes as big as half-crowns as the soft whine of the engine changed tone and we moved off once more. I decided to involve Hagley. It would make a change from nagging him, I thought. "Hey Steve, what was that song I heard you singing the other day – something about your mother-in-law?"

"Weren't me, it was, Paddy," he replied, sullenly, nodding in Paddy's direction.

Paddy grinning at Hagley, his distinctive Irish brogue, pleasant to the ear, replied, "You do know it – you do, you do now."

With that Hagley forced a smile as he called across to Bins, "This one's for you, Binnsy." He commenced, slowly at first, a distinctive tune but his own words, "I love my mother-in-law," and the whole platoon erupted in song,

> "She's nothing but a dirty old whore
>
> She nags me day and night
>
> I can't do nuffink right
>
> Chorus   How I love her, how I love her
>
> How I love my mother-in-law"

Wayne, one of the Americans, amused, reached in his pocket for a pencil and began scribbling, helped by his pal Hank, who dictated missed words.

2nd Verse "I love my mother-in-law

   She's nothing but a dirty old whore

   Last night I greased the stairs

   Put tin tacks on her chairs

   I hope she breaks her back

   Cos I do love wearin' black

Chorus   How I love her, how I love her

   How I love my mother-in-law"

Suddenly, there was a violent knocking from the cab in the front. Flynn started yelling. I feigned deafness, encouraging the men, to sing up – I had always loved a sing-song. Chopper persisted. I continued to ignore him, "Come on lads, I can't hear you – sing up!"

3rd Verse "I love my mother-in-law

   She's nothing but a dirty old whore

   And tattooed on her spine

   Is the Middlesex in line

   And on her fanneee

   Is Jolson singing mammeee" ..... The line accentuated

Chorus finish "How I love her, how I love her

   How I love my mother-in-law"

"Shut up! You lot!" Chopper shouted, at the top of his voice. The singing stopped abruptly as Chopper announced, "Sergeant Legg says, not so loud or we'll give our position away."

It had worked; the men seemed to forget the pains in their feet, but within a few minutes the stamping of hob-nailed boots, on the floor of the TCV, re-commenced – keeping our blood flowing.

*

Now, back at Zeltweg, Nigel and I ceased bulling, it was time for dinner. We sauntered across to the cookhouse and as we lined up, Nigel suddenly announced, "You're very quiet, Lloyd, what have I said to upset you – or were you thinking about Ginger?"

"No, no," I replied, mechanically, my mind wandering, as I thrust my plate forward. The last time I had eaten in this cookhouse was when I spoke to Ginger on the morning of departure. I felt my arm vibrate as something solid was dumped on my plate. I looked to see a heap of 'pom' (potato powder mixed with water) but flavoured with stale cheese to add taste. There was no choice anyway. One had to take what was on offer, or starve.

Nigel looked at his helping, and then back at me, turning his nose up, "It's a case of like it or lump it as usual, Lloyd."

"If you don't like it, complain to the duty officer – if you dare," retorted the cook laughing.

I shrugged, "It makes a change from compo rations, I suppose." We placed our eating irons alongside our heaped plates at a trestle table in the corner of the vast dining area and sat down. It was an unusual offering but there was plenty of it and we were both hungry. Unspeaking and feeling very sleepy, we commenced eating the 'pom', carrots and green cabbage. I watched Nigel amused, as he cleared his plate and looked at me mournfully, the look he had when about to say something profound.

"Lloyd, don't take this the wrong way but I think you are too close to some of the men, particularly Boozer and Dave."

"You cheeky sod, they're my mates."

"That's what I mean. It will become increasingly difficult for you to exercise discipline if you don't distance yourself more."

"That's a matter of opinion."

He went quiet. Maybe there was something in what he said. Admittedly the men seemed to look up to Nigel more than most NCOs. He was three or four inches taller than me, and I was six feet tall myself. Could it be his cultured voice, or that he spoke loudly? I had noticed with the officers, who were invariably ex public school, that they were loud, even when talking.

Nigel went on, "In a week or so Lloyd, we'll be burying the guys that were killed, you know. Jock Campbell will be looking for coffin bearers and they usually prefer taller men. How will you feel if you're chosen for the bearer party?"

"I don't think I could do that somehow – I was too close to Ginger."

I was reminded of his little habits; how he would talk in your face and blink and sniff a lot – probably hay fever. In training, he had suffered in the gas chamber. We all had to remove our masks whilst inside and then walk around a table before departing in an orderly manner. Ginger had run out too early and the training NCO had forced him to go back in again. When he finally emerged, he looked like death.

I looked up at Nigel, sadly, "Poor old Ginger, he must have suffered terribly in that barn."

Nigel said something – I missed it.

"Do what?"

"I said, I can see a way out for you if you'd prefer to miss the funeral."

"Eh! How?"

"Have you seen CO's orders since you've come back?"

"No. I leave that to you, Nigel." I hardly cared and rarely bothered to read orders. There was always someone around, especially Nigel or Dave, to tell me if I had missed something on the notice board. Nevertheless, I was intrigued. "How do you mean a way out?"

I watched, enviously, as Nigel, smacking his lips, tipped his plate, spooning the last of his syrup pudding. "You were a Civil Servant before you joined the army, weren't you?"

"Yes, why?"

He grinned, "My manners are terrible lately. I shouldn't scrape my plate. Dave told me you could type."

"I can touch-type," I replied, proudly. "A lot of good it did me. We had a typing pool in the office and all the letters were typed for me." I was reminded of the daily boredom in the Commissioner's Office. Big Ben would strike every quarter and there was no escaping the monotony of that clock.

He took out his cigarette case, flicked it open and offered it across the table. I shook my head. Removing a cigarette for himself, he stroked his thumb across the wheel of his silver-plated lighter and lit up, at the same time inhaling and filling his lungs.

"Lloyd, did you know HQ Company are looking for a typist?"

"What for?" My spirits rose at the thought of a soft number in the office, but dismissed the idea – it would be boring. It was bad enough watching the days pass in the normal way and I couldn't bear the thought of clock-watching again for my last year in the army.

He leant forward, tapping surplus ash onto his empty plate. "I've got a fair idea what it's all about – I could arrange it if you're interested." I shook my head, as he continued, "Seriously Lloyd, I believe you could do with a change of scene. Just imagine - no more drill – no weapon training – no more guards – no bullshit. And, having seen how worked up you were when you thought Dave was trapped in that barn . . ."

"No I wasn't!"

He recoiled laughing, "Lloyd! You should have seen your face – and the others noticed it too. Let's face it, you all shared the same room in training. You've been through a lot together. Following the cadre, I think you should have been posted back to a different platoon, in a different company even. Furthermore, I believe you will benefit from a spell away from that lot."

Incensed, I blurted, "As we ran out of the barn, Nigel, I thought *you* looked remarkably cool in the circumstances – almost pleased, I thought."

He frowned, "Don't be ridiculous, I was shit scared – same as the rest, even if I didn't show it. As far as I was concerned, it was every man for himself, but you were obviously concerned for your mates – especially Dave. We are NCOs – having mates cramps our style and fosters disrespect. The point I'm trying to make, Lloyd, is – I am not as close to the men as you are."

I felt angry now, "What happened to your training intake then, Nigel? How come it's not generally known, about you and . .?" I clammed up, remembering my promise to remain silent regarding his past indiscretions.

He frowned, looking decidedly uneasy, "I shouldn't have told you."

"Why not? It helped you at the time, getting it off your chest."

"Yes but …"

"I told you, your secret is safe with me. Just answer my question – what happened to your training intake? Why is it that no one else knows about your past? Whether you know it or not, Nigel, some men are suspicious of you because you seem to know too much about what's going on – the typing job tonight, for instance!"

He took out another cigarette and lit it using the stub of his first. "As you know, I ended up in Colchester. The rest of my intake was transferred to the Royal West Kents – ended up in Kenya – fighting the Mau Mau." He smiled, saddened at the thought, "I did myself a favour indirectly." He swung his legs and feet up onto the bench-seat in a horizontal position and sat studying me, half smiling, as he revolved his cigarette between finger and thumb. Occasionally, he would point the cigarette up to the ceiling whilst inspecting the lighted end, deep in thought.

Then he appeared to reach a decision as he took a deep draught, threw back his head sending a smoke ring spiralling upwards, and announced, advisedly, "I'd go for that typing job, if I were you, Lloyd."

"Nigel, I do believe you're trying to get rid of me – I will have one of your cigarettes if you don't mind."

* * *

It must have been the fourth night of the scheme when Nigel told me of his own personal tragedy that occurred during basic training. The Company's rendezvous that night had been a disused railway siding somewhere in the northern region.

Here, the Company cookhouse and dining area had been set up in a huge rail workshop. It had stopped snowing; a fresh cold wind had whipped up to sweep the heavens of cloud and the temperature had dropped like a penny in a pool. I remember wondering how much longer we could keep up this stupid game of soldiers?

Jock Campbell had been in his usual spot, his beady eyes everywhere, as we queued in an orderly fashion, each with one eye on the food, the other watching him. Sentries were posted, relief guards organised and 'stand to' positions identified. In the meantime, NCOs were expected to find shelter for their men.

While Nigel finished his meal, I reconnoitred the area and managed to find the ideal spot for both our sections, a group of small rail storage sheds, each measuring around three paces in length by one and a half deep. They were like huge boxes, constructed from railway 'sleepers' with the back, ends and top enclosed and one long side facing the track, open to the elements.

A large expanse of ground, beyond the open sides of the boxes, provided a good line of fire in the event of a frontal attack, whilst offering draught-proof protection from the rear: ideal. Nigel and I commandeered an empty shelter and unrolled our sleeping bags, just enough room for two. We tossed a coin for the inside spot and he won. Lucky Nigel; another six inches and I would have been out in the open!

It was too cold to sleep and my cheeks, nose and ears had lost all feeling, as I stared into the blackness, the stars growing larger and brighter with each passing minute. As usual, my feet were wet and frozen, in spite of the warmth of the bag and with each breath, I could feel the cold air within penetrating my lungs. My bottom lip had split and was now a blob of congealed blood. I was tempted to zip my sleeping bag right to the top, like some of the others, but thought better of it. Alongside me I heard a gulp.

Nigel's voice broke the silence. "Here, have a swig," he said, handing me a bottle of schnapps, "it'll warm the cockles."

I drank thirstly, choking as it scorched my gullet, before passing it back, "You had best wipe it, cos of my lip."

"I don't care, I've had plenty already." He sounded tiddly.

The moon was full and very bright, turning night into day with more stars in the jet-black sky than I had ever seen over London. A shooting star flashed across the sky with a great long tail, from one side of the horizon to the other it seemed, followed by another, in quick succession. "Cor!"

"Uh!"

"Did you see that, Nigel?"

"What?"

"A shooting star – it was magic."

Nigel's cigarette case flashed in the moonlight. "Fancy a burn, Lloyd?" His lighter flamed into life, illuminating the darkest corners of the box. If Jock saw that, we would hear about it any moment. I drew hard on the cigarette, a rare event for me, as I imagined instant warmth for my lungs.

"Was the ciggy case a present?"

"Yar, Madeline bought it – here have another swig."

I drank – searing warmth. "Madeline? You never told me you had a girl-friend, Nigel?" I handed back the bottle.

The glow of his cigarette brightened, "I haven't, she's history," he replied, sadly.

I cupped the cigarette in the palm of my hand, lest Jock should see the glow, and sucked hard. "Oh! What happened?"

"She was a big spender, Lloyd – a deb." I visualised a beautiful model such as I had seen on magazine covers. "I idolised her, would have done anything for her but it doesn't grow on trees old boy." He drank some more. "Ahh! I hope we don't have to shtand to, Lloyd - I'm in no fit shtate."

"I know, who cares!"

He drew hard and the interior of the box glowed. This refuge, the night sky and the shooting star, it reminded me of an illuminated nativity scene, but it wasn't a stable and we were no angels. I heard him take another drink, intrigued to know more, as I pictured him with a glamorous girl.

"She had a pen ... a pen ... a penshant for casinos," he slurred. "I managed to ex, extra, extricate myself from that but she had this farcking hat. She inshisted on taking it to Ashcot. The geegees took the rest of my money. I was doing basic training at the time, had passed Wozby (War Office Selection Board) and was all lined up for Sandhurst."

He had told me part of the story previously and wanted to know more. "Is that why you missed becoming an officer, Nigel?"

"What, the debt? Oh no! It was more than that." He went quiet, his cigarette a dull red now and vibrating. He had a distinctive way of holding his cigarette – between forefinger and thumb only, with his little finger held high as some people might when holding a precious teacup, except that he would roll the cigarette between the end digits of finger and thumb.

"Lloyd," he said, "this is shtrictly on the QT!"

"Trust me."

He went on to tell me that during training he had been persuaded by an old lag, scheduled for demob, to break into the NAAFI after lights out – that he had been told by the counter assistant that the manager never bothered to lock the safe at night. Nigel's task would be easy. He had simply to keep a look out whilst the other man, name of Cooper, helped himself to the takings – that they would split the proceeds. He took out another cigarette and lit it with the spent butt of his first.

"You ought to watch out with that light, Nigel. If Jock sees it – well!"

"Shure." He stubbed it out on the ground as if he was using a screwdriver.

"What happened, Nigel?" I was beginning to feel sorry for him as I imagined where his story was heading.

"Cooper ! . . said it was a peesh of cake. Ash far ..as I was conshured . . it was like a game of chance."

"Were you tumbled?"

"No, one a the id'jots on guard duty sh aw the light – p, p, panicked an told the guard commander. They caught us red-handed."

Nigel went on to say that he had been lucky. He had been tried by a military court – was found guilty – and sentenced to six months in Colchester Detention Centre. I knew about Colchester and it was well known throughout the army, as a frightening place, much worse than civilian prison, with unimaginable punishments, applied by an evil regime.

It explained a lot about Nigel Pallister – his superb fitness, his perfect kit, boots and brasses and skill on the parade ground. Officers generally, were usually uncoordinated at drill.

I turned my head, once more watching the night sky. Strange, I could feel the frost particles in the air – the nostril hairs seemed to be pricking the inside of my nose like needles.

I might have known that the man lying beside me had been earmarked for Sandhurst. His name for a start – there were no other Nigel's in the Battalion. Then there was his public school accent – and he spoke louder and more confidently than anyone else, another trait. He had been so cool during the evacuation from the barn.

* * *

On the way back from the cookhouse, we visited the NAAFI, delaying our return to the barrack room by a couple of pints. Central heating and clean sheets beckoned. I felt good.

13

At Zeltweg, next morning, the foot inspection produced surprises for senior officers, who throughout the scheme had seemed oblivious to our discomfort. A large number of us were found to be suffering from various degrees of frostbite. These were categorised and treated accordingly with minor sufferers committed to our own camp hospital. Worse cases, including Bins and Pearce were despatched to the British Medical Hospital at Klagenfurt, referred to as BMH, for special treatment. Some, it was discovered later, were flown home for specialist care in a military hospital at Millbank, London. Charlie Company was now very much depleted in numbers.

We had been back two days when rumours began to re-emerge that our Commanding Officer had ordered a Court of Inquiry to establish the cause of the fire. We could have told him had he asked! He didn't need an Inquiry to find that out! Nigel, clever Nigel, knew about the objectives of a Court of Inquiry.

"Is that the same as a Court Martial, Nigel?" I asked, as I removed my stiffened socks from the radiator. "Damn!" One of them had a hole that needed darning. We had all become quite proficient at darning socks, using the repair kit, part of army issue.

"No. The purpose of a Court of Inquiry," he replied, "Is to explore the facts to determine whether a Court Martial should be held." His socks were new – a present from his mother, which he rubbed together between his hands before putting them on.

"How does it work then?" I asked.

"Same as a police investigation, except that the witnesses swear on oath, to tell the truth at the tribunal, rather than in a court of law – and I seem to recall that witnesses are not cross-examined. Well! Shall we say, the questions by the court lack the probing aggression of a prosecuting counsel."

"So! Does that mean the accused can lie on oath, Nigel?" I slid my feet into a replacement pair of socks.

"Hrmph! No one's been accused! Besides, officers don't tell lies, old fruit. Why should they – if they've not been charged with anything?"

"Oh come on – if you believe that!"

"They're a different class, Lloyd – old school tie and all that." He slipped on a pair of size eleven, 'bulled' black, plimsolls. "There are two other things you should know. Firstly, the president and members are usually fellow officers from the Regiment, whose roles are to assist and advise. Second, the proceedings of a Court of Inquiry are privileged and the findings are never published."

This angered me still more. "It seems obvious to me then, Nigel, that the purpose of the Inquiry is to produce excuses for events!" I stood up. My size nines looked tiny beside his elevens.

"Lloyd, you are such a cynic! But you might be right – that's why I think you should go for that typing job in HQ Company. I believe it's to do with this Inquiry and it would be very useful if we had someone on the inside, who is able to see the statements of witnesses – discover the truth of what really happened."

"Are you suggesting?"

"Go for it Lloyd, while you've got the chance."

"You crafty sod!" I felt myself shaking at the thought of what, indirectly, Nigel was suggesting. I didn't want any part of it. "No wonder you were turned down by WOSBY!"

Rehearsals for the funeral began and I joined what remained of 'C' Company for a drill rehearsal. Jock Campbell, for his part, saw this as an opportunity to demonstrate his mastery of another range of drill movements, particularly the slow march, and he was determined to make this funeral one to remember for the hierarchy in Klagenfurt, centre of command for the British Troops in Austria.

Before the rehearsal, my heart missed a beat, as Jock called me to one side. Remembering Nigel's words that I might be asked to carry a coffin, I slammed my feet together and stood before him, trembling. I knew, if I had a choice, I would decline from performing that role.

However, it was not coffin bearing he had in mind! He made another suggestion that took me by surprise, especially since he gave me the choice, unusual for the army. He looked annoyed when stammering with fear I declined. I marched back to my place, still shaking and feeling guilty for having turned down his offer. As we set off for the parade ground, I began to wonder whether Jock would make me pay with extra duties.

Our barrack block was positioned directly opposite the guardroom and entrance to the camp so, if we weren't involved elsewhere, it was easy to see any visitors entering the camp. A day or so before the funeral, civilians began arriving and we guessed these were relatives, who had travelled from the UK to attend. In the meantime, Jock Campbell, who had spent the last few days drilling us to perfection, knew we would perform well.

Within a week of the catastrophe, the remains of 'C' Company and the Regimental band were assembled for the funeral parade in a suburban street in Klagenfurt. Jock seemed unusually subdued as we formed up in three ranks that morning. He was a hard man, but he must have known it would affect us once the procession got under way and we all respected him for that, making us even more determined to perform well.

We had bulled up in honour of our muckers and a casual observer that morning, would have found it hard to believe we were the ragamuffins that had returned to camp at the end of manoeuvres. Following pains-taking hours of spit and polish, our boots looked like patent leather whilst rifles and brasses gleamed and our uniforms were pressed to perfection, fit to satisfy Jock's demands.

The usual chatter of men falling in for the parade was absent and an inspection hardly necessary but the Governor still gave us cursory glances here and there as we took our places and summarily dressed in line. There were no observers and it was deathly quiet, apart from the sounds of chattering birds, as Jock waited for the signal that the band was ready.

There was no hollering or shouting and the command to begin the slow march was uttered in an almost conciliatory tone as the first beat of the bass drum sounded and the front left foot of each man slid forward, an inch high, across the surface of the gravelled road before lowering it with a clump. The procession was under way to the hollow beat echoing off the surrounding houses with the brass instruments sounding a tuneful but sad lament.

The timing was easy, our emotions rising, as each beat of the muffled drum, covered in black, seemed to hammer home the injustice we felt, boom, boom, boom, all the way to the cemetery at Annabichl.

As we progressed, I kept asking myself, again and again. Why? Why had Major Appleby done such a stupid thing? The more I thought about it, the sadder I became. I tried to think of something else but felt it my duty to remember my special mate that day. This ceremony was in Ginger's honour, as far as I was concerned.

"You got the best bed," Ginger had said to me, that first day at Mill Hill, as laden with bedding, we raced into the room to claim our spot. It was he who helped me, the first night, when my spirits had sunk to an all time low. It was he who blancoed my webbing when I was cleaning out the ablutions with Dave. Had he not done so, I could so easily have ended up on 'jankers', a punishment I could not have handled easily. Who knows what might have happened, had it not been for him.

Nothing was ever too much trouble for Gerry Parker and in no time he had adopted the army terms of endearment. To him, everybody was, "My old mucker." I could almost hear him and in my sub-conscious state, saw him, up at that window of the barn screaming, as my eyes filled with tears.

The double beat of the bass drum, the signal for the music to cease, awakened me from my stupor as automatically, in step, we plodded on. The only sound, gravel scraping beneath the soles of our boots as our grieving turned to anger and we wheeled into the cemetery in step, proud, resolute with the gentler breeze drying our cheeks. The next-of-kin had arrived before us and seemed to flutter weightless in the background, with us wanting, yet unable, to mingle and tell them how the fire started, how much we cared for their sons.

Writing letters was a way of life for troops serving overseas to distant relatives and the postal service, by today's standards, was excellent; yet, I am sure it had not occurred to the authorities, that being a mainly London based Regiment, communications between friends and relations at home and those serving in Austria were almost as efficient as Emails are today. The Battalion was like a big happy family. Rumours were rife, not all of them true, but following an event such as this, most were soundly based.

Within weeks of the funeral, letters from home confirmed rumours that the War Office had refused to pay the return fares for the next-of-kin to attend the funeral. The reason given, was, 'We do not meet the expense of relatives attending military funerals overseas from public funds and this is a long standing policy.'

It was rumoured later that the Regimental Association paid the fares of the next-of-kin, which included Ginger's mother but not his fiancée, who also attended the funeral. Had we known that day the pain relatives had suffered through this kind of 'red tape', it would have added a twist to the anger we were already feeling.

Once the formalities of burial were over, I stood in a line with what remained of my platoon, to be issued with the usual packed lunch, before climbing aboard the TCV for the return journey to Zeltweg. I lowered myself onto the seat beside Boozer who sat head bowed, unspeaking, with his beret perched on top of his rifle barrel. The engine fired into life: we lurched sideways like stuffed dummies as we moved off.

Boozer was the first to speak as wistfully, he announced, "We could have called on Bins, if we'd had enough time, couldn't we. You'd have thought …"

"I'd forgotten he was here in hospital – and Pearce of course."

Nigel, sitting opposite, said, "I've heard some of the survivors from the fire'll be moving to BMH soon. Well, should I say, those strong enough to be moved."

"BMH?" queried, Dave, innocently.

"The hospital here at Klagenfurt – others are being flown home for treatment at Aldershot."

"Where have they been for the past week then?"

"Camp Truscott – the American Forces hospital at Linz. That's where the helicopters flew them to." The men looked at Nigel, agog, wondering what he would say next. "I understand the speed and efficiency of the surgeons was a decisive factor in saving lives."

"Do you mean to say, there could have been more dead if ... ??"

"Yah – They had surgeons waiting, and as the helicopters touched down the guys were transferred to the operating table within seventy-five seconds of arrival."

"How come you know so much, Pallister?" shouted Paddy from the front of the lorry.

Nigel smiled back at him, "Contacts old boy." Boozer nudged me and nodded towards the front of the vehicle where Paddy was pulling a face. I was intrigued at how my room-mate was so well advised. Certainly nothing had appeared on CO's orders about this, or Dave would have picked it up. The TCV fell silent, except for the whine of the engine and the rustle of paper as men picked over their food parcels.

"Just imagine – old Bins with frostbite. I wonder if it's cured his stinking feet," said Boozer chuckling.

"It would be a fucking miracle, if it has," said Hagley, who had been quite subdued since the scheme. "I pity the nurses with them cheesy feet of 'is."

"Do you know what they have to do with their feet?" Chopper Flynn, quite subdued until this point, was about to impart his knowledge on treatment for frostbite: we turned to hear from the expert who had probably experienced it himself in Korea.

Fuller, the only man brave enough to call Flynn by his nickname, encouraged him, a touch of sarcasm in his voice, "No, what do they have to do? Go on Chopper, tell em!"

Chopper stared threateningly at his mate, long and hard, before replying. "They have to lay with their feet by the open window and warm them up in stages. If they don't, they could lose a toe or two."

"Fuckin 'ell, really?"

Boozer nudged me, whispering, "That's a load of old bollocks."

Chopper overheard, as shouting, he said, "You think so huh! You wanna ask Adamson in 'A' Company – he lost two of his toes in Korea."

"Get away – and he's still in the kate?"

"Well the treatment shouldn't worry old Binsy," said Dave, "We made him lie with his feet by the open windows one night at Mill Hill, didn't we, Lloyd!"

"Yep!" I smiled to myself at the thought of that powerful man being made to do anything, as I remembered those early days in training and the shock of being thrust together, all from different backgrounds, with each other's distinctive odorous smells and sometimes repulsive habits.

Bins feet were the worst I had ever experienced – that sweet, yet sickly pong of athletes' foot.

"Gerry Parker couldn't stand them, do you remember? That young bird at the funeral – nice bit of stuff – was that his fiancée?"

"Yes," said Boozer, "I remember seeing her during our passing out parade."

I called across to Nigel, louder than I meant to, "Have you heard if any of us are being called to give evidence at the Tribunal?" Well, I thought, he's bound to know?

Nigel shook his head, frowning, as if to indicate such utterances were out of order.

"What do think Corp," asked Fuller, winking at the rest of us, as he addressed Chopper Flynn, "do you think he should be court-martialled?"

"There's no chance. There's one law for them and another for us – and if it hadn't been for that bastard, I'd be a sergeant by now."

"Oh?"

"It was his fault I got this fucking packet," he said, pointing to his face, "It has scarred me for life and one of these days he's gonna pay for it!" There was hate in Chopper's tone, as he added, "I'd gladly swing for that bastard."

We fell silent exchanging glances, fearful of Chopper's intent. Fuller, a Korean veteran himself, stared at the rest of us shaking his head as if to say, 'I was there – it's not true!' Why would he do that, I wondered?

I looked again at Chopper's grotesque features, feeling a sense of pity for a fleeting moment as I wondered what it was that Major Appleby was supposed to have done to deserve such venom.

"Was it him that started the fire?" asked Dave, aloud.

"Yeah, but he's guilty until proved innocent," said Boozer chuckling, to ease the tension.

I looked at Boozer sideways. He was, after all, a Polish migrant – maybe he's not conversant with British justice, I thought. "No, you've got it wrong, Yanek," I said, "You mean he's innocent until proved guilty."

Boozer nodded his head, smiling, a thin smile, "No Lloyd, it's you that's got it wrong. Officers have special privileges, same as politicians. They can do no wrong in the eyes of the law."

14

I was still packing when Nigel walked in, his teeth flashing, with a false grin. "How come you avoided the square-bashing?" he asked, feigning innocence, as he flicked his cigarette case open and offered me a cigarette.

I shook my head fiercely, "You know full well – you put him up to it in the first place; I might have guessed it was you."

He lit up, took a drag and seemingly deep in thought, began rolling his cigarette between fore-figure and thumb. "Is that what the Guv'nor talked to you about at this morning's muster?"

"He didn't talk to me – he ordered me." I replied, scowling. "I told him before the funeral, I didn't want it. I thought that was the end of it. Then he said, you're the only man in the whole Battalion who can touch-type. There's no one else. Move your kit across to HQ Company by sixteen hundred hours today and that's an order. Now you know why I'm packing."

Nigel took another puff of his cigarette, "So that's where you're off to - I'll give you a hand with your kit."

"If it eases your conscience!"

He put the cigarette in his mouth and squinting through fluttering eyelids, picked up my case, smiling, "I say, Lloyd, you'll be able to keep me informed with what's going on in the higher echelons of power, now."

"You seem to do well enough without me," I said, hoisting my kitbag onto my shoulder, "having friends in high places." As we began making our way down the stairs, I warned, "Nigel my illustrious friend, you should be aware, I've had to take the oath to keep my mouth shut about all things confidential, with the threat of a court-martial if I don't."

"Ah! So you *are* involved with the Court of Inquiry then?"

I pulled a face, trying to stop myself smiling. I was really quite pleased with the importance of my new role.

He stopped at the door, stubbed his cigarette out in a bin and turned to look me in the eye. "I was joking actually - take my advice Lloyd, keep your lips buttoned – you wouldn't like the Colchester Detention Centre and it would prolong your service, with time added on." I shivered at the thought. I had no wish to serve any longer than necessary. As an aside, he added, "Mind you, anytime you want to unburden yourself by talking about it, Lloyd, you have my assurance of confidentiality."

I had been given a room of my own in HQ Company, situated at the opposite end of the horseshoe ring of buildings, closer to the NAAFI and within earshot of the parade ground. A solitary window provided a view of the main drive leading to the guardhouse and main gate. If I craned my neck, I could just see Charlie Company lines.

I looked around, pleased with my surroundings: my bed, directly opposite the window, a decent locker and lots of room to spread out. Best of all there was a small polished table in one corner and an upright chair – ideal for writing letters. I was now secretly looking forward to the assignment and was arranging my shirts and underwear on the shelves, when Nigel appeared with my webbing.

"I say, Lloyd, a room all to yourself, I like that." In his arms were my large pack, small pack and ammunition pouches, just as I had left them, freshly blancoed and blocked out neatly with boards, their brasses freshly polished with my helmet on top. "Where do you want these Lloyd, usual place, top of your locker?"

"You kidding – throw them on the floor, I'll stuff them in my kit bag until further notice."

"How come?" he said, as with great care, he lowered them onto the floor.

"It's not done over here." I grinned. "The only blancoing, is my belt occasionally." I threw my boots in the bottom of the locker, "What's more, I'll be wearing shoes and no gaiters from now on." I realised too that shoes would be kinder to my feet. Since the scheme the feeling in my heels, of numbness and pins and needles, had continued with no sign of easing.

Nigel sighed, pretending to be envious, "You jammy bugger, what a cushy number you've landed yourself." He turned to leave, "I'll pop across from time to time to see how you're getting on."

'I bet you will,' I breathed, as he departed.

I had a few ideas of my own as I took hold of Jane's photograph, a casual girl-friend, who had recently begun writing to me. I pinned it on the inside of the locker door, within sight of my bed – someone to mouth goodnight to last thing before closing my eyes. I had no illusions. It was going to be pretty lonely working most of the time in solitary conditions.

I reported for duty the next day and was told to acquaint myself with the typewriter – that an officer would call on me later. That end of the barracks was swarming with them. Wary that one of the officers might re-enter at any moment, I slumped back in the comfortable barrel-backed leather-upholstered chair enjoying the moment. Only

Executive Officers in the Civil Service had chairs like these. This could be a nice number, after all, I thought and to look busy I decided to type a letter to Jane – a sensible way of getting used to typing again. An hour had passed, with boredom setting in, when I stood up to stretch and study my surroundings in more detail.

The office was smaller than I had expected; about ten feet square with iron bars set three inches apart on the inside of a clear window. I shivered at the thought of past residents, the Luftwaffe, wondering what the room might have been used for during the war years. 'A small armoury, perhaps? A secret map room? Or simply a storage cupboard of some kind?' It was certainly strategically placed in the layout of the camp.

Looking out I visualised a panoramic view of the parade ground, the airfield and the mountains beyond, but not today. The scenery had been blotted out by a raging snowstorm. I imagined previous occupants sitting in there, on clear starry nights fifteen years before, watching the Luftwaffe aircraft departing, loaded with bombs and returning hours later their pilots jubilant and unscathed following successful missions against defenceless foes.

Warsaw would almost certainly have been a targeted area and Boozer's family, even. He had told us how Stukas, at the beginning of the War, had killed his mother in a bombing raid: there were illustrations of these aircraft drawn on the hangar walls. The pilot of the raid, that killed his mother, might possibly have been based here. I wondered how Boozer felt coming back to Austria, the country where he himself had been imprisoned in a forced labour camp, together with his father.

I sat down again with my back to the window, cosy and warm, smiling to myself – but for this, I could have been on guard duty tonight – brrr! I could get to like this existence, I thought.

In front of me, the typewriter had its own little mat, positioned centrally on a rectangular polished desk with a black leather in-lay. In the drawers I found a generous supply of stationery, including pens, pencils and paper. There was no other furniture in the room and just one overhead light. On the wall opposite, a clock was mounted, much like a school timepiece in size.

A couple of times I heard crump, crump, crump, the dull thuds of men marching past the window in the snow as I relished the fact that I was in the warm, excused duties. The morning was beginning to drag and I was finding it more and more difficult to think of anything else to write. I completed the letter and signed it off – I would write the envelope later in my own room.

Instinctively, I looked at my watch and chuckled to myself with the realisation of that great clock face staring down at me with its winder key hanging on a chain beneath. I had only another half-an-hour to wait until lunch.

Returning from lunch I grabbed a pencil and a clean sheet of paper and began to doodle. I had always liked drawing. I had never been good with figures and faces: instinctively, I began with a landscape as I imagined it from where I sat looking through the window: the cookhouse, trees, parade ground, fields and the mountain range beyond, with no idea where my doodling was taking me.

Then, absent-mindedly, I drew the barn as I remembered it, side elevation. It was about forty-five yards long, I believe. Our vehicles had been parked out front before the fire but I didn't want to tackle that task. Even so, it confirmed my judgement as to the length of the barn. My first attempt was a failure. I threw it in the bin – then another until finally, I was satisfied. Yes, I felt pleased with that. I suddenly realised my folly, retrieved the spoiled drawings and pocketed them for disposal later.

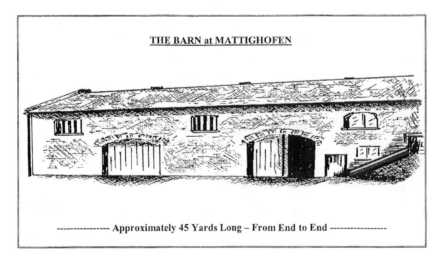

THE BARN at MATTIGHOFEN

----------------- Approximately 45 Yards Long – From End to End -----------------

That night I deliberately avoided any contact with my mates and slipping into the NAAFI, bought myself a paperback, the first in almost a year. The book was the story of James J.Corbett, known as 'Gentleman Jim', an American boxer of some renown. I was feeling like a gentleman myself at that moment, as I looked back along the road at the lights of the guardroom reflecting off the snow and shivered at the thought of the poor devils on guard duty, trudging around the outbuildings and perimeter, throughout the cold night.

Next morning I spent the first hour messing about on the typewriter and then to relieve my boredom, took up the book. I had just got into the first chapter when the door opened and a baby-faced officer walked in. Embarrassed, I quickly shut the book, dropped it on the chair behind me and leapt to my feet.

"Sit down, Corporal Freeman," he said, smiling, friendly, "there's no need to stand up when I come into the room. I want you to feel free from the usual pressures of routine over here."

"Okay, Sir." I collapsed gratefully onto the chair and felt the book cut into my buttocks as I took up a secretarial pose, with hands poised over the keyboard, watching the newcomer as he took stock. He was not over tall, with a shock of blonde curls, a pug nose, ruddy cheeks and thick lips. From his speech and manner he had to be ex-public school – I had yet to meet an officer that wasn't.

"Here take this," he said, handing me a brown folder, "You will be required to keep it up-dated, adding to it yourself, once typed statements are checked and signed off."

"Right, Sir." I looked down at the folder as I eased my buttocks to one side to release a nerve end. The foolscap file was held together with elastic loops stretched across the top and bottom corners. It was entitled 'Court of Inquiry - Barn Fire, Mattighofen – 11th March, 1955'. A large red label was stuck diagonally across one corner with 'Confidential' printed in black.

The officer ducked his head and gestured with an open palm towards the label, "You have already signed the Official Secrets Act, I believe, Corporal?"

I smiled, showing off, "Yes, Sir – the first time, two years ago."

He looked surprised. "Oh rearrlly."

"I was a Civil Servant before joining the army, Sir, so I'm conversant with the procedure." I began to feel important as I slipped back into my, 'trust me, I'm a devoted servant' mode.

"Good, you're the ideal man for this job. Let me know if there are any problems." With that he left, leaving a sweet smell of expensive after-shave in his wake. I liked the look of this officer at first – not a snob, like so many of them, and he had treated me as an equal, almost.

Eagerly I opened the file, my mouth dropping open in dismay, as I realised the full importance of my role and why I had been sworn to secrecy. Inside, was a hand-written statement by **Major APPLEBY**, together with another, already typed and signed by a Sergeant from the Special Investigation Branch, Royal Military Police. It had been taken from **Sergeant EAMES**, our platoon sergeant, on the day of the fire, just five hours after the catastrophe, whilst we were travelling to Camp Roeder.

In it, **Sgt EAMES** was saying….

*'On the 11ᵗʰ March1955 I was asleep in a barn at Mattighofen when I was awoken about 1315 hours by **WO 11 CAMPBELL** of my Company. I was actually sleeping on the ground floor.'*

*'When I looked around I saw about 6 or 7 officers and ORs standing in the doorway. Just after awaking and whilst I was still looking towards the doorway I saw **Captain CLARK** walk in my direction. When he reached a spot about the middle of the floor he stopped and turned around. Just as he turned I saw a flash and heard a bang. Capt. Clark immediately turned back with his hands to his face.'*

'A few seconds after this someone shouted 'Fire'. I looked round and then up and saw fire in some hay about 12 feet from the ground.'

'Within a few seconds of my noticing the fire it had spread across the front of the loft. I immediately got my platoon out and assisted in moving vehicles away from the vicinity of the barn.'

'I did see a lot of men coming down the stairs inside the barn and at least two people trying to get up the stairs. I think one of these was Mr **RAWLINGS** *. I don't know if there was anyone sleeping on top of the hay where the fire started.'*

'I should say from the nature of the flash and bang that it was a thunderflash or something like that.'

Alone in the office, I read his statement with thumping heart, struggling to control my emotions, for these were his actual words written in testimony. The conclusions were obvious but it didn't lessen the shock of seeing it in writing for the first time. I recorded it in the minutes, adding the time and date – the first entry on the file. I suddenly realised it was lunchtime.

My immediate thought was to tell all of what I had just seen read - we had known it from the start. I placed the folder in a drawer and locked the office door. 'Well,' I thought, as I made my way to the cookhouse, 'the driver had been right, it was a thunderflash that started the fire but I must guard against blabbing about it.' As I entered, who should I bump into but Nigel Pallister on his way out? I was in the wrong mood to meet anybody, especially since there was a very real danger of disclosing what I had just seen.

"Lloyd! Just the man," he said, tossing his head in the direction of 'C'Company lines, "We've been having an argument over there."

"Oh!"

"They want to know what you're up to?"

"Didn't you tell them – you know most things," I replied, as I continued walking, "can't stop, got to get back." Fortunately for me Nigel just shrugged and continued on his way.

That afternoon, uninterrupted, I decided to draw a rough plan of the layout inside the barn including the disposition of my mates prior to the fire outbreak. I little realised then, the full significance of these drawings and the impact they would have on me once I became more involved in the Inquiry

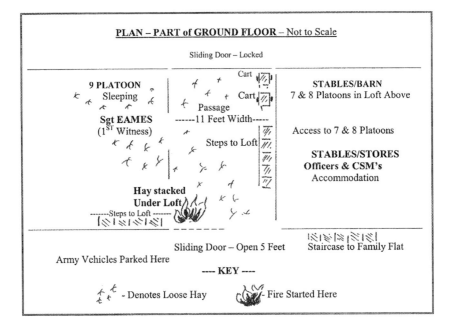

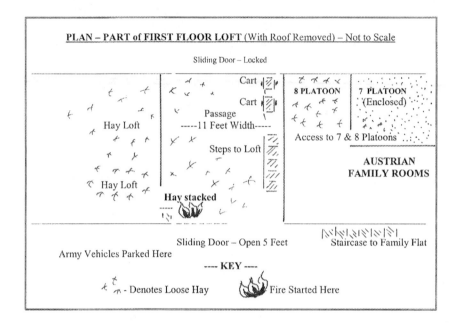

From what I had read that morning, it was clear for all to see, but nagging doubts clouded my mind, especially Leggy's directive that, 'if anyone asks questions about the fire, you know nothing!' I somehow felt this would be a complicated Inquiry – that destiny had determined my role – that one day my disclosures could be useful in establishing the truth of what really happened at Mattighofen. I decided to take note of the statements produced to prove how the fire was caused, the actual words used by witnesses, even though the punctuation might on occasions be a little inaccurate, and in the event of publication, re-produce them in italics.

I threaded a top sheet and two flimsies, interspersed with two carbons into the old 'Royal', and commenced typing. The initial layout took a while to sort out but before long, my fingers were skipping across the keys.

It commenced with, 'Proceedings of a Court of Inquiry', assembled at Zeltweg followed by the date – by order of the Commander-in-Chief. Ah ha, I found myself mumbling, 'So it was the Commander of British Troops in Austria who had ordered this Inquiry!' Here was a much-respected man. He had won fame commanding troops of The Parachute Regiment at Arnhem.

The reason for the Inquiry was stated . . . 'For the purpose of investigating the circumstances under which named personnel (twelve in total) of the Regiment were killed/injured and WD property was destroyed in a fire at Mattighofen 11th March 1955 during a manoeuvre with the USFA in 'Exercise Roundup.'

I completed the heading and sat back to admire my handiwork – fine. The President of the court, I confirmed, was a Major from the Middlesex Regiment, whilst the members consisted of two more officers from the Regiment, a Major and a Captain, and three others 'in attendance' - a Captain from RAOC (Ammunition), a Warrant Officer from RASC (Fire adviser) and of course, **Major Appleby**, whose role was not identified. Was he the accused? Was he suspected? I found it all very strange, but then, what did I know about such things?

I felt I needed to study Major Appleby's statement more fully before typing and that evening took it back to my room, more convinced than ever, that I should retain a copy of anything of vital importance.

Major Appleby's statement commenced with a preamble regarding his role in 'Exercise Roundup' and how strenuous it had been for his men who had slept in the snow, in barns and in guesthouses and how 'C' Company had slept for one hour only in the previous twenty-four, prior to bedding down in the barn at Mattighofen.

His disclosures were so true and it was gratifying to know that Major Appleby had been concerned for us, for there had been moments during the scheme when we wondered if anybody cared at all about our suffering.

15

I awoke next morning with doubts crowding my mind. Having seen Sergeant Eames written statement, taken within hours of the catastrophe, and compared it with Major Appleby's, read last night, it seemed even more clear to me that independent witnesses would be crucial in determining what really happened at Mattighofen.

It was snowing again as I let myself into the office and shut the door, alone once more, to record **Major Appleby's** actual words.

Following the lengthy introduction, Appleby had gone on to say . . .

'A message came through that the exercise was over and as everybody was so tired I did not pass it on but left them to sleep on. Some time later the order to move came through, and I awoke the officers and CSM. They went round waking the men. This was a hard task, as the men would not wake up.'

He continued . . .

*'After about ten minutes in order to speed it up I decided to discharge an American Fire Cracker to wake the place up. I obtained one from **2ⁿᵈ Lt Rawlings** and he helped me light it. I placed this carefully on the ground right against the brick wall of the stable in a position where I did not imagine it could do any damage. It was about a foot away from a very large doorway. As it went off **Captain Clark** came out of the doorway and it went off at his feet blowing dust in his face. Within three minutes or so there was a shout of fire from inside the building.'*

Immediately, questions were ringing in my head. When interviewed by the Sergeant from SIB, Sgt Eames had said that Captain Clark was inside the barn, walking towards him and had just turned, when the explosion occurred – really? Furthermore, Eames said the hay ignited seconds after the explosion! The difference between three minutes and just seconds, is a very long time – is it not? This was the first time I had seen that 2ⁿᵈ Lt Rawlings, the one who had died, was involved. He wasn't alive to agree or deny that he helped light the Fire Cracker!

As for Major Appleby's assertion that it was difficult to wake the men, I knew from experience that Sergeant Major Campbell would have woken us himself. He was not the type to go round shaking men and the power of his voice alone would have penetrated the deepest sleepers' heads sending fearful tremors through our minds.

Evidence produced later by a number of witnesses would indicate there had been a great deal of shouting and shaking before the explosion. Also, I was awake before the explosion, albeit a little sleepy still, as were a number of men in nine platoon, my platoon, and we were nearest to the outbreak.

Sergeant Eames had also stated there were six or seven officers and other ranks standing in the doorway before the explosion occurred. I assumed, therefore, that all of these witnesses, who stood between Captain Clark and the door, would be called to give evidence. I decided to look out for these six or seven and their contribution.

There was no indication that the Major was cross-examined by the court. Strange, I thought? Then I remembered Nigel's words, if true, 'that a Court of Inquiry is the same as a police investigation, except that the witnesses swear on oath, to tell the truth at a tribunal, rather than in a court of law – that witnesses are not cross-examined. Any questions asked by the court are for verification and lack the probing aggression of a prosecuting counsel.'

Appleby's statement continued . . .

*'I went inside and the hay on the left side of the main doorway was alight. I tried to put it out but could not do so. I told **Captain Clark** and the other officers to get the men out quickly.'*

The only other officer available, I would discover, was 2nd Lt Rawlings!

There were no other officers there, apart from Clark and Rawlings. **Appleby** went on to describe his own actions….

'As there were no other fire appliances available I got Pyrenes off the vehicles. (Pyrenes, were fire extinguishers) They seemed to have little effect. I climbed up the back of the haystack and tried to attack it from the top by the roof but it was burning too fiercely.'

Perhaps it was Major Appleby I had seen thrashing at the hay and sending sparks flying immediately after the big bang. Was this was the action of a desperate guilt-ridden man, I wondered? Could it be that the other man running up the stairs, identified by Sgt Eames as 2nd Lt Rawlings, was the other guilty party, already named, for having lit the Fire Cracker?

Major **Appleby's** statement continued . . .

'When I went to the truck for the Pyrenes some of the Austrian employees were there to whom I called out fire. They came with buckets of water and called for the civilian fire brigade. Most of the soldiers were sleeping in the lofts to the right of the entrance, which only had a narrow staircase to get in. As they were coming down the staircase steadily and the Platoon Commanders were upstairs chivvying them along, I did not try to go up myself as it would have delayed their exit. I next warned some Austrian civilians who were living in some rooms at the top of the stable. I also warned the owner of the stable to get his cattle out.'

Feeling the strain of typing, I arched my back and forced my shoulder blades together, groaning as I stood up, switched on the light and looked at my watch. It was five-thirty. Just then the blonde officer walked in. I felt tense.

"How's it going Corporal?"

Foolishly, I pointed at the typewriter and Appleby's half-typed statement, together with that of Sgt Eames. "There are contradictions in these two statements aren't there, Sir!"

He shook his head knowingly; "I know – it's sad to think a fine officer is under suspicion for the stupid act of one man lighting a cigarette."

My mouth dropped open in surprise and without thinking I said, "I don't follow what you're inferring, Sir! Major Appleby has already said he placed the firecracker!" I regretted it the moment the words came out. I had never questioned an officer before.

"Look, Corporal," he replied, his manner threatening, "your task is to type, not to question what you read – is that clear. Anyhow, it's time you called it a day – you can resume this tomorrow."

I placed the cover on the half-typed statement and stood to leave. The officer stretched himself to his full height, yet six inches or so shorter than me, saying, "I'll lock up after you – report here in the morning at nine o'clock and I'll open up the office." His eyes narrowed,

"Remember, Corporal, do not speak to anybody about what you have seen today."

Next morning I continued typing Major Appleby's account in which he explained his actions after the outbreak. His own account could be described as heroic and it appeared that after the outbreak, he had exhausted every fibre of his body trying to rescue trapped men inside the barn. I figured, he must have been beside himself with the worry of what he had done!

My initial anger against him had turned to sorrow, for although it was a stupid thing to have done, I became more and more convinced it was guilt that had driven him on, once the fire erupted. In my short spell in the army, I had never seen a senior officer do anything physical. But this one had!

His actions were inconsistent with that of a commander – keeping a cool head and getting things done through others. Quite clearly, he had been neither cool, nor in command of the situation.

In fairness to him and in his defence, the following statement made in his first submission seemed genuine….

'Although there was snow in the area, the place where I put the firecracker was bare. It was right up against the wall. The nearest hay was about fifteen feet away, through the door into the barn. I cannot remember whether it was the main door, which was open, or whether it was a small

door set into the main door. Whichever it was, it was not wide open but only a foot or so.'

Clearly he was unaware of his facts regarding the door. It seemed from the last paragraph in Appleby's statement that he had placed the simulator in a caring and responsible way, yet, I would question - in placing the explosive *outside* the barn, there was more likelihood of him alerting the inhabitants of Mattighofen to his irrational act, than achieving his objective, that of waking the men in the barn?

If his intention had been to wake the men up, surely he would have placed the explosive simulator closer to the sleepers in the barn? Also, it was more usual to throw these like one would an exploding firework!

Just as I completed typing Appleby's statement, my tormenter appeared with another deposition – that of **Captain Clark,** second in command and the nearest witness to the explosion from inside the barn. It was Captain Clark who had arranged the accommodation with the brewery manager and it was he who had given the false alarm to the CSM when we had first bedded down, when we heard him say, 'No, no, I was only joking.' During discussions following the fire, men said, that when they heard Jock shouting 'Fire', they thought it was another false alarm.

I fed a new sheet plus copies into the 'Royal' and commenced **Captain Clark's** statement, which confirmed he was second in command of 'C' Company and how the first time the Company had arrived at Mattighofen was Thursday 10th March. He told how he had arranged accommodation with the brewery manager but at 1700 the Company had received orders to advance. He went on to say ...

'From 1700 hrs until 0300 hrs next morning the men were on trucks the whole time. The men were very cold and had to bang their feet on the floor and sing to try to keep themselves warm. Initially when we stopped at 1900 hrs we were told that there were enemy on either side and that we were to take up defensive positions, which we did. The umpire stopped this on the grounds that it was incredibly cold – that the men could not carry on.'

'On Friday 11th March the convoy left at 0300 hrs and we took up positions in the area of a timber yard. In taking up positions and with "Stand To" at 0500 hrs there was again no time for rest. At 1100 hrs approx the company left their positions and reached Mattighofen at, I should imagine, about 1145 hrs. I was asleep downstairs in the stable and at approximately 1300 hours I heard the Company Commander say, "We are moving the exercise is over."

He had made no mention of his false alarm order to the CSM, when we first bedded down, when he said, 'We are on the move again,' resulting in us preparing to 'stand to' unnecessarily. I felt suspicious as I commenced typing once more. Told the exercise was over, **Captain Clark** went into the barn to help wake the men.

His statement said . . .

'I went into the barn and into the area of seven and eight platoons. I had physically to pull people to their feet to awaken them. I then came downstairs and did the same with nine platoon. My intention was then to leave them and let them gradually rouse themselves as there was no vast urgency.'

To me, this seemed to confirm the men in nine platoon would have been awake <u>before</u> the explosion. If this was to be believed, it should be obvious to the court that men from nine platoon would be crucial witnesses and in consequence be called to give evidence. Would they be called, I wondered?

Captain Clark continued . . .

'I then went towards the door of the barn. As I was approaching the door, I saw a flash and heard a bang from in front of me, towards or beyond the aperture of the door. At no time did I see anything lying on the ground in front of me. I cannot say exactly where the explosion took place. I must have been seven feet from the door at the time.'

At this point I remembered, Sergeant Eames, in his statement, said he had turned round and seen Captain Clark with his hands to his face and that there was smoke inside the barn around where Capatin Clark was standing – that in his opinion the explosion had taken place inside the barn.

In his evidence, Captain **Clark** went on to say ...

'I immediately ran out of the door to try and find out what had happened. When I came round the corner I could find no one.'

Strange? Where was Major Appleby who had indicated he was outside the barn? How come Clark didn't collide with Appleby who by his own assertion had just placed the firecracker?

Captain Clark continued . . .

'I immediately retraced my steps with the intention of carrying on rousing nine platoon. When I got to a position in the area of the platoon I saw a trickle of smoke and a glow coming from the top of the high pile of hay . . . . . . In my opinion the time between the explosion and when I first spotted the fire was between twenty and thirty seconds but it could have been longer . . .'

Sergeant Eames and Captain Clark had both indicated the fire had ignited within seconds of the explosion. At first glance twenty to thirty seconds seemed a long time but as I read this, an idea was already forming in my own mind regarding the time it took from the explosion, until the time the fire was first spotted.

Captain Clark went on . . .

'I carried on pulling 9 Platoon to their feet and pushing them out. I concentrated on this Platoon because I foresaw a collapse of this high hay onto their bodies, which were immediately underneath. I did not see the Platoon Commanders. When I succeeded in getting the last man of 9 Platoon out I then myself went outside the door.'

Sergeant Eames had already said he continued getting his platoon out when the fire started – so we had two now, **Eames** and **Clark** shepherding us, nine platoon, out once the fire started? I wondered how many more would claim that privilege?

I stood up, rubbed my aching knuckles, and looked out of the barred window. The snow was beginning to melt. On the road beyond, I spotted a prisoner from the guardhouse being marched in double quick time accompanied by a Regimental Policeman, reminding me of the dangers awaiting me, if I dared to reveal anything of what I was reading and typing. I had written home expressing my views regarding the cause of the fire, but had made no mention of my current role for fear that my letters might be opened.

My father had already written telling me of the storm of protest raging back home. The local weekly publication had given great prominence to the catastrophe and how the fire had claimed the life of a lad from Tottenham, whilst three others had suffered serious burns, two from Edmonton and the third from Winchmore Hill.

16

That night I received a surprise visit from Nigel Pallister. "How goes it?" he asked, as he sauntered into my room carrying his plates and eating irons.

"Fine! You?" I nodded for him to sit down on the only chair, whilst I perched myself on the end of the bed and looked at my watch. "A bit late aren't you?" I had already eaten.

"Yah," he said, sitting down, before tossing his plate and accessories onto the bed. "We were late working on the block in preparation for CO's." He looked weary, as he took out his cigarette case and offered me one. I declined, as I watched his lighter fire into life and his lips pucker with the first intake of smoke.

Suddenly I was reminded of the idea that had crossed my mind earlier. Clark had said, *'the time between the explosion and when I first spotted the fire was between twenty and thirty seconds...'*

"Have you a box of matches, by any chance, Nigel?"

"No, why?"

My tongue seemed to thicken – warning me against divulging Clark's words! "Err! Nothing – I just need a box, that's all!" I changed the subject, chuckling, "I've heard about the CO's inspection – I'm not sorry to be missing that."

He drew hard on his cigarette, persisting, "I want to know why you want a box of matches? You a non-smoker too!"

"I just thought I might fancy a fag once in a while, that's all." In truth, at that moment I felt unusual pleasure inhaling his smoke. Was the pressure of this case getting to me? I changed the subject, "It's a piece of cake here, Nigel," I lied. "No parades, no guards and no bullshit but I miss the banter." The monster within was bursting to get out as I fought back a natural desire to tell the whole story. A wagging tongue had always been my greatest weakness yet instincts told me to keep off the subject of the barn fire.

He stood up and paced the room, "You're not missing much, Lloyd. It's the same old routine. Jock gets worse by the day; he's been chasing us up hill and down dale all this week. I believe he's after the title of 'best company'." He looked down, "Anyway, what are you up to these days?"

I laughed, unconvincingly, "Not a lot – bit of this, some of that, but not enough of that."

He laughed, "You never did get enough of that, did you?" He sat down again. A couple of minutes elapsed and an uneasy silence. "You're a good liar, Lloyd!"

"I will have one of your ciggies, Nigel."

"Sure!" His lighter fired into life as I sucked at the dreaded weed, instantly regretting my decision.

Suddenly, he jumped to his feet, announcing, "Lloyd, I know much of what you're doing."

I felt woozy! "Let's change the subject, shall we." I believed him, in spite of the secrecy surrounding the Tribunal, but I was determined to keep my own counsel. If he did have friends in high places, I felt any utterances from me would have repercussions.

"How are you getting on with Bates?"

"Who?"

"Master Bates – he's the go-between that hands you the statements to type each day."

"So that's his name. Why Master Bates?" With trembling hands, I stubbed the cigarette out in a boot polish lid, disgusted with myself for smoking. Cigarettes had always had that effect on me.

Feet astride, he stared down at me, grinning, "Same school old boy. My mother was the one that called him that – and it stuck. But in reality she didn't know how we would twist it. Thereafter, we all called him, 'Masturbates'."

I sensed that Pallister wanted to tell me more as trembling at the thought of my scheming mind, I flopped back on the bed clasping my hands behind my neck. "That still doesn't explain how you get so much inside information? You don't exactly hob-nob with the officers, Nigel, and you've never mentioned him before. How do you know so much?"

He fingered the curtains, appearing flustered, as he peered out into the darkness. He turned to face me, looking fearful, "Sorry, sport, I can't reveal that."

The day's revelations had put me in a foul mood and spurred on by Nigel's attitude, my idea was already taking shape, as I probed deeper. "Actually," I lied, "Your little friend, Masturbates has been quite chatty. I wonder if he knows about your little holiday in Colchester Detention Centre?" I asked, sarcastically.

"You wouldn't . . ."

"Try me . . . old sport!" I retorted, threateningly. "How about your mother – does she know the truth about what you did?"

I could see Nigel was worried, as with shaking hands himself, he lit another cigarette. I sensed my last remark had hit a raw nerve and pressed home my advantage, "What would she have to say, if she knew you had blown it – led astray in training by some old lag – all for the sake of this money-grabbing, horse-loving, whore from Harrow. What was her name – Madeline?" I was closer to a break-through than I had realised.

"Look," he said, condescendingly, "I'll skip dinner - how about us discussing this over a drink, eh?"

"Piss off! You fixed it for me, getting this job, so that you could feed your own thirst for being mister know-it-all in the barrack room. Then you come over here with, 'how goes it'? And you expect me to tell all. I feel like I'm being used and frankly, Nigel, I don't think I can trust you!" I knew this would strike a raw nerve.

He slumped back in the chair, feigning despair but his eyes registered a look of triumph. I felt elated, yet a little sorry for him now, as he teased, "It's really quite simple. I thought you of all people, Lloyd, would have guessed long ago." He was friendlier now, his eyes focusing on his cigarette, as he twirled it between finger and thumb, but I could see he was expecting me to solve this myself.

I hedged, "You never write letters, Nigel, but you seem to receive plenty. Has it got anything to do with the one-way postal traffic? Someone back at Mill Hill, is it?"

He tossed back his head, smiling, as he sent a smoke ring souring upwards, "You're getting warm – if I didn't know you better, Lloyd, I'd have thought you'd been reading my post."

I smirked! "I might have, you'll never know. Go on, tell me?"

"Our two mothers are friends, Bates's and mine. Masturbates tells mummy everything and as you know, I hardly ever write. His old lady passes on all the Battalion tittle-tattle. Fortunately for us," he laughed aloud, "Mother doesn't miss a thing. Besides, it gives her something to write to me about."

"Bloody obvious – I might have guessed!"

He turned looking at me earnestly, "You should see your face sometimes, Lloyd, it's a picture!"

I jumped to my feet, slapping him, laughing. "I was on the right track then – all those letters – you bastard! And you've never said a word before."

In the NAAFI, we sat at a corner table, with a couple of full bottles of Gosser each, and two full glasses, absolutely essential to prevent time wasting at the counter waiting for refills. In the opposite corner, knitting long green woollens, sat a grey-headed lady, the wrong side of sixty, with hair set like a cottage loaf. She was wearing the distinctive dull green uniform of the WVS. Occasionally a soldier would sit down opposite her for a brief chat or to exchange a book.

Around us, men sat at tables, enveloped in smoke, chatting, drinking and playing dominoes or cards. Now and then, an argument would erupt or someone would burst into spontaneous song, or a glass would crash to the floor, greeted with loud applause.

Over drinks, we agreed that in future we would divulge anything we considered important, without compromising our positions. I suddenly remembered my earlier idea as I stood up, and took a draught of beer, with, "I'll be back in a minute!" A little unsteady on my feet, I tottered across to the counter for a box of matches. Nigel looked at me quizzically on my return.

"Come on," he asked, "why the matches?"

"Later!"

Nigel, drained his glass, leaned forward and in a whisper announced, "Lloyd, you should know that Major Appleby has been stressed out. He feels guilty for having started the fire."

"I know."

He poured another glass and moved his chair closer, so as not to be overheard. "Yes, Lloyd, but what you don't know is, he was prepared to take the consequences - but his colleagues in the mess persuaded him to brazen it out."

"You can't blame him, I suppose. It was a stupid thing to do and I feel sorry for him." I couldn't believe I was saying this, and was suddenly aware I had drunk too much, as I thought of Ginger, "Just think, what it's done to Gerry's folks back home?"

"He is a very popular guy in the mess, Lloyd, and ..."

"I know, you told me before, remember?"

"His fellow officers are convinced the whole incident was coincidental – that it was a discarded cigarette that caused the fire, not the explosion."

"That's what they want to believe – let me show you something," I said, removing a live match. "Has your watch got a second hand?" He nodded, his eyes, like a child's, full of wonder. "When I strike this match, I want you to time how long it takes to burn out completely." He frowned. "Don't look at me like that, I'll explain in a minute." I struck it and the match flared as, holding the last sixteenth of an inch with my fingernails, I watched the flame burn. "Ouch! I felt that," I said, dropping the charred remains.

"You're mad, Lloyd!"

"Yeh! Okay, how long did it take, Nigel?"

"Twenty-seven seconds," he replied bemused.

"I thought so. Nigel," I said, triumphantly. "I read a statement that said it had taken thirty seconds from the moment of the explosion until ignition, I felt it was rather a long time – that a certain party was covering up for Major Appleby. I was wrong. I can see it all now. It was bang! Flying spark! Ignition! The time it takes from striking a match to burn its full length."

"But it could have been a discarded cigarette, Lloyd?"

"Think about it! First of all, the men were sleeping, so how could they discard a fag end, when they weren't even smoking. Secondly, how remarkable that the hay caught fire within seconds of the explosion – it would have been a chance in a million for the hay to have flared up from a smouldering cigarette, at the moment the Firecracker exploded?"

"Oh! It was a Firecracker then, Lloyd?"

"Just forget I said that. We all know it sounded like a thunderflash, Nigel, but someone else said it was a Firecracker."

"What is a farcking Firecracker anyway?"

"I'd never heard of one until …"

"Until? Don't leave me in suspense, Lloyd?"

"No, I shouldn't say any more, Nigel, but I'll say one thing, Captain Clark was very considerate. He went to great lengths to describe our suffering throughout that night before we bedded down."

"How about the time we'd spent skirmishing, the day before, in four foot drifts, wet through – he didn't mention that I suppose?"

I shuddered, remembering the last hours before the fire.

* * *

We had been told that morning that action was likely – that we were closing on the enemy. Personally, I thought the so-called enemy must have been closing-in on us, in view of the slow speed at which we had been travelling. We had heard only that morning that Bins had become a dad. To celebrate, it seemed, he had spent most of the morning munching hard tack biscuits. I had called out to him.

"Building yourself up, Dad?" The compo cans of cheese looked tiny in his great paws.

Through biscuit covered teeth and gums Bins, garbled, "Wan' some?"

That was when Chopper Flynn, from deep inside the vehicle, told us all to shut up, that Sergeant Legg, from the front seat in the cab, had called for complete silence. The stamping ceased as we exchanged glances. The engine had been cut as it freewheeled down a gently sloping road. The slightest sound was amplified in the eerie silence. At last, it seemed we might see some action.

Even the hardest and most carefree of us looked excited for we had all longed for this moment – to get out and stretch our limbs and to fight. We were proud, we were soldiers, we had guns and we had been trained to use them. I think we all felt the same – we would show these two Yanks accompanying us that we were fit and hardy. Moreover, the suffering of long spells of cold had made us angry and aggressive – it was time we gave vent to our feelings upon the so-called enemy instead of to one another.

Soundlessly, the vehicle came to rest against a snow bank as we looked at each other grinning, our adrenalin racing. So this is how the real thing would feel – perhaps? I felt strangely scared. It was only a game, we were only armed with blanks and so were the enemy, our American allies, yet we all felt a little scared.

Leggy appeared at the back, his cheeks on fire, as quietly, he spoke to Nigel and myself, the nearest NCOs.

"Get the men to check their guns, drop into the snow behind the bank on the right and wait. Pass it on." I turned to find the rest were already eagerly preparing to de-bus. Without hesitation we launched ourselves into the snow and waited as Leggy beckoned us NCOs forward to join him. Even he looked excited, re-kindling memories of Korea, perhaps. Then, speaking softly, he began.

"Right, 'B' Company are fighting a rear-guard action two fields away - their positions will be obvious once we go over the top of that rise ahead." We heard a bren gun open up, just as Leggy spoke. "We are going to move up within the dip and attack the Yanks on 'B' Company's right flank. Move forward Indian file, five yards apart, remember. Any questions?"

"Lovely sound, the bren!"

Leggy chuckled, "Right let's go!"

Back with my section, Boozer nudged me, his head nodding in the opposite direction. "Bloody hell, they're all here!" Looking ahead beyond our lorry, I could see the vehicles of seven and eight parked and the rest of the Company milling on the road. Even further ahead I could see a couple of Jeeps parked, Captain Clark and his entourage and Jock Campbell himself – they were all there. So this was a Company assault. I had never, in training, been involved in anything this big. I felt very excited at that moment.

The American radio operators, typically, had strapped on snowshoes - nothing had been omitted from their equipment issues. Seconds later we moved off, the two Americans in their Michelin suits, in the middle, with radios strapped to their backs. We had a mile or so to march in snow, three feet deep in places, with seven and eight platoons strung out, heading in the same direction. At last we were doing what we had been trained for, as we yomped in sodden ammunition boots, picking them up nimbly in the deep snow, enjoying the exercise and grinning with excitement.

Within fifteen minutes, the two Americans were sweating and breathless in their heavy suits and massive Arctic boots as Bins and Pearce, the two biggest men in the section, without any order from me, relieved them of their radios to lessen their pain.

"They'll be sorry they joined us, those two Americans," mumbled Dave to me as our visitors, breathless, began to lag behind.

An hour later, perspiring from the exertions of marching, some of the time through four foot deep drifts, we were marched back again without a shot fired.

"What happened Sarge?" I asked, chuckling to myself. That beret of his was the most ridiculous shape.

He grinned, "The Yanks must have pulled back - we'll find out more once the umpires reach their conclusions."

"Umpires? It's hardly cricket?"

He smiled, "That's the army for you." I liked Sgt Legg and felt easy talking to him, as he strode ahead joining the rest of the men who stood by the vehicle, full of cheer, waiting for the next order – an order in keeping with his image as he addressed us cheerily, "Right men, saddle up!"

Back on the lorry we were once more on our way, rocking gently from side to side, our shoulders comfortable buffers between brittle bones, as we exchanged pleasantries for the actions shared, albeit non combative.

"We never got our game of snowballs did we?"

"What price your Mickey Mouse boots now Yank?" The two Americans smiled. They looked exhausted.

The diversion had lifted our morale and the hardships of the past few days had been forgotten for a while. Bins and Chopper passed tins of compo around and at last the Americans seemed to relish the taste.

I finished the remains of a tin of sliced peaches and looked back at the sun, a great spent orange, dipping fast below the horizon.

We had been up since five and, feeling tired and hungry, were heading for Mattighofen and we hoped, a good nights rest. It was here, having alighted from the vehicles in Mattighofen, the day before the fire, when Jock had done his little pirouette in front of the Austrian audience when he conferred with Clark. After that we were ordered back on the lorries and moved out again to spend the rest of the night, most of it exposed to the elements, presumably protecting the snowbound wood yard.

* * *

In the NAAFI, I felt myself being shaken. I raised my head and tottering slightly, stood to leave. Nigel looked at me sympathetically, "I think you've had one too many, old sport. Do you want me to see you back?"

"No thanks! *Old sport*! I've got another statement to type and it's strictly confidential."

"Not tonight you haven't." He smiled, "You're pissed! You're not back on duty 'til the morning."

"Bugger off Nigel!"

17

Next morning, back in the office, another piece was waiting to be typed. **Sergeant Eames** was on the stand, so to speak, the twenty-fourth witness to give evidence at the Tribunal. This was in addition to the statement given to the SIB, at the scene, hours after the fire. I wondered what changes were in store as I started to type?

Extracts from his statement, taken under oath stated . . . .

'I am acting as CQMS for 'C' Company and was doing this job during the scheme. I was awoken by the CSM . . . I got up and started getting the Company HQ people moving. I saw Captain **CLARK** *in the barn. There was an explosion, which I heard but did not see.'*

I was astounded. He had not exactly changed his version but the initial account had been watered down? Two hours after the catastrophe, when interviewed, he remembered seeing the flash. In front of the

Tribunal, he didn't mention it? Coincidently, the SIB Sergeant who had interviewed Eames originally, seldom appeared in other transcripts. Had he been removed from the case?

Sgt EAMES tribunal statement went on . . .

*'I turned round and saw Captain **Clark** with his hands to his face. There was smoke inside the barn, around where Captain **Clark** was standing and in my opinion the explosion had taken place inside the barn. Shortly afterwards, a matter of seconds only, I saw that a fire had started in the hay, about twelve feet up from the ground and about ten feet in from the door.'*

At least, I was pleased he was clear that the explosion had taken place inside the barn and that the fire had erupted within seconds of the explosion.

Sgt Eames concluded . . .

'I got the Company HQ personnel outside and then assisted in moving the transport.'

Here was another contradiction? In his statement to the SIB, he had said . . .

'I immediately got my platoon out and assisted in moving vehicles away from the vicinity of the barn.'

His platoon was nine, my platoon? Surely he would have remembered which personnel he helped to get away? Why had he changed his statement? Had he been in collusion with Captain Clark, who had already said that *he* was getting nine platoon out? I recalled how in his first statement he had said . . .

'When I looked around I saw six or seven officers and ORs (ordinary ranks) standing in the doorway.'

This assertion was not repeated at the Tribunal. As the weeks progressed, the only evidence from anyone near the doorway had been that of Captain Clark? Apart from the sergeant major, I wondered – how about the other quote of 'five or six officers or ORs' who Eames had said originally, were standing near the doorway? They had mysteriously disappeared. I could see this was developing into a cover-up and Boozer had been right all along when he had said, 'Appleby is guilty until he is proved innocent!'

In spite of my brief, to type and not get involved, I was becoming more absorbed in the whole affair now as I pieced together the jigsaw of witness statements and wondered what importance the Tribunal would apply to Sgt Eames's original testimony – or if they had even read it?

Bates suddenly appeared and without a word slapped another typed report alongside the typewriter for filing. Reading it, I discovered that when we were returning to Zeltweg the day after the fire, an investigation team meeting had taken place in the charred ruins of the barn at Mattighofen. It involved a Captain from the Special Investigation Branch – Royal Military Police, a Commandant from the civilian Crime Investigation Department at Linz, a highly qualified fire expert, and another Austrian, the official interpreter.

The police report handed to me, identified as Appendix 'C' in the tribunal documents, appeared in a communiqué from Headquarters British Troops in Austria to The Under Secretary of State. Originated by the SIB, It was dated 15th March 1955 – just four days after the fire.

It confirmed that the fire had started inside the barn in the hay above and immediately to the left of the main entrance door – that, when interviewed, **Major Appleby** had already given a statement to the Tribunal.

"Really!" I found myself saying, aloud, as I wondered whether the fact that **Appleby** had already been interviewed, prevented cross-questioning of him by the SIB – Nigel's advice regarding cross-examination rules, had returned to haunt me.

Extracts from the S.I.B.'s interim report read . . .

Point 11. stated *. . . 'On my attached plan will be seen a cross marking the approximate position of a FIRECRACKER. This is a battle simulator, American type and at the moment, the action of this particular object when set off is not fully understood.'*

The word Firecracker was typed in capitals, as if to emphasise the point that it was <u>not</u> a Thunderflash. The thunderflash was a British battle simulator, which was later proved to be far more powerful than the American equivalent called a Firecracker.

Point 12. stated ... '*This firecracker was set off by the Company Commander,* **Major Appleby,** *in the following circumstances.*'

The description was lengthy and self-explanatory, repeating much of what had been said to the Tribunal.

Point 13. stated ... '*Major* **Appleby** *had the idea to set off a thunderflash and attempted to obtain one from Private* **Turner,** *a signaller. He was unsuccessful but did manage to obtain a firecracker from 2nd Lt* **Rawlings** *(deceased). This firecracker was apparently lit by Rawlings but placed on the ground by Major Appleby.*'

Point 16. stated ... '*I cannot, at this stage, accept it is absolutely certain that the firecracker was responsible. A spark would have to travel upwards, through the gap in the door, to the top of the haystack, a distance of at least 20 feet. This is undoubtedly more than possible...*

On reading the second and third sentences, I knew that the SIB would have been totally convinced of the possibility, had they spoken to members of nine platoon who would have confirmed there was an abundance of loose straw littering the floor of the barn right up to the door. Furthermore, we had felt the full force of the gale blowing through the open door – and loose straw, as it burns, becomes lighter. A flaming strand could easily have floated in the up draught, wafted to the point of combustion. Similarly, it would have had the same effect from a spark.

Point 16 continued *… but every member of the unit must first be seen and interrogated to prove beyond doubt that no soldier was occupying the hay where the fire began and therefore a cigarette or match could not have been responsible.*

Regarding the last point made, no soldier was occupying the area in which the fire started – it was simply a great pile of loose hay.

Point 17. stated *… 'No interrogation has been made of Major Appleby; when seen by me on 14th March, he had already given evidence on oath before the Court of Inquiry.'*

This statement appeared to substantiate the reason why Major Appleby could not be questioned. Strangely enough, Major Appleby's statement to the Court of Inquiry was made the same day. How very convenient that the Court of Inquiry had taken Appleby's statement first? Or had they?

Point 17 continued *… 'He (Major Appleby) assisted in describing the position of the door to the barn and identified on my plan the spot where he placed the firecracker. His statement will not be attached to my final report but will of course be included in the Court of Inquiry proceedings.'*

The SIB Report Plan, agreed by Appleby, clearly showed the door of the barn open with a gap of five feet, identified with a small cross on the plan, opposite the door, indicating where the combustible had been placed. Quite obviously Major Appleby did not query the size of the gap or the position of the Firecracker.

In Appleby's first interview, or was it his second that day, after he had seen the SIB, he confirmed with the Inquiry, that he had placed the firecracker carefully, right up against a wall. He identified the distance between the combustible and hay but he couldn't remember whether it was the main door that was open or whether it was a small door set in the main door. Whichever it was, he asserted, it was not wide open but only a foot or so, thus decreasing the likelihood of a spark flying through the opening to where the hay was stacked.

Had the order of interviews been reversed to suit his defence when he realised he had already confirmed with the SIB that the door was open five feet and that the placement of the firecracker had been more matter of fact? This, I felt was confirmation that Major Appleby may not have given evidence to the Tribunal before seeing the Captain SIB, as stated.

Coincidentally, Captain Clark also confirmed with the SIB that the gap opening in the door was five feet.

I quickly endorsed my own drawing, showing the spot on the plan and the door opening. Amazing! I sensed, at that moment, that one day my little drawing might be useful.

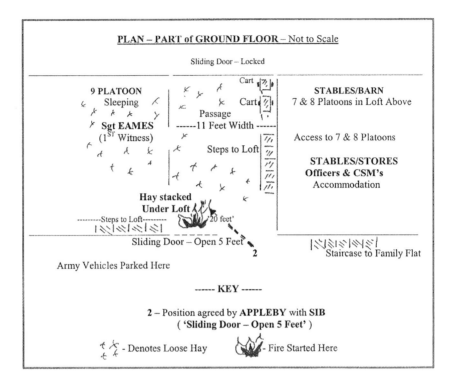

When I visited the NAAFI that evening, I found myself besieged by my old muckers, Boozer, Bins and Dave, crowding round, wanting to know what I was up to. It was good to see Bins back from hospital.

"How's your feet, Binnsy?" I asked, by way of an opener.

Bins grinned and jigged on his toes imitating a boxer's shuffle, whilst flicking the end of his nose with his right thumb, "Great! I'd love t' go back – you should see the crumpet down at BMH, Lloyd."

"Good news too, Lloyd, it's cured his stinking feet."

"Wonderful." I now felt important, as they began questioning me about my involvement in the Tribunal. Boozer spoke first.

"Well, Nancy boy, are you enjoying all that typing?"

"How did you know I was typing?"

"Come on, Lloyd," said Dave, oozing confidence, "we know why you were selected and what you're up to."

"Oh! You know what I'm up to – what's that then?" I immediately suspected Nigel had said something, as I looked to Dave for an answer. Dave looked a little sheepish as he turned to Boozer for support. There was an uneasy silence. I swivelled my head taking in all three. "You may have an idea what I'm up to but listen here fellas, it's more than my life's worth to let on."

"We fink it's got summat to do wiv the Tribunal," said Bins.

"It could be, but I can't say anything, honestly – anyhow, what are you lot drinking?" I could just about afford a couple of rounds.

I hurried back from the bar, "Help yourselves," I said, lowering the tray of drinks onto the table. I sat down and began to fill my glass from one of the bottles. Two of the bottles were already being tilted at forty-five degrees between the lips of Bins and Boozer.

Boozer, his legs astride the seat, with his elbows propped on the chair-back, lowered his bottle and stared at me, with, "They say that Ginger's mum is having a right go at her MP. She was disgusted the Government wouldn't pay her fare out for the funeral and she's angry because she's still not been told how the fire started."

"And Rawlings's ol' man's been 'aving a go as well," said Bins.

"It's probably just a rumour – you lot haven't changed," I replied, laughing.

"It's not, Lloyd, " said Boozer, "Ginger's mum's been in touch with one of the blokes and told him she's seen Rawlings's dad and he has told her what to write – and she told him she's written to her MP. She's even been asking the blokes who it was that did it?"

"Have they told her who…?"

Bins interrupted, "Yer Lloyd, and 'ave you 'eard – they say Rawlings lit the funderflash for Appleby. He died, poor bastard, but Appleby should be fucking court-martialled for what he done."

"You think so, huh?"

"You don't sound convinced Lloyd – you're cutting yourself off, like the rest of them. I tell yuh, the men are really pissed off – they want answers!"

I felt emotions surfacing, as I took on a more serious note. "I'm not cutting myself off, believe me. Like you, I know who did it but I can't talk about it, okay." I was on the point of leaving when Boozer burst out.

"Guess who's got himself a job as storeman?"

"Storeman – do tell me?"

They all laughed speaking, at once, "Reg Fuller!"

"No! – 'Fingers' – in the stores – you've got to be joking. Who set him up for that?"

"We're not sure. It's all a mystery."

"Fancy putting 'Fingers' in the stores! How is Chopper these days?"

"Ain't you 'eard the latest?" said Bins. "He's bin busted - and ee's bin goin' on about Appleby gettin' off Scot free ever since."

"Hang on! Chopper busted! How come?"

"He got in a fight in the Copper Kettle," said Boozer, "Hit a Kraut with a bottle. Could have killed him."

"Blimey – it's all happening in the old Company then."

"Yea," said Dave, "What's more, Fuller reckons, Chopper's even more incensed now. He's looking on Appleby's conviction as a kind of crusade, now he's one of us."

"Chopper doesn't like Appleby, that's for sure. He was sounding off about it on the way back from the funeral – do you remember?"

Bins lowered his glass and frowned, "Wha' was that then?"

"I thought you knew? He said he would gladly swing for him. He reckoned Appleby was responsible for his injury in Korea – don't you remember?"

"How would I know that, knuckle 'ead, I was still in 'ospital wiv fros'bite?"

"Oh! Right – I forgot!"

"It's a long story," said Boozer, "But I'm not sure there's any truth in it. Fuller reckoned it was someone else that gave the order, not Appleby.

They say, that back in Korea, a three tonner went off a road and got lodged on some rocks or something like that. Chopper's section had to put a line on it and pull it back onto the road. Chopper reckons he warned them it was too heavy and would end up in the valley below but an officer ordered it. And he thinks it was Appleby."

Dave joined in. "Yeh! They fixed a steel hawser to it and pulled. I couldn't help laughing. Chopper said it was impossible – like a tug-o-war with a hundred sumo wrestlers, he said. Well you can guess what happened?"

"Tell me?"

"They managed to shift it about a foot – next thing it catapulted into the valley, just as Chopper said it would."

"Yeah but Chopper's injury? Did he forget to let go?"

"No, no! They let go the steel hawser – it must have cracked through the air like a whip and ripped his face open."

"Ooh! Poor sod." I felt sick at the thought of it. I disliked Chopper intensely but I could understand him hating Appleby, if indeed, he had given the order that led to his injury. It was so disfiguring, I just could not imagine Chopper, in his twenties, ever finding a girl with those looks.

"Fuller says that Appleby wasn't even there – that Chopper must have suffered memory loss or something, but ever since, has held Major Appleby responsible."

Bins chuckled, "When Fingers told us, Chopper'd 'ad plastic surg'ry, I fought to meself 'is arse an' Chopper's face were a fuckin' good match."

"Fuller confides in Binnsy," said Dave, who until now had gone quiet.

"Of course, I'd forgotten those two have something in common." I looked at my watch and back at Bins, laughing, "It's still there!" Bins looked crestfallen. He and Fuller had served their penance, for crimes committed, in the same borstal, albeit at different times. Bins, however, was now a reformed character and totally trustworthy. I slapped the gentle giant on the back, smiling, "No offence meant, mucker. It's time I was getting back – give my regards to Jock."

I left them drinking and returned to my room feeling more relaxed, as I pondered over what had been said. So it wasn't a bullet after all, that had caused Chopper's injuries? Flynn was a dangerous man and I wondered what all this would lead to – whether losing his stripe would make things worse?

My post arrived early next morning. Jane was writing lots of late. A bright girl, she had written previously telling how she had read about the fire at Mattighofen. In her letter that day, she enclosed an article which described how, a labour politician, Austen Albu, on the opposition front bench had asked the Secretary of State for War whether he would make a statement on the barn fire in Austria in which a number of British soldiers of the Regiment had lost their lives or were injured.

The government spokesman, in reply, described the incident expressing sympathy for the relatives of the dead and injured before offering thanks to the courageous efforts of Americans and Austrians in rescuing men of the Regiment. The final paragraph of his statement, reported in Hansard, said . . . 'Inquiries into the accident cannot be completed until the injured men are fit to give evidence and Hon. Members will appreciate that I, therefore, cannot yet give a report on the circumstances which caused the fire.'

"Bullshit!" I heard myself saying, as I tossed the letter on the bed in despair. I left my room, wondering what Bates had lined up for me?

He was there waiting when I arrived.

"Good morning, Sir." I said, breezily, chuckling to myself. The conversation with Nigel had been a revelation - the two mothers back home gossiping about life in the mess and funniest of all, his nickname at boarding school. I wondered what they called him in the mess? He said something I didn't quite catch.

"I beg your pardon, Sir?"

He looked irritated, "I said, type this and add it to the file!" With that, he turned and left the room leaving me staring, excitement mounting. I had been looking forward to reading this evidence.

18

A signaller, **Private Turner**, was the only known army witness prepared to admit that he saw what happened. Interviewed by the Captain from SIB three days after the fire, he had said . . .

'At about midday we received news that the exercise was over and I went to inform Major Appleby. I eventually found him and told him about the exercise. I went to the 15cwt W/T truck and a few moments later, **Major Appleby** *came to me and asked for a thunderflash, he stated he wanted to wake up the company.'*

Major Appleby had said in his statement preamble that he too had slept for an hour yet Turner's statement inferred he had some difficulty finding the Major. Where was he, then? It was never confirmed where Turner found him! In a plan drawn up at the Tribunal, it was shown that the officers and sergeants shared an old stable within the barn, beneath the Austrian family's flat. Was he not there then?

It will be seen from Turner's statement that from the time of telling Major Appleby the exercise was over, until he was asked for a thunderflash, was, quote, 'A few moments.' It would seem that Major Appleby had already decided he would detonate an explosive simulator to wake the men, in spite of the fact that he, in his statement, had said … *'I awoke the officers and CSM. They went round waking the men. This was a hard task, as the men would not wake up.'*

Clearly, Appleby had not given the others much time to wake the men, before reaching the decision to wake them himself with a BANG! Great idea! Good fun! But irrational in view of the frequent warnings given by the CSM of fire risk!

Could it be that the officers generally were in a buoyant state of mind? Certainly, from the statements gone before, there were a number of men of rank milling around inside the entrance to the barn, when the explosion occurred. Bearing in mind they had NOT been subjected to the same hardships of guards and loss of sleep, I could not imagine them bedding down in the middle of the day, with an end to the manoeuvres in sight?

The signaller's statement continued . . .

*'I did not have one (a thunderflash) and I heard him ask **Mr Rawlings** for one who produced instead a firecracker. I saw Mr Rawlings hand this*

*over to Major Appleby who also got Mr Rawlings to light the fuse with a match. I saw **Major Appleby** place the firecracker by the lintel near the open part of the door of the barn. I moved back to my vehicle after the bang and it seemed only a matter of seconds before the alarm of fire was raised and we started to try to put out the fire. I did not see the firecracker explode, I just heard the bang and I can only guess that this was what caused the fire.'*

Turner said he returned to his vehicle – after the bang – so he must have been close to the barn when it exploded. He also confirmed that he did NOT see the firecracker explode. Clearly he would have seen the explosion if it had taken place outside the barn as stated by Major Appleby. He was not asked who else was around at the time.

Turner confirmed . . .

'Major Appleby placed this firecracker in the centre of the open part of the door. He did not throw it but placed it on the ground against a raised doorstep which seemed to be intended to keep the barn weatherproof.'

At the Tribunal, I noticed that Turner's statement involved more detail, in particular, the presence of another signaller in the 15 cwt truck, Private Randall. Was this the missing signaller who had said, as we all left the barn, that a thunderflash had been thrown, I wondered? This signaller, Private Randall, who was present outside the barn, was never called, in spite of having had a conversation with Major Appleby, regarding clarification of a message, just before the firecracker was placed?

I noticed also, that at the Tribunal Turner had made no mention of looking for Major Appleby in the first instance, as he had done to the SIB? Major Appleby, invited to ask questions of the witness, simply restricted his questions to what messages he received on the radio. Nothing else.

Closer investigation indicated why Major Appleby had wanted clarification of messages. In his own statement, he had recalled receiving a message 'that the exercise was over.' He let the men sleep on! Sometime later he said, 'the order to move came through,' and he woke the officers and CSM.

Under cross-examination, Turner confirmed . . . .

'I did not receive any message over the air about our moving. **Private Randall** *was operating the set at the time and I passed on the messages to Major* **Appleby** *as* **Randall** *gave them to me.'*

'The last message, which I received and passed to Major Appleby, was that Exercise Roundup had finished and that we were to await further instructions. The message before this was that the **Adjutant** *was coming round to give further instructions. This I passed on wrongly to Major Appleby as that "he was required on the set where the* **Adjutant** *would give him further instructions." Private Randall corrected this when Major Appleby came out to the truck.'*

The Tribunal had interviewed the Adjutant, so I checked back on his statement to see if there had been any mention of messages relayed to Major Appleby. Interestingly, the **Adjutant**, had said . . .

' *. . .at about 1215 hours we were informed that the exercise was over. Soon after, the G3 from Aggressor Force HQ (manoeuvre jargon) visited us by helicopter and told us that we were to concentrate in Mattighofen preparatory to dispersing from the exercise. I was about to go round companies and give them orders when I was told that there was a fire in the 'C' Company area.'*

There was no mention of a call to Major Appleby? So who sent the message to the signaller that the exercise was over, I wondered? Furthermore, there seemed to have been no message "to move personnel" as indicated by Appleby.

When Appleby cross-questioned Signaller Turner he did not query Turner's description of where the firecracker had been placed or the size of opening in the doorway. Later the Major was given an opportunity to inspect the spot – the signaller wasn't. Reconstruction of events leading up to the explosion, especially the spot where Turner saw Appleby place the firecracker, was never re-enacted, as crime investigations are today?

Instinctively, I marked the spot on my plan where **Turner** said **Appleby** had placed the firecracker.

Questioned by the Court, Turner confirmed . . .

'The doorstep is one and a half inches high as far as I can remember. To the best of my belief, the firecracker was on the inside of this step when Major Appleby stepped away from the doorway.'

I now turned my attention to typing the statement from **Sergeant Legg,** our acting platoon commander. He confirmed that the fire erupted immediately after the explosion. He also described Captain Clark's reactions when the firecracker exploded.

Part of **Legg's** deposition read . . .

*'I can remember the **CSM** coming in just before the men bedded down, and saying that we were to pack up and move, but almost immediately Capt **Clark** said that he was only joking and the men carried on. Sometime later, but I cannot remember when exactly, someone woke me and told me that the exercise was over. I got up and went to my platoon area to tell the men and get them up ready to move. Some of the men were very sluggish and some had sleeping bags pulled right over their heads. However I had got them moving in a very short space of time.'*

This was important, as far as I was concerned. Sergeant Legg stated that he had got us moving in a short space of time – all this, before the fire outbreak? His account alone had shown that some men of nine platoon were awake before the explosion.

Captain **Clark**, in his statement, said of seven and eight platoons

. .

'*I had physically to pull people to their feet to awaken them. I then came downstairs and did the same with nine platoon.*'

All this before the explosion – somehow, it didn't add up? Surely the court would explore these statements more closely? Having, in his words 'got the men moving in a short space of time,' Sergeant Legg went on . . . .

'*I was standing with my back to the door, when I heard an explosion behind me. I turned round and I saw Captain Clark with his hands to his face, silhouetted against the opening in the door. He seemed to be just about leaving the barn at the time. Almost immediately someone shouted fire and I saw that the pile of hay between my platoon area and the door was on fire some ten feet or more above the floor. My men could see the fire and very quickly got up, picked up their kit and got outside.*'

This was getting ridiculous! From what I had seen so far, it seemed that a senior officer and two sergeants had all been involved moving nine platoon personnel in some way or another with conflicting observations regarding the disposition of the platoon at the time the fire erupted.

Sergeant Eames, in his first statement to the SIB had seemingly just woken up when he witnessed seeing the explosion. Then he had, quote, 'Immediately got my platoon out'. He had subsequently changed his version at the Tribunal, saying he had got HQ personnel out and then assisted in moving transport from outside the barn – no mention of nine platoon?

Then **Captain Clark** talked of waking nine platoon before the explosion and then after the fire outbreak, quoted, 'I carried on pulling nine platoon to their feet.' .

And now **Sergeant Legg** was saying . . . 'My men could see the fire and very quickly got up, picked up their kit and got outside.'

Surely, I thought, members of nine platoon will be summoned to give evidence?

Sergeant **Major Campbell** recalled . . .

'About 1300 hours the Company Commander told me the Company had been ordered to move. I did not know at this time that the exercise was over, and I entered the barn to arouse the Company. I saw that the second in command and the platoon commander were with nine platoon so I went upstairs to arouse seven and eight platoons.'

Amazingly no one had told him the exercise was over! Yet others knew it had ended! Major Appleby at this time knew the exercise was over but had not told the Sergeant Major this – why not?

I sat pondering over the statements of Sgt Eames, Captain Clark, Sergeant Legg and the Sergeant Major. Before Clark became involved with nine platoon, he had already been upstairs rousing seven and eight platoons, as he said – "physically pulling men to their feet", before going back down to nine platoon. So what was the Sergeant Major doing whilst Clark was upstairs? Jock Campbell wasn't the type to leave officers to wake his men for him. This was before the explosion and he would have been quick to do the job himself.

The Sergeant Major went on to say . . .

'As I was calling I heard an explosion and the shout "Fire" from downstairs. I came back to the top of the stairway to see what was happening, and saw that a fire had started, in a pile of hay just inside the main entrance, some ten or eleven feet above the ground. This was about five yards in from the front wall of the barn and in the edge adjacent to the path through the barn.'

He then went on to describe how he had seen two people in the path trying to extinguish the flames and had gone back to both seven and eight platoons and ordered the men to file out as the place was on fire. He then dashed off in the direction of the brewery to raise the alarm before assisting in removing transport to a safe area some two hundred yards away.

The sergeant major concluded . .

'When I returned the barn was blazing from end to end.'

The commander of seven platoon, **2ⁿᵈ Lieutenant Machin,** the only other officer in the Company, provided yet another aspect of what happened prior to and during the outbreak. He too recalled Captain

Clark's false alarm, just prior to the men going to sleep, when he told the CSM, 'we are on the move again,' before confirming that he was only joking! He confirmed the officers were sleeping in a stable or hen run, in the same building as the barn, but not part of the main barn. His actual words continued …

'Some time later I should think at about 1300 hours, I heard the **American Umpire** *come in and say that the exercise was over and Major Appleby got up and went outside.'*

So, now I was reading of an American Umpire coming in to advise the exercise was over!

Machin continued …

*'I saw him, Major **Appleby**, through the doorway talking to 2nd Lt **Rawlings**. I then heard an explosion and almost immediately a shout of "Fire". I got out of my sleeping bag; I was still fully dressed and I picked up my bedding and dumped it outside quickly. People were coming out of the barn then and it did not seem necessary for me to go inside, so I assisted the CSM in getting the transport away.'*

So, where were the drivers of the vehicles?

Machin continued . . . .

'When I came back from this as far as I remember men had stopped coming out of the building and were standing in small groups. I started trying to reorganize my platoon and also get 8 and 9 Platoons sorted out.'

The American Umpire could not have been far away when the fire erupted, yet he was never called to give evidence.

Machin went on . . . .

'I could not find all my men, but it did not strike me that they might be inside as they could have been mixed up with the civilian population or have gone away with the transport. I then saw a crowd of civilians around the far end of the building and I went to see what was going on. When I got to this place I saw two hands protruding from the bars across the windows and a head up against the bars.'

During the next few weeks, I immersed myself totally in my task as one by one, men were called before the Court of Inquiry and their handwritten statements were handed to me for typing. They had all been taken from personnel who had been asleep in the loft area furthest from the outbreak. I felt incensed. Apart from Sergeants Legg and Eames, no statements had been taken from the other ranks of nine platoon, who were nearest to the fire when it erupted.

My only consolation was that, without exception, all the survivors of seven platoon confirmed that Gerry Parker had returned specially to warn them of the fire. His action would have saved many lives. He was a true hero.

The task had now become a little repetitive and I yearned for something more significant – the last piece in the jigsaw as far as I was concerned. I remembered reading how, the day after the fire, the military police had met up with a Commandant from the Austrian C.I.D. from Linz, and a fire expert, yet their statements were not to hand. Surely they would have completed a report? Why had I not seen it?

I stood up, stretched and crossed the floor to the window from where I could see the aircraft hangars and disused airfield reaching out to the foothills of the mountain range beyond. A thaw was under way. The blanket of white on the lower slopes had been replaced by large splashes of emerald green where young firs, fed by the streams and rivulets of the melting snow, were springing into summer with an abundance of new growth. The low clouds of winter that had so often covered the tops of the mountains had cleared to reveal brilliant white peaks, glistening in the midday sun.

In front of the hangars a section of men, kneeling in a line, were firing dummy rounds from two-inch mortars to the familiar tubular sounds of bloop, bloop, bloop, followed by dull thuds as the practice shells landed a couple of hundred yards distant in no man's land. Range firing was a part of the army that I enjoyed and I was missing it – missing too the camaraderie and the barrack room banter.

I smelt his after-shave, before he opened his mouth.

"Have you finished the last lot already, Corporal?" It was 'Masturbates', himself.

Bates was standing there with another typed report in his hand, "Yes, Sir – I mean not quite, Sir. There's a little left to do."

He placed a typed report on the desk. "File this as it is – there's no need to read, or re-type it." Pausing as he opened the door to leave, he added, "You've done a good job Corporal Freeman – when this is complete, there's just a chance I could make this a more permanent position for you – if you want it?"

"Thank you, Sir."

As he departed, I cursed aloud for having just squandered an opportunity to get back to Charlie company my first love and, with summer coming, my ticket back to Vienna. I had no desire to stay in HQ Company for my remaining year in the army – too boring.

As for the latest report just received? There was no likelihood that I would file it without reading it first.

19

In my hand was the report I had been waiting for – objective and impartial. Already typed, presumably at HQ British Troops in Austria, it was the translated report by the Austrian C.I.D., dated 14th March. It confirmed that all implements stored in the barn had been destroyed and that the barn itself had been burnt down to its walls. The first estimates of damage costs, including inventory, was estimated at 1,945,000 Austrian Schillings (ANS) and identified the insurers as Danubian Insurance Company.

Officers from the Gendarmerie Investigation Department arrived at the scene at 1720 hours on the day of the fire. Commandant, Lieutenant Schneider was in charge of investigations and his Inspectors, Johann Braun and Walter Grünbaum, reported that upon arrival efforts to control the fire were still in progress and all Occupational Forces had already departed.

An extract from the report stated …

'At approximately 1250 hrs the farm hand Achim Gottsburg went to the barn and was waiting there in front of the staircase leading up to the living quarters of the foreman Heinz Mann, in order to take the latter's orders for work. At this time military vehicles were parked at the southern side of the barn and soldiers of the Occupational Forces were either standing with their vehicles or were up in the barn. At the foot of the stairs in front of the barn door Gottsburg's work mate, Friedrich Dennerling, was also waiting.'

'Shortly before 1300 hours Gottsburg heard from the direction of the barn a sharp loud bang, which in his opinion, was louder than a rifle shot. A few seconds after the bang he heard soldiers in the barn shout "FIRE". He immediately went to the open barn door and from there he saw that the haystack on the left of the hayloft at the southern entry, was burning in its centre. The soldiers, who were in the barn, were trying to put out the fire while others were attempting to take the vehicles out of the danger zone. Gottsburg and Dennerling, as well as other people who were coming for help did their best to try and put the fire out with buckets of water, but as the fire was rapidly spreading across the whole hay loft and even to the adjoining rooms, they had to give up their attempts and started taking out the cattle and the agricultural machinery.'

The report confirmed that Friedrich Dennerling ...

'Was waiting at the staircase to the flat with his work mate Achim Gottsburg and a British soldier, whom they thought was an officer. It was at this moment that Dennerling heard a sharp bang from the direction of the barn door. At hearing this he said to Gottsburg, "What are they trying to frighten us?" The soldier who had been standing near them, after the bang, ran into the barn, but immediately came out again, shouting "FIRE". Dennerling went over to the entrance of the barn and saw that the hay stack to the left of the entry, was on fire in its centre, within a radius of about one metre. The soldiers were trying to put out the fire with forks.'

The report went on to describe the valiant actions of Austrian volunteers to fight the blaze and prevent loss of life and stated in part ...

'Judging by the circumstances under which the fire broke out it is to be assumed that the fire was started through the negligent handling of a detonator, which was discharged by one of the soldiers. It is known that the fire broke out immediately after a detonation had been heard.'

Here, once more, was confirmation that the explosion had taken place within the barn and the fire outbreak occurred within a split second of the explosion.

The report concluded ...

'*British soldiers considered rescue work hopeless and impossible but Austrian rescuers saved many lives by climbing through a small window into the attic and then brought soldiers out.*'

The two Austrian witnesses, Gottsburg and Dennerling, had been standing just yards away from where Major Appleby stated he had placed the firecracker. Clearly they would have seen the blast, had it been set off where Appleby claimed.

A further three Austrian civilians, either inside or close to the barn, claimed they heard the bang coming from within the barn, witnessed the fire outbreak and ran to help.

A translated report by Austrian fire experts concluded there was no doubt as to the source of the blaze – in the hay stack three metres up, just inside the entrance. It ruled out all other causes such as electrical installations or self-inflammation and concluded the blaze could only have arisen by a subjective cause. It went on … '*Judging from the centre of the blaze intentional arson can be ruled out as the spot where the fire broke out was inaccessible from the floor. The blaze therefore must have started through an incendiary, which was brought over a distance of a few metres into the front of the haystack. It can be assumed that this was the detonator from a fire arm or similar weapon which was discharged inside the barn in close proximity to the place where the fire broke out.*'….

It concluded …

'The fire in the barn on 11.3.1955 was, with certainty, caused through the setting on fire of a haystack through an incendiary or detonator developing high temperatures and discharged at a distance of a few metres.'

I was now fully convinced from the evidence I had seen, there was absolutely no doubt that the battle simulator, placed by Major Appleby, had started the blaze. I felt my hands trembling as I filed the report. Suddenly, without knocking, Bates walked in startling me.

"I have here an addition to the statement by Major Appleby – just type it and file it with the sketch on the next page following his first statement."

"An addition – how do you mean Sir?"

"Don't ask questions, just type it – the usual number of copies."

Major Appleby's additional statement began . . .

'Having heard the material witnesses and revisited the scene of the fire, I should like to add to my previous statement.'

It continued . . .

'The doors to the barn were hung on pulleys on a rail and the doors did not quite reach the ground. There was no ledge at the foot of the doors, no ground rails for them to run along and the movement of the doors had made no mark on the ground immediately underneath them. Any ledge would hinder the entry and exit of farm carts. The doors were hung inside the barn. The thickness of the barn wall at the base was at least one foot and

the cracker was placed between six inches and one foot around the corner from the door, i.e. on the outside wall of the stable, and any debris from the cracker should not have been able to turn the corner, travel through a half open door and seemingly rise some fifteen feet upwards, a total distance of twenty feet. The cracker was a small grey one between two and three inches long with a fuse in the middle and does not produce one quarter of the bang of the WD issue thunder flash.'

At the end of his statement Major Appleby had also included a sketch of where he placed the firecracker. In the sketch Appleby had shown the door with a tiny opening in the middle; yet all the evidence portrayed it as a solid door, which was open at one end – the end nearest to where he alleged he placed the firecracker. Was this the drawing of a desperate man? He had previously agreed with the SIB that the door was open with a gap of five feet. I made a copy of his drawing.

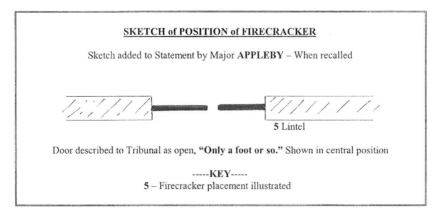

Obviously, Appleby was trying in desperation to place a barrier between the simulator and the source of the fire. The adjudicators never questioned this? Were they really oblivious to the two Austrian witnesses and the signaller standing a few feet away – and all of them heard the explosion coming from inside the barn?

All the evidence pointed to the firecracker as being the cause of the blaze, yet it seemed to me the real purpose of the Tribunal in accepting this additional statement and diagram, had been to disprove it, without producing an alternative credible cause.

Summary of Reported Placing of Firecracker and Witness claims of Placement/Ignition and Explosion Heard

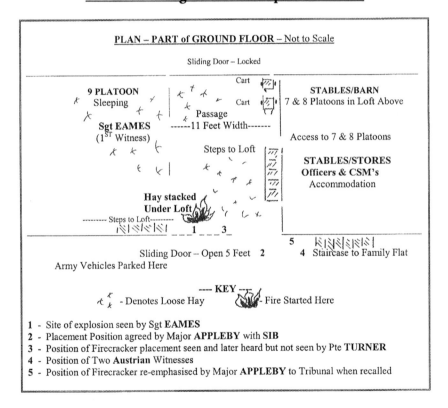

1 - Site of explosion seen by Sgt **EAMES**
2 - Placement Position agreed by Major **APPLEBY** with **SIB**
3 - Position of Firecracker placement seen and later heard but not seen by Pte **TURNER**
4 - Position of Two **Austrian** Witnesses
5 - Position of Firecracker re-emphasised by Major **APPLEBY** to Tribunal when recalled

I brushed the typewriter down and was about to leave the office when Bates walked in. Unspeaking, he bent over and picked up the file then leant back, flicked it open and studied the minutes at the front, his face more serious, concentrating. "You've done a good job here, Corporal," he said, with a cursory glance in my direction.

"Thank you, Sir."

"There's no need to minute the last entry," he added, pointing to Appleby's latest submission, "we'll sort that out." He closed the file, "Your role here is now more or less finished, Corporal."

"Oh!"

He smiled, and with a hint of sarcasm, announced, "Tomorrow, you will return to 'C' Company – your Sergeant Major needs you back in the unit."

"Okay, Sir." I wanted to ask why but thought better of it.

"I somehow think you'll be pleased to get back, won't you?" He seemed more conversational than usual.

"Yes, Sir – this is not really my cup of tea."

"I thought not." He became more serious and looked intently at me as he lectured, "I must remind you though, if you communicate with anybody about what you have seen here, you could face a Court-Martial – is that understood?"

I stood up, not wanting to answer that question.

He looked at me a little strangely before glancing around the tiny room as if seeking some object or other. Feeling embarrassed, I left him standing there clasping his precious confidential file that would retain its secrets for the next fifty years or more.

I had a busy night ahead of me.

Next morning I awoke to the sound of scuffling boots outside my window and then seconds later the bugler raised the gleaming instrument to his lips. I turned over and smiled to myself admiring my kit on the floor opposite. Packs, pouches and webbing, freshly blancoed the night before and spread out on sheets of newspaper, were now dry.

My best uniform too, hanging in the open locker, looked good having been ironed to perfection, my last task before climbing into bed. The solitary stripe and crossed swords stood proud on the sleeves of my jacket. That too had been carefully ironed, including the tailored box pleats, sleeves and back.

I grinned to myself, reminded of the training NCO's words during my induction. 'Bullshit baffles brains', he had said. My boots too had been bulled to perfection. Breakfast was off the agenda as I completed the task of cleaning the last of my brasses; cap badge and lapel badges included and a last dust over of my boots.

There was just time to wash my hands and get dressed and as I looked in the mirror straightening my beret, I heard the crunching sound of men marching past outside my window. I looked out to see Sergeant Major Campbell accompanying the marchers heading for the parade ground.

A cold shiver ran down my spine. I had been awake for a long time last night worried regarding the decision to return me to my unit. Now, I considered, why the sudden change in direction? 'Your Sergeant Major needs you back in the unit,' he had said. What was it all about, I wondered?

My convalescence was over.

20

In 'C' Company lines, the air was suddenly punctuated with the sound of chattering voices and studs on concrete as men ran, walked and slid their way into the barrack block and mounted the stairs. They were back. I felt myself smiling as I stood in the doorway of my old room looking for familiar faces as men raced back to their beds for a quick lie down. Dave suddenly appeared, recognised me, detached himself from the bunch and came over.

"Lloyd! You're back!" I clapped him around the shoulders and backed into my room with him just as Boozer burst in.

"Fancy seeing you, Lofty – what are doing back here?"

Then Nigel appeared, "Piss orf, we've got things to talk about, Lloyd and I."

"Oh get you." They disappeared to collect their plates and irons – it was lunchtime.

"So you're off the case then?" Nigel said, smiling, as he extended his hand, "Welcome back, sport."

I pumped it, solemnly, "Thanks, you could say that."

Nigel looked at me questioningly, "Jock was looking for you."

"I know – he wants to see me later."

He shut the door. "Sit down – a quick chat before lunch."

I remained standing and stamped my feet, improving the fall of my trousers.

"Oh yes, I like the creases and the boots – you must have been up all night."

"Very well near."

"Cigarette?" He asked, slumping onto his bed.

I shook my head and leant, half-sitting against the window sill, looking back across the room towards the door.

He frowned, as his lighter fired into life. "There have been fresh developments, Lloyd - you've heard, I suppose?"

"Sorry, I think I know all there is to know – what have *you* heard?" I undid my belt, placed it carefully across my bed and then released the rear buttons between jacket and trousers. "That's better."

Solemn faced, he announced, "Questions have been asked in Parliament by several MPs. Their constituents are clambering for answers …."

"I thought you had something new to tell me!"

He looked disappointed, "Who told you?"

"You surprise me, Nigel, there are enough people talking about it."

"How about the Austrian Police report? Have you seen that?"

"Yeah – dated fourteenth March, if I remember rightly. They not only confirmed it was an incendiary that started the blaze but they also named two civilian witnesses who were standing at the foot of the stairs by the barn door when it went off. And, the explosion came from inside the barn."

"Case proved, Lloyd!"

"That's what I think – lunch – coming?"

I dallied a while outside Company office and read the notice board. Volunteers were wanted for various sporting events in celebration of Albuhera Day. The Regiment had distinguished itself, long ago, in the Battle of Albuhera during the Peninsular Wars and ever since had been given a day off in recognition for the heroism of a our leader, Colonel Inglis, who, dying from grapeshot wounds to his neck, rallied his men with the words, *"Die hard my men, die hard."*

The thoughts of my first weekend pass for Albuhera during training served to rally me at that moment – with less than a year left to serve. I thought of Gerry Parker and remembered how the training NCO had delayed his departure by making him re-blanco his belt before releasing his pass. Gerry had been so anxious to escape for a couple of days to see his fiancée. He wouldn't be going home to see her now – not ever, poor man.

I took a deep breath, rapped the door of the orderly room, marched in and snapped to attention. Jock stood by a desk in the outer office, jaws twitching, inspecting me from head to toe, just as he had the day I arrived in Vienna. In the background, a clerk greeted me with a smile.

"Step into my office!" Campbell snapped.

I turned smartly, marched in and stood by his desk waiting. A minute later he walked in, closed the door, picked up the phone and swivelled the dial, yet maintaining eye contact as he waited, his eyes unfeeling, boring into mine. Then he growled, "I've got Corporal Freeman in my office now."

There was a long pause. "He's relieved of his post then?" Again silence. Suddenly, he smiled, not at me – it seemed a look of triumph as I stood there, knees knocking. "I wouldn't be so sure, if I were you," he said, clasping the phone to his ear, "he's fooling nobody this time." Then he laughed aloud – a cocky laugh, watching me as he replaced the receiver.

Picking up a loose cigarette from his pen tray, he lit it, drew hard and exhaled, smiling – the first time he had ever smiled at me, "Do you know why I sent for you?" he asked, as he chewed on an imaginary stone.

"No, Sir." I had seen this before in training. NCOs would revel in watching men squirm and then smile as they put them on a charge. Did he know about the drawings - the discussions I had had with Nigel? I could feel my hands shaking?

He smiled again, showing his teeth, quite yellow. "We need you in the team for Albuhera Sports Day?" I felt my whole body sag with relief as he went on, "Last year 'B' Company won the cup – they think they're gonna do the same this year!" He drew on his cigarette once more, "Fat chance – we're gonna stuff 'em," he said, triumphantly, as he released more smoke, "And I want you to get the men fit." His mouth opened and he rolled his tongue around his molars. "You can do that between training sessions."

"Training sessions, Sir?" I groaned.

He smiled again, "I hear you're a boxer?"

I nodded.

"You're to join the Battalion Boxing Squad in training for the BTA Championships. You'll be excused all duties for the next three weeks and you'll be given the best of food in the cookhouse – don't abuse it, the CO is expecting great things from the whole team. Any questions?"

During the next couple of weeks I joined five other stalwarts from the Battalion boxing squad, training to decide the champions of all British Troops in Austria. The Commanding Officer had uncharacteristically agreed for us to be excused duties but his original belief, that men would abuse such privileges, was well founded.

Each day, dressed in maroon tracksuits with boxing gloves strung around our necks, we would leave camp, supposedly road running to improve our stamina, with some sparring involvement at stopping off points on route. Instead, once out of sight, we would take to the hills at the rear of the airfield and seek out a suitable hideaway in the green pastures. Then we would strip down to our shorts and sunbathe in the early spring sunshine before going through the motions of training with a few friendly boxing bouts.

At the end of the day as we ran jauntily back into barracks, 'Punchy' O'Shaughnessy, the provost sergeant, would be waiting to greet our return with, "I bet you lazy fuckers have been up in the hills lying in the sun all day."

On returning to the barrack block I would face constant jibes from those, envious of boxers on excused duties, but never brave enough to volunteer themselves. During the evenings I attempted to get the men fit for the Albuhera sports, my first involvement in physical training since qualifying as a PTI, but not very satisfying since it was only short term.

One night after dinner, Chopper Flynn, now Private Flynn, fell in alongside me as I walked back from the cookhouse. "I'd love to be training with you lot for the BTAs!" It was a typical remark, frequently heard by others envious of our perks.

"There's nothing to stop you," I said, in a challenging tone.

"If only," he said, sadly, pointing at his busted face, "the doctor would never pass me fit to box – it could open up all over again."

"Did you ever box?" I asked.

"Yeah, in Hong Kong – before Korea and this lot," he said, gritting his teeth angrily, as he pointed at his scarred face.

Too embarrassed to look at him intently, I suddenly felt compassion for this man, who I had never got along with, but who seemed anxious to be friends – I sensed he wanted to tell me about his wound, as I asked, "How did it happen?"

Chopper seemed to revel in describing the incident in great detail, much of it just as my mates had disclosed, a few weeks earlier, in the NAAFI, but he made no reference to Major Appleby. He may have been waiting for me to ask, 'who gave the order that led to the accident', but I felt reluctant to elaborate for fear of becoming involved.

Back in the room Nigel seemed anxious to find out what we had been discussing, as closing the door, he asked, "You didn't tell him anything about the Tribunal, did you?"

"Don't be daft – there's no way I'd tell him anything. Mind you, he was certainly trying hard to be friendly. It may seem strange but I felt sorry for him, somehow. He is so disfigured. Has he any relatives that care about him?"

"I have no idea but he has been badgering me on whether I think Appleby will get off."

Each night on returning from training Nigel would express concern regarding the Tribunal shortcomings. All along it had seemed to me that Nigel wanted Appleby to get off, but it seemed more apparent of late that he wanted Major Appleby to answer for his stupid act at Mattighofen. Nigel would usually start by saying, 'He'll get off, Lloyd! I know he will!'

I would respond, 'That's wishful thinking on your part!' Then a debate would ensue, during which I would end up feeling embarrassed for having divulged too much of what I knew, leaving him smirking in a self satisfied way.

Then one day, following some aggressive sparring with the boxing squad, I returned to camp fired up, just as Nigel caught me with my guard down.

"I tell you, Lloyd, he'll get away with it!"

"What makes you so bloody certain he'll get off, know-all?"

"Apparently, Lloyd, Bates is pissed off with the farcical nature of it and has told his mother so. The Austrians are not best pleased to get involved in the latest tests. As far as they are concerned it has been proven, especially they said, since the British officer had already admitted it."

"What tests?"

"Haven't you heard, Lloyd, we've asked the Austrians to carry out more tests on explosives – that could sway it?"

"Oh! Those." I knew nothing of the tests that Nigel was referring to but pretended I was aware.

"Lloyd, I for one will be fucking annoyed if he gets away with it – from what I've learnt so far, if he gets off it will be a travesty of justice."

"Nigel, there's so much I haven't told you but I'm pleased to hear you say that."

"Believe me Lloyd, I have never felt any different, it's just that I'm a realist!"

There was an uneasy silence as I turned away and looked out of the window, wondering about these latest tests that Nigel was referring to. It was a pleasant evening and the barracks seemed awash in a pink glow with generous daubs of light green embroidering the deciduous trees that lined the pathways and roads. The hangars and outbuildings beyond looked mauve in that light, whilst in the distance, I could just make out the dark shapes of the mountains. On the ground below I could see miniature black mountains piled high beneath the trees.

"Those heaps - are they what I think they are, Nigel?"

"Yar, May Bugs. The lads were out again yesterday evening, swatting them with their bed boards, taking bets on who could kill the most."

I had already experienced the wretched things earlier in the week. At dusk, these giant sized brown beetles, would fly in swarms tangling themselves in our hair and when swatted would leave a bloody deposit on heads and hands. They were quite grotesque.

Nigel grabbed his plates, "I'm hungry - where are your plates?"

"I've got 'em, let's go!"

The next two weeks passed quickly and although those of us in the boxing team had not trained too hard up in the hills, the good food, sunshine and duty-free existence, must have worked. We returned from the tournament at Klagenfurt, five of us undefeated, clutching a cup apiece, champions of British Troops in Austria at our weight. Thus, our Commanding Officer could bathe in the glory of the team's success for several months to come, whilst enhancing the Regiment's reputation once more and remove the stigma of the barn tragedy.

The Albuhera celebrations too achieved the same objective. The big day of the inter-company sports finally arrived and as the Company, participants and supporters, waited for the events to be called, Jock dumped a crate of Gosser beer alongside us, speaking in unusually friendly tones, "Help yourselves – when that's gone, they'll be another waiting."

'C' Company won the team trophy as predicted and Jock, already the worse for drink himself, stepped forward, puffed up and proud, to receive the cup. He promptly filled it with yet more Gosser and toasted his champions before passing the cup around for each of us to take a swig or two.

Reg 'Fingers' Fuller won many friends that day when, having crept up behind Jock surreptitiously, he poured the remaining contents over the head of the most feared man in the Company who just stood crossed-eyed, grinning like a big kid, too drunk to care.

Afterwards it was said that our leader had shown a great sense of humour but no doubt Fuller, now a storekeeper, was thankful he didn't have to face Jock Campbell when we paraded next day. Remembering how, after the fire, Jock had sat all night mourning the losses at Camp Roeder, I wondered whether in fact he had seen the sports day as an outlet to drown his sorrows and get closer to his men. There still remained those that blamed him for having delayed the escape of some of the lads by insisting they collect up their rifles before running to safety.

That night the celebrations continued at a cracking rate in the NAAFI. We all discovered that Bins had talents previously unknown, when he gave a Palladium style performance of Frankie Lane singing 'High Noon' followed by Johnnie Ray with 'Such a Night' to rapturous applause, before being dragged off the table and saved the indignity of a broken leg or something more life threatening.

Eventually, the only sober men left in the camp, the Guard Commander and his force, cleared the NAAFI and we returned to our beds in various states of drunkenness singing all time favourites. The actual words of 'In the shade of the old apple tree' would never sound the same again. Our Russian neighbours in Fohnsdorf, further down the valley, no doubt wondered what the commotion was all about.

All talk of the tragedy at Mattighofen had ceased by the time the Company began preparations for range firing at Warmbad, near Villach, in the south. On the eve of departure the post arrived.

Jane was writing about life in the rush hour in London, with tube trains full to capacity and so called city gents, less chivalrous than she had experienced before and certainly less gentlemanly than "her darling Lloyd". I felt good.

More fashions, she wrote, were beginning to appear in the shops but the prices were escalating. I conjured a vision of her in something red. We all looked forward to the mail, particularly letters from loved ones, with desire for a woman, always present and common to all.

Jane had kept a lookout for news of the fire and the aftermath but things had gone quiet for a while, she wrote. However, she promised to keep watching and to inform me of any developments. Meanwhile, she hoped I would return home on leave soon. She went on to say that her friend's soldier boyfriend, serving in Aden, had gone out there about the same time as I had to Austria and would be going home on leave around July – that she couldn't wait for me to come home.

Although homesick, I had not even thought about leave. There was always a flow of men taking leave or returning from leave but it seemed to us National Servicemen, more of a privilege enjoyed by the regular soldiers who were also paid more than us. Jane's letter raised my hopes that one day I too would be going home to a loving reunion. I choked up.

21

In contrast to the cold of winter, the Austrian summer was surprisingly hot and having suffered from exposure during manoeuvres with inferior kit, it came as a pleasant surprise to be issued with Khaki Drill, or KDs for short: this attire was far more comfortable than the thicker battle dress (referred to as BDs) and just in time for our trip to Warmbad. Excitedly, I wrote home.

'They are just like the outfits I remember seeing in War films of the Desert Rats in North Africa. The KDs have no ties or sweaty collars. We have lightweight sand coloured jackets and shorts to match, with long, woollen, maroon coloured socks, turned over at the tops, which we hold up with string or elastic bands. The join between boot and sock is covered with a khaki wrap around puttee. These not only look smart but they also

prevent bites from the troublesome ticks which, we have been told, are

common in certain parts of Austria.'

'Unfortunately these new issues will mean additional pressing and

cleaning because they crease and stain easily. Still, I'm pleased to say we can

change often because we have a regular laundering and starching service

provided. I know Dad, I can just hear you saying – it wasn't like that in my

day. By the way Dad, my mates are always anxious to hear what the papers

are saying about the fire – keep looking out for us and send me anything of

interest. I'm sure you don't need me to tell you, most of them think it'll be a

cover-up. I'm not so sure.'

I had not told my family about my involvement in the Tribunal.

It was late in the afternoon when the convoy of TCVs slowed. Dressed in battle order, we looked out at our first sight of Warmbad, better known for its warm health-giving springs, providing public baths for the wealthier Austrians. We skirted the town, leaving civilization behind, and began a hilly ascent, eventually coming to a halt on the edge of an encampment. Leggy appeared at the back of the vehicle and lowered the tailgate, smiling. He seemed to be in holiday mood.

"Right de-bus and form up in three ranks," he said, with a grin, "I hope you've got plenty of sun oil – it's gonna be hot up here." The proprietary brands of today were not readily available then, so olive oil was the popular choice generally used when sun bathing, often with painful results for the fair-skinned.

I had never seen Jock so relaxed, as we stood waiting in line. He must have been pleased to get away from battalion routine, I imagined, as he stood facing us preparing to give one of his homilies.

"At ease – stand easy!" He began, "We will be here for a week – maybe longer. It depends on the weather and how quickly we get through the programme. Warmbad is a spa town for the locals but we are here for a purpose and confined to camp during our stay." It was the first time I had him heard use the term, 'we'.

"There will be a daily parade," he said, as he strolled along the front rank, studying each of us in turn. "Button it!" he smiled, in a friendly manner, tapping Boozer's jacket with his stick. "You will be sleeping in the tents laid out behind me. Inspections will take place daily." Immediately behind Jock, we could see rows of tents, each big enough to take eight men, set up in perfect lines on a flat, mowed-green pasture, as big as a football pitch.

He went on, "Tent sides will be rolled back and secured at each corner. If it rains, it won't be necessary to trim the tents but I don't expect any – the forecast looks good." He turned his head ninety degrees – no teeth grinding – relaxed jaws. Now I was convinced his mood had changed and he seemed more like the highly respected Sergeant Major the regulars talked of having served under in the Korean War.

"Company orders," he said, "will appear on the notice board across the way. Acquaint yourselves with these, daily." I heard Bins murmur in the back row. It went unnoticed.

Jock continued, waving his stick in an arc, "Fatigue parties will be detailed to maintain the ablutions, at the far end, beyond company lines." I could see two more large tents, with water butts supported on stilts alongside, for washing and toilet facilities; the actual toilets were in fact wooden boxed seats with holes in the centre, supported on cross beams suspended over a huge man-made pit; thunder boxes, we called them. These were protected from the elements by a huge, all embracing shed-like structure.

"The area beyond," he said, in his usual clipped manner, "Is out of bounds!" I wanted to ask why? But only an idiot would do that – Jock could react without warning to such questions. I could see, from where I stood, the ground shelved steeply revealing thickly planted coniferous woods, which no doubt covered the entire hillside down to the valley below.

Across the valley, in the far distance, could be seen a picturesque range of mountains, covered in mist, with one of them distinctly bulbous at the top and lighter in shade than the rest. Could this be the famous mountain that Nigel had told me about during the journey, I wondered?

I remembered taking Jane to see the film, 'The Glass Mountain' and now, I realised, I could be looking at the real thing. During the next ten days I would learn its many moods – one day, dark and ominous, the next shining, as if carved in ice.

Jock raised his stick again, pointing, like a holiday guide, "On the right, through the trees, is the firing range. During the next ten days you will each have an opportunity to fire an assortment of weapons over measured distances. If you do well enough, it will mean an increase in your pay."

"Yeh, about two bob a week," mumbled Paddy.

Jock's stick swung towards the rear rank, as he snapped, "Was that you Molloy?"

"Yes, Surr."

Jock's face cracked in a smile, "Take his name, Sergeant Legg, we have our first volunteer for picket."

To the right of the encampment were more conifers interspersed with young maturing deciduous trees; silver birches, most likely. These occupied a large expanse of ground alongside the firing range, acres and acres of mown grass. Regular humps spanned the greensward, parallel with each other indicating measured distances across dead mans' land between the humps and the targets and butts in the distance.

Behind where we stood was rough scrub, bushes, the occasional tree and rocky outcrops stretching for a distance of several hundred yards, before meeting up with steeper rising ground and more rocks. Apart from the entrance to the camp, the surrounding landscape provided a natural barrier, with little need for fencing. Nevertheless, night patrols were necessary to protect ourselves from unwanted visitors.

With the parade over, temporary guards were posted and accommodation allocated in the tent lines. Nigel was given the task of organising a working party, unloading more compo rations from the supply truck. Meanwhile in the cookhouse, the evening meal was well under way, using stores left over by the outgoing company who had returned to Zeltweg prior to our arrival. The dining area consisted of a huge marquee, with open sides and trestle tables set up within.

That first night, no thanks to Paddy and his little remark earlier, I was the automatic choice for second in command on guard duty, together with another five men from the section. I didn't mind too much though, for it would give me an opportunity to reply to Jane's latest letter.

The guardroom, yet another tent, was separated from the company lines. In it was a trestle table, a couple of chairs and a paraffin lamp, plus sleeping accommodation for members of the guard. Rests of up to four hours were taken between shifts, with members of the guard involved in a couple of patrols, each lasting two hours.

Regardless of the shift timing, most men achieved little more than four hours sleep during a night-guard. For the guard commanders, what with organising, posting and gossiping, it was even less and usual for us to split the last six hours of the night, taking turns in charge.

For every guard there was invariably a duty sergeant and duty officer to check and make sure the men were alert and operating according to instructions. These were documented and read to the men upon commencement. Checks usually took the form of a visit, in the dead of night, whereupon the waking NCO would 'stand the guard to', requiring members to present themselves fully dressed and alert.

That night, before sunset, I posted the first stag whilst the Guard Commander sorted the rosters and paperwork. At that early stage, the area surrounding the encampment had not been fully explored and there was little time for me to accompany men into unknown territory. For the men on patrol therefore, it was virgin territory, and for them, an interesting and varied hinterland to discover; much better than manning static points in concrete or sand-bagged surrounds. It was also warm and very comfortable for the men on patrol and they were in high spirits, looking forward to the week's activities.

The evening went quickly enough as the first two men were relieved, then the next and about ten o'clock it was suggested I sleep awhile and take charge for the last shift from two o'clock onwards. It suited me: I always wrote better in the dead of night with fewer interruptions. It was too warm to sleep at first but eventually I must have dozed off and it was just after one o'clock, earlier than planned, when I was woken up to take my turn.

I was surprised at my own freshness, probably driven by my desire to write that reply to Jane. I sat down at the desk in the light of the oil lamp, eagerly took up my pen, pad at the ready and – cogitated. Struggling for words, I eventually managed, 'Dear Jane', but got no further. My first distraction was the moths, dozens of them it seemed, circling the paraffin lamp. Next, the other NCO, a few feet away, was snoring like a blubbering whale. Then a fox, outside somewhere, was howling like a child in distress.

A large moth dropped exhausted on the open pad as, sweeping it aside with the back of my hand, I was forced to remove the soiled page and toss it in the paper bin. I took a deep breath and made a calculation before starting again.

'Dear Jane, I have just 345 days to go before demob – roll on. The countdown to freedom is well under way now...'

Suddenly Dave, who had been patrolling the northern perimeter, burst in breathless and in an excitable state.

"Lloyd, come quick!"

"What is it?"

"You must come, quick!" His breath was coming in short pants, "You won't believe it!" I tried to guess what it was. Excitement? Fear? Either or both, I couldn't be sure. Dave was not the type to make imaginary claims of things moving in the night, as some men would, so I guessed it wasn't his eyes playing tricks in the moonlight, but something in his tone gave me cause for alarm.

"Right, I'll stand the guard to."

"No! No, don't do that!" He seemed alarmed at my suggestion.

"What is it then, Dave - tell me?"

"No! You've gotta come with me, now." Clearly in a state of shock, he turned about and chased off into the night.

I threw my pen down and dashed out after him. Catching up with him, I grabbed his shoulder and spun him around, "Dave, you must tell me what's happened – we may need help?"

"Shh!" he hissed, "Keep your voice down. You'll thank me for this, I promise you," as tearing himself away, he sped off once more, with me following close behind.

It was a balmy starlit night with a full moon and the whole camp sleeping peacefully. The only sounds were the cicadas rubbing their back legs together creating their high-pitched tropical sound, like loose points in a carburettor, whilst muffling our footfalls. Together, unspeaking, we slipped noiselessly across the brilliantly lit scrub towards the distant black curtain. Looking sideways, I inwardly marvelled at the sight of the highest mountains, a long way off, still snow-capped with the glass mountain, quite distinct, glistening in the moonlight.

My eyes were now becoming accustomed to the darkness and it was possible to see into the depths of every shadow as my imagination conjured visions of what this was all about: badgers at play in the moonlight, perhaps a deer, or even a wild boar. On the high banks, beyond the fringe, tiny lights of fireflies blinked in the darkness.

All at once, Dave stopped dead, took hold of my arm and pressed his face into mine with his forefinger to his lips, urging silence. He crept forward to a line of bushes, then eased his way through into a tiny meadow of long grass. The noise of the cicadas stopped abruptly. I hesitated for a second and then followed in his tracks.

Why was I creeping? I had no idea what this was about, as I followed Dave's example and crept on through the damp grass to another line of bushes. To my surprise, Paddy, the other guard, was waiting. He too signalled for me to remain silent, before turning back to peer through the hedge himself.

My throat was locked in nervous anticipation as I ventured forward. Suddenly, I could hear splashing water and laughter – female laughter. I stepped up, parted the leaves and gasped. There before me, in one of the warm spring pools bubbling up from the bowels of the earth were two naked, shapely young women, splashing and threshing, the moonlight reflecting their glistening breasts as they rose and fell in the water, bouncing up and down gleefully.

Then, like startled fawns, they stood up in slow motion and paused for a moment, looking directly at us, revealing the full length of their wondrous bodies with slim waists and wet buttocks, shimmering in the warm health giving waters, as we stifled our breathing.

It all happened in a split second: as Dave cleared his throat, the two beauties screamed simultaneously, leapt to the bank and grabbed their clothes in one movement and fled, leaving us with mouths agape, eyes popping.

Paddy was the first to speak, as he turned, shouting, "What the fock were you doing Dave – clearing your troat like that?"

"Sorry, mucker, I couldn't help it."

Paddy was devastated. "Do you tink they'll be back?"

"No chance," I said, dallying awhile. Then I remembered the time "Jesus! It's time for the others to take over."

Reluctantly, we returned to the guard tent, where Dave and Paddy couldn't wait to tell the relief guards what they had seen. Throughout the rest of the night, I knew for certain where I would find the others, if needed. My letter to Jane was very short and I was at pains to avoid recounting my experiences down at the pool. It had certainly concentrated my mind in emphasising how much I was looking forward to our reunion.

Imagine the Sergeant Major's surprise, in the days that followed, when the number of volunteers for guard duty exceeded his wildest expectations. In fact, once news of the warm spring had become common knowledge, each evening, there was a continuous procession of men to the distant pool, seeking the impossible in the magical health sustaining waters.

Sadly, the nymphs were never seen again.

Throughout the next week the weather was perfect for firing, with brilliant sunshine and clear blue skies from sunrise until sunset. Each day we were marched to the firing range where the previous wartime occupiers, the German Army, had provided magnificent facilities, which the civilian grounds-men still maintained.

Whilst the conditions were perfect, individual performances were varied and successful results were dependant upon good eyesight, a steady aim and confident handling of the weapon. Dave, already a marksman from his performance during initial training, achieved it again but it was one man who astounded everyone with his uncanny accuracy with the .303 rifle, scoring more bulls than anybody else.

I led my section down to the butts to perform the dubious task of papering up holes in the targets, once the officer in charge had taken down scores. We were unaware of who was firing on any particular target but guesses were rife as to who might be achieving outstanding results on one target in particular.

It was after a comment made by the presiding officer that the mystery marksman's identity was discovered. "It couldn't be anyone else but Private Flynn firing on that one," he said, as he took notes. Chopper's reputation was well known by the officers and sergeants, especially those who had served with him in Korea.

We were discussing it that night after dinner in the marquee, which also served as a bar, when Bins related the conversation that had taken place in the butts. "I was pasting up, wan' I, while Fingers was doin' the paper 'anging. Then he started firin' and the fuckin' rounds ripped frough the targit, dead centa. Yuh couldna put a finger between 'em."

"How did you know it was Chopper firing, then?"

"The officer said so, when we arst 'im. Fingers knew straight away – 'e reckoned Chopper was a sniper in Korea."

"Well, I thought Dave was good – it would take a good shot to better him," said Boozer. At that moment 'Fingers' Fuller ambled by and Bins called after him.

"Ain't that right! Chopper was a sniper in Korea."

"Yep! I've seen him knock over gooks two hundred yards away."

"So the injury didn't damage his eyesight," I said, conversationally.

"No," he replied, looking over his shoulder, "And it didn't do a lot for his fucking brains either."

*

"Lloyd!" I recognised Boozer's voice, in the darkness behind me, as I made my way back to my tent.

"Yeh! What?"

He caught up with me. "Can I have a word in your shell-like?" He said, stubbing a cigarette out under foot, as he steered me out of earshot from the tents. We walked on silently before stopping on a gentle rise, about fifty yards distant, and turned to look back at the tent lines, with the trees behind us.

"If you're thinking about visiting the spring, forget it," I said, "There's no chance of those birds coming back while we're here."

He chuckled, "I'm not that desperate – sit down! Less obvious in this moonlight, Lloyd." We lowered our bodies and sunk back on our elbows, looking back at the tent lines. Some of the men had left the sides rolled back, watching the stars from their beds, before dozing off. The sloping hoods glistened white, like shop awnings, in the moonlight. Behind us, an owl hooted in the night,.

"Did you know," I said, "owls don't go towit-towoo, like people think? That noise is in fact, two owls. One calling, the other, answering."

"Get away! Pull the other one?"

"It is true, I tell you."

"Look," he said, "I haven't come out here for a fucking nature lesson."

"What have you come out here for then, Yanek?"

"Don't breathe a word of this," He said, "I'd hate Bins to think I'd told you, but I'm worried, Lloyd."

"You! Worried? He might have seen you tag onto me."

"No – he's in his tent across the other side,"

"Go on!"

Boozer lowered his voice to a whisper. "It's something Fuller said to him." Instinctively, I remembered the conversation that night in the NAAFI, when Dave had said that Fuller confides in Binnsy.

"Oh!"

He turned, his face clearly visible in the moonlight. Unlike him he seemed worried. "Lloyd, there may be nothing in it, but Fingers seems to think Chopper is planning to kill Major Appleby, if he gets off."

"What a berk! He can't be serious! He'd never get away with it, Yanek."

"He seems to think he will – that his killing would be covered up, for the sake of the Regiment's reputation."

I laughed, "So how will he do it – poison his booze?"

"Shoot him, I suppose."

"How?"

"With a gun, stupid."

"I mean how could he do it, without being seen, and how would he get hold of the ammunition in the first place?"

"There's plenty around here, Lloyd."

"Yes but we have to make a declaration every day. It's a court martial offence, remember, taking rounds off the range – empty cartridges even."

"So – what's in a declaration, if you mean business?' He said.

"So, why are you telling me all this, Yanek?"

"I just felt someone ought to know – and I trust you."

"Thanks – we should do something, I suppose, but Chopper would deny it. Besides, I don't think Appleby will get off."

"You don't seem very interested, Lloyd?"

"What can I do about it? Just keep your ear to the ground and let me know if you hear anything. One thing I would say, Yanek."

"What's that?"

"Tell Binnsy to keep it to himself or Fingers will clam up."

Throughout the rest of that week, I couldn't take my eyes off Chopper Flynn: I even wondered whether Fuller was involved in some way. On the other hand, I reasoned, if Chopper was considering an assassination attempt, he was hardly likely to broadcast it or involve Fuller in his plans – unless?

Nigel Pallister had once warned me I was too close to the men. Now, I couldn't help thinking, how wrong he had been. The discussion with Boozer, I felt had proved that my closeness had paid off. I was in a quandary myself now but decided to keep quiet.

22

By the time we returned to Zeltweg, there was not a pale face to be seen. Even Boozer, the white-faced clown, was sporting a tan the colour of polished oak. Nigel, unrelenting, couldn't wait to read CO's orders and the outcome of the 'Court of Inquiry', but he faced disappointment – there was no news. I felt the same as Nigel, but chose not to show it.

The responsibility of knowing what Chopper could be planning in the future was beginning to weigh heavy and when passing Boozer, I would raise my brows mouthing, "What do you know?" Invariably, there was no response. I tried to convince myself that no news is good news, but the possibility of a cold-blooded murderer in our midst worried me.

Within weeks of our return from Warmbad, news broke that we were off to Vienna once more to replace French troops on National Guard duty in the City. Not only that, but agreement had been reached between the five nations that Austria was to become independent and self-governing once more. The date had been fixed, which meant that ours would possibly be the last changeover and the very last ceremonial parade of British troops in Vienna.

It was the day of departure for Vienna. I had been looking forward to returning but Boozer's forewarning had become a constant worry at the back of my mind. Nigel's frequent references to the 'Court of Inquiry' didn't help. He was still talking about it whilst packing. "We won't know the outcome, Lloyd, until we get back from Vienna," he said, forcing his helmet into his kitbag and bouncing it on the floor, to compress the contents.

"Do you think so? I thought we'd hear pretty soon. They're watching out for it in the papers at home, in case the Army keep it from us – so is your mother, I guess."

"Yar. I just hope they wait 'til we get back, before publishing it."

"Oh! Why?"

"Well, Major Appleby's Liaison Officer at the ceremony in Vienna. He's bound to be on the saluting dais for the march past." He lowered his voice to a whisper, "And knowing how Chopper feels."

I felt the hairs on my neck bristle, "You know!"

He looked at me, suspiciously, "Know! Know what?"

I shrugged, "Nothing." I couldn't believe that Boozer would have said anything, but then Bins, no he wouldn't ....

Nigel interrupted my thoughts. "After his outburst, coming back from Klagenfurt, he's sure to be gunning for Appleby."

"You don't miss much do you! And you don't sound too bothered, either."

"Lloyd, there's not a lot we can do about it – that man's crazy enough to do anything."

I felt even more worried now at the thought of what Chopper might do. Murder wouldn't solve anything. Murder? That word sounded too awful to contemplate. I felt I should warn somebody – but of what? I had frequently heard men say they would shoot this 'shit' or that 'bastard' but it was just talk. Chopper could be no different to the rest. I grabbed my shaving kit and sauntered off to the washroom.

My arms felt leaden as I went through the motions of shaving. I dried my face involuntarily and patted on after-shave before pausing to look at my reflection in the mirror. The tan had penetrated through several layers of skin producing a semi-permanent Caribbean veneer and an inner glow. I looked fit and felt fit, but inside, my mind was churning at the thoughts of what lay ahead.

Stripped to the waist, I took a blob of hair cream; I loved that smell, as I slowly revolved it in the palms of my hands before massaging it into my hair and scalp producing a healthy shine. I seemed to be doing things in slow motion this morning as I took up my comb and passed it through the lustrous growth of hair, with its sun-bleached, blonde highlights.

Gone was the shorn look of induction. It was considered more mature for men in the Battalion to show a little hair below their berets, provided there was no unsightly growth showing at the temples and nape of the neck. I moved closer to the mirror, absent-mindedly stroking my chin.

Just then Bins emerged from the toilet. "You look luvverly – she'll wanna shag you, when you git 'ome."

"Piss off! Ouch!" I had missed a whisker or two on my Adam's apple. Still, it was passable for first parade.

I gathered my toiletries and strolled dreamily into the room to find Nigel had already placed his belongings outside, and was rolling up his bedding. I panicked, "You're in a hurry, Nigel, aren't you?"

"Haven't you heard, we've got to have our stuff outside by nine o'clock."

"Who said so?"

"Leggy looked in while you were ponsing about in the washroom."

"Do the others know?"

"Of course, I care for my men," he said, pulling a face, "not like a certain somebody round here. By the way, Fuller's been having a strop with the blokes as usual – insisted they make a separate trip with their sheets and pillow cases."

"Oh!"

"He's in his element in the stores – it's given him the power he always wanted."

"Nigel!"

"Yar."

"I've just had a thought!"

"Go on."

"You don't suppose Chopper worked it for Fingers to get a job in the stores to suit his own ends?"

"If you don't stop farcking about, you're going to end up just like him – busted. Get a move on!"

I swept my kit from the top of the locker and commenced stuffing it into my kitbag, "Will you take my bedding down if you've got time, mucker?"

"Say please!"

My hands were sweating now as Nigel left me packing and disappeared with two lots of bedding. Outside, I could hear the rest of the company hollering at each other, excitedly, as they trundled down the stairs with their bedding. Suddenly, there was a flurry of movement outside the barrack block and I heard men running.

I looked out of the window to see Sergeant Major Campbell approaching at a leisurely pace, his back rigid, the colours of his campaign ribbons looking bright against his sand coloured khaki drill jacket, his chin jutting forward with the tell-tale signs – eyes afire, in a mean mood. His brown knees looked a touch knobbly above his hose tops but his cap badge, brasses and toecaps shone brighter than any man's.

Jock entered the billet, hollering, "I want all kitbags outside, now!" Then beyond the door, I heard his footsteps coming up the stairs. I quickly stuffed my helmet onto the last items in the kitbag, snatched at the cord fasteners and gulped – he walked in and stopped dead in his tracks watching me in silence, no doubt disgusted that one of his NCOs was still packing.

I felt my hands trembling as slowly I raised my eyes. His hands looked large and strong, the hairy knuckles of his right, whiter, as he tightened the grip on his stick. The crown of office, set in a leather wristband and shining brightly, stood out on his right arm; his arms looked surprisingly thin poking out from the sleeves of his jacket, each sleeve folded to four-finger regulation width, the lowest crease finishing immediately above the elbow, as he hovered silent, like a falcon, jaws grinding, eyes narrowing – then his voice stabbed the air.

"Corporal Freeman, what . . . are you playing at . . . man?" I snapped to attention and opened my mouth ... "Pull yourself together, Corporal! – I want all kit outside, NOW!"

"Sir!"

His footsteps faded, as Nigel re-appeared, "Jock's outside chivvying them along . ."

I laughed weakly, "No! Really!"

"Your bedding's in – Fingers was in a foul mood."

"Who was daft enough to put him in the stores?"

Bins put his head round the door, "Come on bootiful, they wan' yuh kit outside now!"

"Do me a favour, take my kitbag," I said, as I finished tying it.

"Here give us yuh case!"

"No! Leave that, I'll take it myself." The precious Tribunal drawings and notes had been secreted inside the lining.

Dave looked in and hovered, staring, "You're not leaving her photo on the door are you Lloyd?"

"Christ no – thanks mate." I grabbed my case, threw it upright onto the bedsprings and fumbled for my keys. I felt the sweat on my forehead pressing against the band of my beret as, unlocking the case, I laid it down and painstakingly removed the cherished photo of Jane from the locker door.

Dave looked concerned, "You're only just in time."

Outside on the forecourt, I avoided Jock's hard stare as I deposited my case, last in line but first off the vehicle at the other end, I thought, as I turned and dashed back to the safety of the empty room. Nigel was sitting calmly on the iron bed, a cigarette in one hand, an empty boot polish lid ashtray in the other; we had already cleaned up the room prior to packing.

"Why not have a ciggy Lloyd – it'll calm you down." I shook my head – not after the last time. I had felt quite sick. Today, I could feel my hands shaking, what with the stress I was feeling and the latest brush with Jock. A cigarette would have added to my misery.

The first task facing us on arrival in Vienna would be a guard mounting to take over from 'B' Company. Had I been singled out for guard duty, I wondered? Nigel lying on the bedsprings now, his ashtray on the locker top, had tactfully opened a paperback to read, whilst absent-mindedly projecting smoke rings in the air. I asked him, "Has the Vienna main gate guard appeared on Company orders, do you know?"

"Eh!" He folded the book upon his forefinger and looked up. "Yar. I can't remember who, but it's not us, Lloyd. I think it's someone from Support Company."

"Did you say Support Company, Nigel? What are they doing up there? I thought it was only us at Schönbrunn?"

He folded a corner of the page and slammed the book shut, impatiently, "It's our Company mainly – but there's a hand-over taking place with the French in Heroes Square!"

"So?"

"Well, it's possibly the last parade of British troops in Austria and all the six footers in the Regiment are involved. They want to make this the best show ever, with Jock playing the lead role as usual – the CSM of 'B' Company's too short and dumpy – he'd look out of place – besides, he's not as smart as the Guv'nor."

"Blimey! All six footers you say? The size of some of our blokes, we'll look like giants up against the Froggies."

Nigel kept quiet. He was chomping his teeth together, a habit he had when working on something. "Will you stop that Nigel – it bloody annoys me."

"Sorry Lloyd. I can see you're in one of your moods."

I began whistling quietly to myself, thinking. Suddenly Nigel slapped the book down on the bedsprings and looked up at me, enquiringly, as if searching for something deep in my eyes. "Lloyd, listen a minute!" His own eyes narrowed, "Do you remember telling me that Sgt Eames told the SIB immediately after the fire, there were six or seven officers and other ranks by the door when the thunderflash exploded?"

"Sh! Keep your voice down," I hissed. I looked out of the window at the forecourt below. It was quiet. The men were back in their rooms waiting for the call to parade. I shut the door. "Now. Carry on," I said, lowering my voice.

Nigel, speaking quietly, repeated, "Sgt Eames said there were six or seven officers and other ranks by the door, yes?"

"I don't remember telling you, Nigel, but it is true. That's exactly what he said – you got that from your mother, I suppose?"

"No matter who said it, Lloyd, the point is, there must have been other witnesses who saw what happened, if there were six or seven by the door, right?"

"Right!"

"So they must have given evidence – did they?"

"My lips are sealed."

"Getting all mysterious are we?" he said. "Well, I have worked out my own scenario of what actually happened."

"Do tell me?" I said.

"It was lunchtime – I believe they'd all been pissing it up down at the gasthaus – and came back in high sprits wanting to startle us by letting off a firework," said Nigel, triumphantly.

My spine chilled, at the thought, as I whispered, "It was more than a firework but you couldn't be closer to the truth, Nigel. I've never told you my theory, have I?" I took a deep breath and sighed, wanting to release air from a great blown up balloon within.

"Trust me. You said that to me during manoeuvres, Lloyd, do you remember?"

"Yes." I peered out of the window again – then opened the door, to check that no one was on the landing, before closing it again. "To hell with the secrecy act!"

"Tell me your theory then."

"There were only seven men in the Company above the rank of corporal, right?"

"If you say so."

"Well – count them yourself. The officers were Appleby, Clark, Rawlings and Machin. Then Campbell, Eames and Leggy – that's all, right."

"Right!"

"If Major Appleby's telling the truth, he was just outside the barn. So too was Rawlings. I'll come back to that – do remind me! So, that's two, not part of the group. Machin, said, he was still lying down. Campbell, said, he was upstairs waking the men. That's four in total, right?"

"Go on, I'm with you," said Nigel, lighting another cigarette.

"The other three, Eames, Clark and Leggy – all of them, said, they were all waking our platoon in some shape or form – quite ridiculous, I'm sure you agree?"

"Yes, so, what are you saying?"

"When Eames made the first statement to the Special Investigation Branch, before any collusion took place, he was simply describing the group already named. There was no one else standing inside the barn – we were, all of us, sleeping."

"Of course, it all adds up – so why would they lie?"

"I believe that at least six of them knew what Appleby was doing because they were all standing by the open door enjoying the prank whilst we slept. Their statements were concocted to distance themselves from the action to cover up for Appleby – in other words, none of them wanted to say they saw what happened because as you've been saying all along, Nigel – Appleby's very popular in the mess and the Battalion. And another consideration, they could all have been found guilty of being involved."

"Where were our TCV drivers, Lloyd? Were they asleep in the barn? I always thought they slept with their vehicles, didn't you?"

"It's irrelevant!"

"Well, why would Jock and Machin be in such a hurry to move the vehicles, once the fire started, if the drivers were to hand?"

"It's a good point, but I am talking about the moment the fire erupted." I took another look out of the window – men were coming and going still, but Jock was nowhere to be seen, so I carried on, "Now, Machin said he saw the umpire tell Appleby the scheme was over but that conflicts with the signaller's evidence. Turner, the signaller, got the message that the scheme was over and went looking for Major Appleby. In Turner's statement, he said he *eventually* found him. Where did he find him? It was never asked – never confirmed. Where was he then – which suggests your piss-up theory?"

"Lloyd, your imagination's running riot, now."

"You're right – incidentally, the sender of the message to Turner was never identified, nor was the American Umpire. For some reason the authorities, I feel, wanted to keep the Americans out of it. It must have been an embarrassment for us – it was, after all, in their sector."

"So, where did Eames figure, Lloyd, if he observed the others by the door?"

"I'm inclined to believe that Sgt Eames's statement to the SIB is probably more accurate – but he colluded with the others afterwards. When giving evidence to the Court of Inquiry, Sergeant Eames omitted to say, he saw six or seven officers and other ranks standing by the door."

"Appleby and Rawlings were outside the barn, remember, you said to remind you, Lloyd – there was something else?"

"Yes, there were more independent witnesses outside the barn that morning and they verified that the explosion came from within the barn. Turner actually saw Appleby place the firecracker by the lintel near the open part of the door of the barn. Appleby was invited to ask Turner questions, but restricted these to clarification of messages alone. It was only after Appleby had been back to the site, that he refuted Turner's claim, on the basis that no lintel existed."

"So, it's his word against Turner's!"

"Suggesting that Turner had a lapse of memory or was lying, Nigel – yes?"

"I guess so."

"Appleby's memory was none too good either, Nigel. In his first statement to the Tribunal, he couldn't remember the set-up of the doors – said they had an opening of one foot and that he had placed the firecracker safely, against the outer wall. Later, the same day, he confirmed with the SIB that the door had an opening of five feet. Furthermore, it was confirmed that the position of the firecracker, was on the ground opposite the open door and twenty feet from the seat of the fire."

"I see what you mean, Lloyd."

"Initially, Appleby, full of remorse, admitted he had started the fire and was prepared to take the consequences. But, it was obvious from the evidence that he lied, on oath. Now I believe other forces were at work – that he was encouraged to lie, for the sake of the Regiment, the British Army and the War Office because they would be committed to a substantial pay-out if we were found to be negligent."

"In other words, Lloyd, you are saying it was a cover-up."

"Yes, a bloody great big cover-up!"

"In that case, Lloyd, don't you see, he will get off."

"I'd like to believe not – I still believe in justice, for the sake of the men that died, Nigel."

"The Tribunal doesn't decide you know – they only present the facts. It's up to the Commander in Chief down at BTA headquarters to decide. And he's no mug, Lloyd. They won't fool him. I agree he should be found guilty."

I flopped back on the bedsprings, mentally drained, as my thoughts returned to Chopper Flynn and the alternative. "Nigel, you said the parade would consist of six-footers – that rules out Chopper – he's far too short."

"Exactly. And remember, he's a crack shot and he usually forms part of the armed escort."

"But if Appleby's found guilty, Nigel, then hopefully Chopper won't put his own neck on the line."

"Has Flynn got any relatives that you know of?"

"I've checked with Boozer. Bins told him that Chopper was an orphan – hasn't got a father, doesn't know his mother."

"In his state, little to live for really, then."

23

The journey from Zeltweg to Vienna was less stressful than my first and when the train stopped at the Semmering check-point, I thought back to that day, seven or eight months before when, alone, I had faced Russian troops with their burp guns for the first time. I looked across at Nigel who was still reading, seemingly disinterested.

"I've only just realised, Nigel, it's eight months since I first took this journey – it seems a great deal longer than that."

"Ugh!"

I had become nineteen since the first train journey to Vienna but felt much older now. How scared I must have appeared to the Russians, when they had wandered menacingly down the length of the train checking everybody in turn. Now it was different. I was in the company of eighty seasoned warriors, led by a battle-hardened Sergeant Major who was scared of nobody.

Unafraid, I openly watched the handful of Russian troops who lounged around on the platform, in their everyday ill-fitting uniforms, looking very uncomfortable in the summer heat.

"Scruffy lot aren't they, Nigel. They must envy us in our KDs."

"Mmm."

"Probably as jealous of us, as we were of the Yanks, with their quilted uniforms, on the scheme – do you remember?"

"Yar."

"It all seems a long time ago."

Nigel remained engrossed in his book. I felt bored. The Russians seemed quite friendly and I was tempted to give them a wave as I waited for the train to move off. I guessed my mates felt the same yet none of them smiled, treating the Russians with grudging respect.

The train pulled away for the last stage of the journey, meandering between the peaks, traversing bridges and crossing gorges surrounded either side by spectacular scenery with the mountains now clothed in various shades of green, the smoothness of the slopes regularly interrupted with outcrops of granite, their summits still capped with pure white snow that glistened in the sunlight. On the hillsides, cows wandered aimlessly, gorging on the lush grass, their udders full to bursting.

The train slowed as we approached Mödling station. Sergeant Legg could be heard coming down the corridor, stopping at each compartment, calmly giving last minute instructions. He reached our own and slid the door back, just as the Russians had done six months before, but unlike them, Leggy was smiling.

"Once we arrive, don't let the men off the train until we say so."

"Okay, Sarge." Nigel looked up from his book, nodding agreeably.

"Make sure they're properly dressed wearing belts and berets, okay. Once off the train, line 'em up on the platform by platoon for further instructions. Any questions?"

I stood up and glanced out of the window, then back at Leggy, "How about transport and kit, Sarge?"

"There's a working party from 'B' Company taking care of the gear and with luck, it'll arrive at Schönbrunn before us." I thought of my case, hoping the locks would remain secure. He went on "There's transport laid on for us but we'll tell you when to board, okay." We could hear the excitement in Leggy's voice. Clearly, he was thrilled to be back. We walked down the corridor relaying the message. Boozer was in high spirits. Not only had he learnt to speak English like a native, but he had also mastered card games and had just relieved a few of his mates of their pay.

He looked at me, grinning, "Do you wanna borrow a few quid, Corporal?"

"You serious?"

"You fucking creep," said Hagley, circling the end of his nose with thumb and forefinger, "It's, Corporal now, is it?"

"It'll cost you - with interest though." shouted Boozer, salvaging his reputation.

I re-joined the NCOs further down the train.

The barracks at Schönbrunn hadn't changed and it was good to know our way around but new discoveries awaited us. For a start, there was an additional recreational facility in the grounds to look forward to – a good-sized swimming pool with a couple of diving boards.

The first morning back at Schönbrunn went quickly enough – starting with an inspection by Jock, followed by another of his homilies, demanding a special level of smartness and skill at arms drill, leading up to the big parade. Weren't we, after all, 'the best Company, of the finest Regiment in the British Army' and if not, he, Jock Campbell, was going to make sure we were.

Nigel had been right about the six-footers as Jock called out the names of the tall men and informed us that within a day or so, we would be joined by another contingent of giants from the Battalion, who he intended to drill relentlessly to meet the high standards of Charlie Company. It worked – we suddenly felt a little taller.

It was, he said, 'To be our finest hour.' Where had I heard that before? In addition, he told us that a company of French troops would be practising on the parade ground here at Schönbrunn. That they too would be drilling for the hand-over in Helden Platz (Heroes Square). And that it could possibly be the last big parade of British troops in Austria.

The faintest of smiles crossed his lips, as he warned, "They will be sharing the NAAFI with us and I don't want any Nationalistic rivalry. Anyone fighting with French troops will be severely dealt with."

After pumping us up with his little speech, Jock then proceeded to drill us for an hour until we were fit to drop, with special emphasis on arms drill. The next couple of days were confined to combat and weapon training, well away from the parade ground, leaving the French to practise their drill, whilst we awaited the arrival of a dozen heavies from other companies.

Boozer remarked, "Jock kept us away from the square cos he was worried we'd take the piss out of the Frogs."

Dave, shorter than most, and excluded, wanted to know, "What's wrong with them?"

"They are terrible! They're light infantry," he said, punching the air, with his arms swinging back and forth at great speed, "They bomb along at a hundred and sixty to the minute – it'll be over in a flash and we'll show them up with our turnout and drill, especially with our slow marching." Boozer, surprisingly, was so proud to be in the British Army.

By the fourth day the remaining big men of the Battalion had arrived and serious drill got under way, leaving the rest of the company operationally involved on guard duty and fatigues. For the first time since joining the army, along with the rest, I was being made to feel special.

In the meantime, we began bulling our kit in earnest. Boots, especially our boots, were going to shine as never before. Our webbing, normally green in colour, was to be scrubbed clean and blancoed white, whilst the much despised Royal Military Police were to supply us with their puttees and eye-catching white straps.

Whenever possible, in between drilling, I kept more than a casual eye on Chopper Flynn's activities, noting any changes in his routine duties that might appear on Company orders. I saw Dave in the washroom. Totally unaware of what Boozer had told me, he remarked that Chopper, unlike him, had been spending a lot of time in the barrack room watching our marching routine on the square.

I made a remark that I regretted, the moment it escaped from my big mouth, "He's probably upset he's not on the parade – he's another short arse, Dave."

He looked crestfallen, "So, that's what you think of me, is it?"

"Sorry, mucker, I didn't mean that."

"I'm going across to the NAAFI, is there anything you want?" He asked, resignedly.

"No thanks, Dave, I'll be over later – sorry, I'll buy you a Gosser, promise."

Boozer was still in the barrack room as Nigel and I were passing. I pulled away and wandered in for a word. Boozer sat alone at the centre table, a cigarette draped from the corner of his mouth, polishing his rifle.

"Bullshitter," I teased, "What do you know?"

He looked worried. "Thank God, I've seen you – I've been wondering whether I should tell Leggy."

"Why?"

"It looks like he's going through with it, regardless, Lloyd."

"What makes you think that?"

"You remember the scheme, when we nearly went over the top in the TCV?" he said, blinking to avoid his own smoke.

"Remember it – Yanek, I'll never forget it."

"And the Yank lost his watch" he said, nodding his head.

"You mean, stolen. Don't tell me – Fuller!"

He blew down the length of his cigarette to dispel loose ash, whilst retaining the fag in his mouth. "Yes, it was Fingers, all along,"

"I might have guessed."

"Chopper saw him pinch it – in fact, the daft bastard is openly wearing it now." Yanek, gingerly, pushed his rifle to one side and stubbed out his cigarette between fingers and thumb, "Sit down, Lloyd – use my bed, I haven't made it up yet." He placed the half-smoked cigarette on the locker top.

"So what's it got to do with Chopper?"

"Well, Fingers has told Binnsy that Chopper wants him to help with his plan – has threatened to shop him – if he bleats."

"So Fingers was daft enough to let Bins know he had stolen that watch."

"No! Bins saw the watch and guessed – all he said to Binnsy was that Chopper had something on him and had threatened to shop him, if he didn't play ball."

"Oh!"

"He's told Binnsy what Chopper intends to do. Now Bins is dead worried that he's become indirectly involved. Lloyd, I've told Binnsy that you know all about it – I've told him you can help."

"Oh! I hope you've done the right thing, Yanek."

"Lloyd, he trusts you." Yanek took out a fresh cigarette, "Want one?" I shook my head. He lit it, took a draw and commenced, talking through smoke. "Chopper has told Fingers that he withheld a couple of rounds of ammo down at Warmbad. He said he has stashed them away in a pair of his rolled up socks – that one is for Appleby, the other for himself, if he has to.

"So," I asked, "What's Fuller got to do?"

"Apparently, Chopper has got it all worked out. He will join the parade party on escort duty." I watched as Yanek nonchalantly flicked ash onto the floor. He looked at me chuckling, "Don't worry, Lloyd, I'm on floors. Listen! Chopper's gonna shoot Appleby when the parade reaches its climax and we present arms."

"Cunning bastard!" A shiver ran down my spine – this would be cold blooded murder. "It's so obvious we'll be making enough noise to muffle the shot, and all eyes will be on us anyway. The perfect crime – except?"

Yanek's normally smooth brow had darkened. "According to Fingers, Chopper's confident the shot won't be heard and he's so bloody accurate, one bullet will do it. He's told Fingers that Appleby will drop, unnoticed, like a sack of spuds and it'll take minutes before anyone realises what has happened. The parade will continue uninterrupted, giving him ample time to hide the weapon until he recovers it and cleans the barrel back at the barracks."

"That's clever...Except!..An expert armourer would detect that his weapon had been fired recently, even if cleaned immediately."

Yanek smiled, triumphantly, "He thinks the Russians might even be suspected; one of their embassy buildings is right on the edge of the square itself."

"Of course – I'd forgotten that."

"Just think, Lloyd, the murder would be covered up to prevent a major international incident, especially if it's thought the Russians had done it."

"You'd like that, wouldn't you Yanek!"

"I would," he said, his eyes narrowing, "I hate the fucking Ruskies more than the Nazis – you know that."

"So where does fucking, Fingers, figure, then?" I said, laughing to ease the tension.

Yanek smiled weakly, "I'd laugh, if it wasn't so serious," he said. "Chopper knows that a spent round, after the killing, could be linked to his rifle. He wants Fingers to supply a spare rifle from the armoury, without booking it out, to be returned immediately afterwards. So, any investigation to link a spent cartridge or bullet with his own rifle would fail, unless Fingers shops him – which is unlikely, in view of Chopper's threat."

"Clever – it'll be the perfect assassination," I said, "Except, he's got to find a spot to take aim, unnoticed. Then he has to dispose of the empty cartridges. And he has to hide the rifle between the time Appleby's shot and returning it to barracks and the armoury."

"It seems he's got all that worked out, Lloyd. At least, that's what Fingers reckons." He paused, drawing at his cigarette, thinking. "He could drop the empty cartridges down a drain – there's plenty of those in Vienna."

There was nothing more said, as we both lapsed into silence.

"Let's go across to the NAAFI – I owe Dave a drink." I said.

Boozer jumped to his feet and grabbed hold of my arm, "Hang on, Lloyd. I want to know – what are we going to do about it? We must stop this!" I had never seen Yanek so worried as he was now.

"This could resolve itself – if we are lucky," I pleaded, "The outcome of the 'Court of Inquiry' could be announced before the parade – you never know!"

"Yeh – and pigs might fly!"

In desperation, I said, "I've got an idea, I'll talk about it on the way over."

24

With just three days to go before the parade, drill had become more intense with Jock Campbell, probably one of the best drill instructors in the British Army, orchestrating it. Now, like club-footed ballerinas, we were expert at retaining balance whilst marching on the spot, knees high in slow time, whilst manoeuvring in line in an arc of ninety degrees and keeping perfect distance within the ranks. Our rifles were feather-like in our swollen hands and our timing manipulating them perfect: and with legs and feet working together in total harmony we had, I am sure, surpassed Jock's wildest dreams as he stood beaming with satisfaction.

"Tomorrow morning," Jock announced, smiling, "we will have a full rehearsal with the Regimental band. We parade at o'nine hundred. There will be a parade-kit inspection tomorrow night – dismiss!"

At that moment, vehicles were arriving loaded with instruments and band personnel. I felt excited. I was right marker in the leading platoon. Nigel was to perform the same role in the second platoon. All thoughts of Major Appleby and Chopper Flynn had been put on hold.

Nigel strode into the room, holding the latest kit issue. "You'd better get down to the stores, the new puttees are in." They were obviously new, with the white straps looking stark on the khaki wrap-arounds.

"They'll look fantastic in contrast with our maroon socks. I'll just finish these toe-caps."

"Your rifle's come up well," he said, "what did you use on it?"

"Brown Kiwi and cold water," I replied, proudly, "Same as the officers use on their belts, you should know."

"Won't that make a brown stain on our KDs?"

"Sure, but it'll come off in the wash, and it won't show on the day."

I called at the stores an hour later to find that 'Fingers' Fuller had barricaded himself in, with the usual bunting, synonymous with store men of his type. The exterior windows had been plastered with newsprint, between windows and interior bars, to prevent prying eyes. I hammered on the locked door – no reply. I turned and kicked it hard with the sole of my booted foot and heard scurrying from inside.

"Who is it?" shouted Fuller. I didn't answer. Had I done so, it would have resulted in abuse and perhaps a refusal to open. I kicked the door again. There was a distinct pause. I heard a bolt slide back, a key was turned releasing the lock and the door opened a crack. "Oh it's you – whadda yuh want?"

I slammed my boot in the gap and shoved the door open with my hip, "What are you afraid of? Why didn't you open up the first time?"

"I was expecting someone else," he said, sulking, as he stepped away and retreated behind the counter. Unshaven and in need of a haircut, he looked unwashed and his eyes were red rimmed, as if he had woken from a deep sleep. He was wearing a vest and denim trousers with unlaced plimsolls on his feet, shoved on in a hurry no doubt. I detected a pungent smell of body odour and sweaty feet. "I s'pose you want yuh puttees?" He said, leaning across the counter, his gold watch shining in the artificial light.

"Yep! Who were you expecting, then?" I asked, suspiciously.

"Never you mind," he said, reaching under the counter, before slapping a pair of puttees on top. With that he slid an open book towards me and stabbed a podgy finger against my name. "Sign 'ere!" he said, handing me a ball pen.

I grasped the puttees, signed, pointed the pen at his wrist, and looked into his eyes, accusingly, "Nice watch, I've seen one like that before, somewhere."

"Well that ain't it," he said, unflinching, as he snatched the pen from my grasp.

I stepped back and cast my eyes around the natural art exhibition inside Fuller's den-of-iniquity. The walls and interior windows were adorned with magazine cuttings of nude and scantily clad women, with huge bottoms and overlarge busts, posing in sexually provocative positions. "It must be difficult to concentrate, with all these." I said, waving my hands in a sweep of the gallery.

"Jealous?"

"You must be joking! With these distractions it would be so easy to hand over equipment and forget to book it out," I said, looking at him sideways, "but you wouldn't do that now, would you?"

He raised his voice, angrily, "What you tryin' to say, Freeman?"

"I don't need to spell it out – you know full well what I'm talking about, Fuller."

"You've got your puttees, now fuck off!"

On the eve of the big parade, we gathered in the huge mess hall for breakfast, our talk confined to discussing the event. One of the men, who understood a little German, had heard it mentioned on the Austrian radio network. The locals, it seemed, were fascinated with military parades and would gather in hundreds to watch the International guard changes in the Helden Platz. We were even more determined now, to make an impact on the local population.

As we returned from breakfast, a few men broke away to read Company orders. I carried on walking. There were no duties to worry about, not for the next two days, and I guessed that our welcome would be one fit for heroes on returning to Schönbrunn, after the parade. I dallied awhile with Boozer and Bins in their barrack room and it was Bins who ushered me into a corner, hissing, "What's 'appening, Lloyd? It's gettin' too close fo' comfort. I couldn't live wiv meself, if I faught," he whispered, thumbing his nose.

"Trust me!" I signalled, with fingers crossed, lying aloud, "It should have been taken care of, by now." I had meant to discuss Boozer's warning with Nigel but the urgency and excitement of the parade had taken precedence.

At that moment Dave Allen, breathless, dashed into the barrack room. He looked aghast as the words tumbled out, "He's got away with it!"

"Who's got away wit' what?" Paddy shouted, from mid-way down the room.

"Major Appleby," Dave, mouthed, "it's on CO's this morning."

"What!" Our mouths dropped open in shock.

"What was that – I didn't hear?" The barrack room became a whispering gallery punctuated by voiced disbeliefs.

"Who said so?"

"Never!"

"I don't believe it!"

"Well if that's fucking justice, then I'm a monkey's uncle!"

I felt cold and sick with anger, as I looked at my watch. It was an hour to dress rehearsal. I turned for the door, "I must tell Nigel!"

"Hold on a minute!" It was Boozer.

I stopped and stared back at him stonily, "Trust me!" With that I dashed from the room. Seconds later, I felt myself shaking with anger, as I opened the door to our own room.

Nigel, sitting on the bed, looked up, distraught, "I know!" was all he said.

I strode across the room and turned, before resting my buttocks on the windowsill. "There's something I must tell you, Nigel – and it's urgent.

"No Lloyd! There's something I must tell you. I didn't want to before, because I knew you would take it badly."

"Oh!"

He took a deep draught from his cigarette and asked, "You remember me telling you our lot had asked the Austrians to conduct further tests?"

"No! I don't remember!"

"Yes you do!" He said, in that knowing way of his.

"Nigel, I don't!"

"It was back in Zeltweg, before the Albuhera sports, just after you re-joined the Company," he said, knowingly.

"A lot of water's gone under the bridge since then, Nigel."

"We asked the investigation section of the Landes-gendarmerie-kommando for Lower Austria to conduct further tests into the cause of the fire," he said, cupping loose ash into his free hand.

I reached behind me, retrieved a boot polish lid from the sill and handed it to him, "Here use this! Nigel, listen a minute. I saw their *first* report. As far as they were concerned, Major Appleby had admitted placing the firecracker and they were satisfied with the cause, so why more tests?"

He shook his head, resignedly, "It seems the British contested the original findings and wanted specific tests."

"Like what?"

Nigel tipped his head back releasing a smoke ring. "They wanted to identify the reaction of explosive sounds on the original witnesses to see whether they could differentiate between them. These included a M116 British thunderflash, an M80 American Firecracker, a revolver, a rifle and a Very pistol. Witnesses were made to stand in the same position as they did on the day of the fire. But, this is important Lloyd. In view of the fact the barn had been completely gutted and the original doors destroyed, they admitted, it ruled out sensible deductions regarding the sound of the explosive samples. Apparently screens were erected to lessen the sound with detonations enacted inside and outside the barn."

"How ridiculous, with the barn now roofless, the sound would have been directed upwards – so what did they have to say, Nigel?"

He placed the cigarette between his lips, reached into his breast pocket with his free hand, and pulled out a typed sheet. "This is hot – for Chri' sake don't breathe a word of how you came by it," he said, handing it to me and touching the end of his nose with his forefinger – "Read it for yourself, it says...."

The sound impression of the witnesses concluded the detonation heard at the time of the fire could have been the explosion of a hand grenade simulator M 116.' .....

"A thunderflash in other words," said Nigel.

"This is just what our lot wanted to hear – because Major Appleby had said, under oath, it was an American Firecracker"

"Exactly, Lloyd, and the fact the British expressed doubts as to the possibility of such a simulator causing an outbreak of fire, relative experiments were carried out with other explosives. For the purpose of these tests, approximately a half cubic metre of hay, previously stored in the barn and dragged out when the fire raged, was put back for the flammable test."

"That's ridiculous, the hay would have been wet!"

"Quite – and this was stated in their report – hear this," he said stubbing out his cigarette. . . .

'The hay on this occasion was much wetter than it had been at the time of the fire owing to its being stored in open air in the meantime.'

"Obviously, Nigel, if the hay was wet, it would make this particular experiment totally invalid."

"I know, but the findings suited their cause, to disprove the fire was caused by the American firecracker – the one used by Major Appleby......."

It says here ...."

'The test revealed that detonators of the type M 116, when exploded either on, or in the hay, and placed in a horizontal position, in each of the five experiments set the hay ablaze. On the other hand, charge M 80 ...'

"The American firecracker, in other words,"

'did not set the hay on fire nor did a tracer bullet, which was fired into the hay.'

"So they disregarded the fact that the original hay in the barn was tinder dry?" I said, holding out the document for him to take.

He shook his head, "It's a carbon-copy of the original. Keep it – it's yours." Frowning, he added, "If the finger is pointed at me, I shall deny I gave it to you, okay?"

"Of course."

Nigel went on, "The Austrians made the point that the hay was still wet. Our lot obviously chose to ignore it when reaching their decision," he looked at his watch in dismay, "Hey! Look at the time."

We had just five minutes. I reached for my beret; "You said it would be a cover-up at the very beginning, Nigel – you were right."

He stopped at the door, grasped the handle and turned whispering, "Appleby admitted it. He was prepared to face the consequences. But I believe others, in high places, were anxious to disprove it was the thunderflash that started it."

"He said it was a Firecracker!"

He nodded his head, smiling, "Of course – I quite forgot." He opened the door, "It's time we got on parade."

"Hold on Nigel – I almost forgot. Fuller has blown the gaff to Bins! Chopper is out to shoot Appleby, just as we present arms. It'll be cold-blooded murder. We've got to stop it somehow!"

"What! Fucking hell!"

There was an awkward silence, as we left the room and walked down the corridor and the news that Appleby was cleared sunk in. My eyes stung as I found myself stammering out the words, "I feel sorry for the families, Nigel."

"Get a grip, Lloyd," he snapped, as he crashed one foot behind the other, adjusting his step to mine. We marched to the end of our landing and turned, self-satisfied with the alternating hollow sound of our twenty-six studded soles hitting the concrete floor simultaneously and reverberating along the empty corridor beyond. The barrack rooms were empty, the rest of the men having fled to join the parade.

I looked up at him, forcing a smile. We were back in the world of robotic adherence. There was little we could do to change things. He sighed, "I'm sorry too, for the lads that survived, poor bastards. They have to suffer the pain of physical scarring for the rest of their lives. Every time they look in the mirror, they'll be reminded."

"What about Chopper – how are we going to stop him?"

He grinned, "Trust me, Lloyd!"

The rehearsal went well. Stirred by the band, there seemed a greater determination in slapping rifles and stamping our feet and the crisp sound of our drill was perfect. Jock was in a buoyant mood and not once did he ball out anybody for sloppy drill, as he called us to halt. The band, dismissed, marched off the square as Campbell reminded us that the sergeants would be round later to inspect our kit.

Of special importance, he told us to place several coins in our rifle magazines for a thunderous sound as we 'present arms'. If only he knew how important the noise might be for an assassin!

News of the 'Court of Inquiry' findings spread through the ranks like the speed of the barn fire itself and with the dress rehearsal parade over, we made our way to the notice board to confirm it for ourselves.

Standing at the back of the group I read the notice feeling irritated by one of the more literate in front, who seemed to enjoy reading it aloud for all to hear. He read, "It's titled, Barn fire at Mattighofen." ....I read ...

'The Commander-in-Chief, British Troops in Austria finds that on the evidence produced, no officer or other rank of the Middlesex Regiment, can be held to blame for the fire, or the casualties that were the result of the fire that took place on 11th March, 1955.'

He turned and looking over his shoulder, mumbled, "It's a farce!"

After lunch I dallied awhile to read Company Orders again and smiled to myself, just as Bins sidled up alongside, "Anyfink new, Lloyd?"

I couldn't believe my eyes, as I turned to him, smiling, "Let's go – I'll tell you in a sec."

"Wha' did I miss, wha' dit say, wha'dit say?" He asked, as we marched towards the barrack block.

I felt the relief in my voice, as I announced, "Chopper's been taken off escort duty tomorrow – Dave's going in his place. He'll be pleased."

"Great! It worked then. Well done, mucker." Bins looked worried for a moment, "I 'ope Chopper don't fink it was my doin' – e's a fuckin' nutter."

"Relax, Jim," I said, "it's been taken care of." I breathed a sigh of relief but knew it wouldn't take long for Chopper to guess who had triggered the change. As we turned into the corridor, I lowered my voice cautioning, "Whatever happens, don't go blabbing to Dave that we organised it."

"Dave'll be dead chuffed – e'll see the p'rade," whispered Bins, as he turned into the barrack room. I kept walking – there was more work to be done on my rifle, boots and brasses.

25

There was a distinct chill in the morning air at Schönbrunn; washed and shaved, but dressed in denims and wearing plimsolls, we made our way across to the mess hall where the cooks had prepared a satisfying breakfast with double helpings of sizzling bacon, eggs, fried or poached, fried bread and tomatoes – chips too for the gluttons among us. There must be no fainting on account of empty stomachs; this one was too important and the reputation of the Regiment and the British army was at stake. The atmosphere in the cookhouse was electric, with men sparking off each other, enthusing about the day ahead.

With full stomachs, and a new spring in our steps, we hurried back to our rooms; behind us the sky had taken on a pink tinge with the promise of a hot day to come. My involvement with Dave, Boozer and Bins had naturally thrown us together again, just like our first ten weeks induction at Mill Hill, as we strode back to the barrack block. Boozer looked relaxed, as he announced, "I feel really excited about this parade."

"I shall be quite chuffed watching you lot for a change," said Dave, smiling.

"Yeh, I can't wait," said Bins, his huge shoulders rolling and head bobbing, as he bounced along beside us, grinning. He had still not lost some of that 'Teddy Boy' strut. "I'm gonna get pissed t'night in the NAAFI."

"Don't forget, put a couple of Austrian schillings in your mags."

"Cor blimey, yeh – I'm glad yuh reminded me."

A new calm had taken over in my relationship with Nigel. I had fully expected him to alert senior officers of the danger facing Major Appleby, so it had not surprised me when Chopper had been replaced on escort duty. However, I felt a little guilty for having withheld the full story from Nigel – Boozer's warning regarding the direct threat that Chopper posed and the special plan set up with 'Fingers' Fuller, in the armoury. But I felt more relaxed now that Chopper would not be anywhere near the parade, as I strolled into the room.

"Have you seen Company orders this morning, Nigel?"

He looked up from bulling, "Yar. Good news – you can relax now, old sport." Dropping his head, he huffed on a toecap and lightly swept a duster across it.

"It's time we got dressed, have you seen the time?"

"Stop flapping," he replied, "we've got bags of time."

Not another word was spoken as I nipped out for a last pee and then commenced dressing. Our KDs had been starched to perfection and to avoid creasing them, we put on our maroon socks, boots and puttees, whilst still in our underpants, before slipping into our shorts – and then it was time to button my jacket as I turned to Nigel, "My hands are sweating, are yours?"

"Here," he said, as he handed me a damp flannel, "use this."

"Cheers, Nigel, you think of everything."

"On the contrary, Lloyd, it was you who reminded me about, you know who," he said, adjusting his beret. He looked bigger, somehow with his beret on.

"You've no idea how relaxed I feel now, Nigel." I reached for my own beret, "Do you think Appleby will be there, still?"

"Almost certainly, I'd say – you can't spoil the show because of one maniac."

Suddenly a voice boomed out from the end of the corridor. "Two minutes to go, you lot!"

We carefully sheathed our gleaming bayonets and donned pure white freshly blancoed belts before checking each other. Perfect. Lastly, our rifles were lying on our beds; with white lanyards strung tight, they had been polished so well they shone like glass. We picked them up gingerly with clean white handkerchiefs, to avoid leaving sweat marks – once the parade commenced, any scuffing would pass unnoticed. Nigel looked at me with a grin, "Let's go, Lloyd."

Treading carefully as if walking on glass, lest we crack the bulled polish on our boots, we left the room to be joined by the rest of the Company as they poured from the barrack rooms, immaculate, all of them. Senior NCOs gave us all a quick inspection with little need to rectify the turnout of any man present. Nothing could go wrong now.

The three TCVs stopped in the road alongside Helden Platz and the tailboards were lowered. From the rear of the lorry, I peered over the tops of waiting men who had already disembarked. Beyond them, high on a building, alongside Heroes Square, I could see two twentieth century villains staring down at us – huge portraits of Lenin and Stalin.

Then, with one hand on the edge of the tailgate, the other holding my rifle, I bent my knees and jumped to the ground as light as a grasshopper, fearful of staining my KDs or cracking the thick layer of shine on my boots. Little was said as we milled around waiting for the order to form up, all of us a little nervous.

We had been blessed with a cloudless sky, bright sunshine and a gentle breeze, ideal conditions for a parade. Jock, with the faintest of smiles dancing around the lines of his face, ordered us to form up for a last inspection. Jock Campbell was not a short man but as we 'stood-easy', waiting, I felt quietly amused to see that this domineering man had to look up at us as he walked along the line scrutinising each in turn. To the civilian onlookers pouring onto the square, we must have looked like a company of giants.

I swung my head round to look beyond the statue of Franz Joseph to the far side: the hierarchy were already taking their places on the dais. I thought I saw Major Appleby but couldn't be sure, unless? Yes, that was him right enough, guiding the dignitaries to their places.

I looked back at the vehicles to see our band alighting from their truck. It was the first time I had seen them in full regalia – fantastic! They looked resplendent in their white, brass-buttoned jackets, black trousers with a red stripe down each side, and black caps. With the shine of their instruments, drums and white lanyards, the fifty or so men looked very impressive. The colour party was there too: the adjutant with sword unsheathed, two officers carrying the Regimental Colours and three warrant officers.

The French contingent, dressed in navy blue baggy trousers, white anklets and dark blue, 'cut-down kitbags' for berets, had already formed up. In a flash they were off, like Olympic walkers, heel, toe, heel toe, as they sped onto the square, marching at a hundred and sixty paces to the minute, led by their band, moving at the same speed with their instruments flaying the air from side to side.

Suddenly I was aware of someone, poking me from behind. "What's up?" I mumbled from the corner of my mouth.

Boozer, whispered, "Look! Our escort, in the band lorry – far side!"

I looked. Oh no! There was no mistaking – Chopper Flynn. I half turned, mumbling, "What's he doing here?"

"No idea."

I turned to face him. "But, I thought . . ."

"Face the front!" That was the Sergeant Major. What could we do?

The French were already practically running through their routine on the square. Time was running out. The space off the square was limited. To shout would cause a disturbance. Jock's orders were serious, quiet and snappy. "Stand to attention! Get into line! Right . . . dress! Slope . . . arms! Left . . . turn! Stand still. Check your slopes!" I could feel my left hand on the rifle butt trembling. "By the left, quick . . . march!" The band struck up and we burst forth to loud applause from the civilian onlookers.

It was too late now! I could do nothing; surely someone would stop Flynn from firing the killer shot. It was an impossible situation. With the minutes ticking away, we marched onto the square with the Adjutant and his party carrying the Regimental Colours and our band, resplendent, in close pursuit. In a daze I heard the double beat of the drum, the signal for the band to stop playing.

The only sound now was the rhythmic crunch, crunch, crunch of two hundred studded boots on concrete. Time was running out. My hands were sweating, my spine chilled to the marrow.

We came level with the dais and I visualised Chopper Flynn's twisted features lining up with the target as Jock's clipped voice, ordered, "Company . . . halt!" 'Check . . one, two!' Then deathly silence, apart from the clip-clopping of the colour party, who were still marching. They too came to a halt in front of us.

I prayed it was all a dream as mechanically I followed orders and turned to face the dais along with the rest of the Company and stood rigid as the men, eyes to the right shuffled their feet, adjusting their line, using me as their marker. All was quiet as once again we heard Jock's distinctive order, "Eyes front!"

Directly in front of us were the inspecting generals of both countries, one of them our own Commander of British troops in Austria. It was he who had cleared Major Appleby of any blame, in the name of the Regiment. I could see Appleby clearly now – about to be murdered and nothing I could do to stop it. Chopper had never, ever, missed! The crowd held their breath expectantly. In the silence, I imagined him quietly loading that first crucial round. A marksman, I knew, he only needed one bullet to kill Appleby.

It was a stupid act of Appleby's, I thought, 'but he doesn't deserve this!'

In a daze, I heard "Present!" … arms!" In just three seconds he would be dead. My nerves screamed, counting, 'one,' as we grasped our rifle stocks, pause, 'two, three…one,' as our hands cracked high against the lanyards sending white dust flying, pause, 'two, three, CRASH!' A hundred heavily studded, right boots hit the ground and a hundred left hands struck rifles, sending white dust floating through the air, to the sound of a hundred coin-filled magazines vibrating loudly.

Was that a shot I heard? I couldn't be sure. I looked at the dais through the dust-laden air. Appleby was gone! He must have fallen back! There was no movement out there as the generals saluted and the band struck up playing our National Anthem.

There was a lot more marching and counter marching yet to come, before the ceremony would end.

As we marched off the square, large numbers of our own Military Police were milling around but there was no sign of Chopper and as we came to a halt, Campbell, enthused, "Well done men, load up. You've got the rest of the day to yourselves. Normal duties will resume tomorrow."

I looked across at Nigel, mouthing, "Where's Chopper?"

He just grinned, "I told you to trust me, Lloyd."

Back at Schönbrunn, we jumped down from the TCV – Bins, Boozer and myself, to see Dave Allen alight from one of the vehicles and come bouncing towards us, obviously excited, "Did you see what happened?"

"Fat chance, we were on parade, remember?"

"There were Red-Caps everywhere – Chopper's been nicked – hey look!" We turned to see a couple of Military Policemen marching Fuller across to the guardroom.

"What happened?

"Is he dead?"

"How the hell did Chopper get to Heroes Square in the first place?"

"Wait a minute, one at a time. Chopper paid one of the other escorts to change places with him."

"Christ! We didn't think of that – did he manage to shoot you know who?"

"I believe he actually pulled the trigger – but Fingers must have removed the firing pin."

"Great! I told 'im to – but I didn't fink 'e would!"

Nigel suddenly appeared, "What are you lot hanging about for – you've got packing to do?"

"What are you talking about?"

"Haven't you read Company Orders? The Battalion's off to Cyprus in the autumn and you lot are joining the advance party in Colchester. You're all going home for two weeks leave from tomorrow."

----- The End -----

Epilogue :

In Parliament, the Secretary of State for War rose to his feet.

'I refer to the findings of the Court of Inquiry into the barn fire in Austria on March 11th in which four British soldiers lost their lives and others were seriously injured. I should point out that the proceedings of a court of Inquiry are privileged and I cannot publish the findings verbatim. A summary will of course be circulated.'

'There is insufficient evidence to determine the cause of this fire. Some possibilities can almost certainly be dismissed. An examination afterwards indicated that faulty chimneys or an electrical fault in the wiring of the barn were unlikely to have been to blame. Similarly, spontaneous combustion of the hay in the barn seems most unlikely. On this occasion the hay had been cut and stacked for at least five months, whereas internal ignition seldom takes place more than three months after stacking. Nor is there any truth

in rumours that the firing of a Very-light pistol or a cooking apparatus was the cause of the fire.'

'This leaves two possibilities which cannot be entirely ruled out but neither can be said to have been very likely, let alone a certain cause. First is the possibility of a lighted cigarette end. Because of the presence of highly inflammable hay in the barn, orders were given that there should be no smoking and the examination of witnesses produced no evidence that this rule was disobeyed. It seems certain that no one was sleeping in the hay where the fire started, and the fact that the fire began at a point about ten feet above ground level makes it very unlikely that a cigarette end discarded by a passer-by could have been the cause.'

'There remains the possibility that a battle simulator, that is a kind of fire-cracker, was to blame. Very shortly before the fire was discovered the company received orders to move, and two officers let off a cracker outside the barn to awaken the company. This cracker was ignited outside the barn about nineteen feet from where the fire began.'

'The position at which it was set off makes it unlikely that a spark could have travelled directly into the hay stacked inside the barn and subsequent experiments with similar crackers add to the doubt.'

'Several of these crackers, which are of American manufacture and much less powerful than the British thunderflash, were set off in the middle of dry hay and failed to ignite it. Further, the fragmentation of the crackers never went beyond twelve feet and signs of scorching were negligible.'

A year after the fire

The Commanding Officer recommended posthumous awards for bravery for 2nd Lieutenant Rawlings, who was alleged to have supplied the 'Firecracker', and Private Parker, both of whom went back into the burning barn.

In his hand-written letter to the Brigadier the C.O. wrote.

'My aim during the past twelve months has been to protect this Company Commander from the sequel to a very unfortunate coincidence and it has not been easy. I am convinced the fire was caused by a soldier lighting up as he came down the stairs and thoughtlessly tossing away the lighted match.'

In September 2005 'The Die-Hards' Newsletter reported …

'In the presence of HRH Field Marshall The Duke of Kent, British and Austrian dignitaries met at Schönbrunn Palace in Vienna, for the occasion of the 50th anniversary of the departure of British troops from Austria when a similar parade had taken place. On that occasion the British Empire medal had been awarded to Franz Omezeder of Mattighofen in recognition of his services in saving the lives of a number of British soldiers who had been trapped in a fire in a storage barn, in the village, when on exercise.'

Author's Comment

There was no mention that the barn had been full of tinder dry hay, or that men had died, whilst many more received serious injuries. The fact that a Military Court of Inquiry was held to determine the cause was omitted. So too, was the fact that the officer commanding the last ceremonial in Vienna in 1955, was the same man who had placed the 'Firecracker' outside the barn on that fateful day.
